MW00945481

MERCHANTS OF MILAN

BOOK ONE OF THE NIGHT FLYER TRILOGY

EDALE LANE

PAST AND PROLOGUE PRESS

CONTENTS

Merchants of Milan

By Edale Lane

Published by Past and Prologue Press

Edited by Melodie Romeo

Cover art by Enggar Adirasa

First Edition January 2020

Printed in the United States of America

❀ Created with Vellum

DEDICATION

I am dedicating book one of the Night Flyer series to my first and best teacher, Patty Grice Burns, my mother, who passed away in December 2000. When I was a small child, she filled our home with classical art and music: a table sized replica of Michelangelo's David, the Blue Boy and Pinkie on the wall, a bookcase overflowing with classics and mystery novels, and my favorite – a huge collector's volume of everything Leonardo da Vinci every wrote, painted, sketched, or designed accompanied by their historical context and significance. She passed that bound treasure to me in her will.

Mother adored da Vinci and we would spend hours poring over the images and text in the large book. She taught me about his genius as an inventor and art innovator and we studied details of the Last Super, the Mona Lisa, and other masterpieces. Therefore, I think it is highly appropriate to publish this Renaissance novel in which Master Leonardo while never appearing in the book plays a central role, in her honor and memory.

A professional educator for many years, Mother's degree was in history, although most of her career was spent as an English and Literature teacher. I was fortunate enough to sit in her classroom where we read Treasure Island and practiced proper grammar and usage. Patty Burns had been a saxophone player, a drum major, and a soprano choir member and soloist who passed on her love of music to both of her daughters. But in addition, she was my biggest cheerleader and supporter, always encouraging me to strive to reach my goals and make my dreams come true. Of all the knowledge she bestowed upon me, the most valuable lesson she conveyed was for me to believe in myself. I love and miss you Mama, but have all confidence you are somewhere smiling at me, praising my success. Thank you for everything!

PROLOGUE

$\mathcal{M}$ilan, Italy, June 1502

"TELL ME ARTISAN DE BOSSI," Don Benetto Viscardi broke the silence at the formal dining table. "Do you find the canard à l'orange and pecorino cheese to your liking? What of the fava beans and pears?" A slight lifting of the wealthy merchant's chin cast haughty slate-gray eyes over a Roman nose onto the guest seated to his left. Benetto's chiseled jaw was clean shaven and his hair, an alloy of iron, nickel, and granite, flowed smoothly to the top of his shoulders in keeping with Milan fashion. His belly bulged enough to proclaim his status without being so great as to hinder his movement.

The fifty-four-year-old patriarch of the Viscardi family raised his wineglass to thin lips as he regarded the inventor he had employed for the past year. Luigi de Bossi was his inferior in every way, from his disheveled attire and unmanageable walnut curls to his thick, square brown beard. True, he was younger with a sturdier build, but his dusky olive complexion attested to a humble lineage. Clearly the man had brains and talent or he would never have served as an assistant to the esteemed master, Leonardo de Vinci; nonetheless, he had proven to be... unsatisfactory.

Luigi smiled, his deep-set chestnut eyes sparkling with delight at the delicacies before him. "I must say, Don Viscardi, this is a feast indeed–quite a savory and appetizing fare. But what is the occasion?"

Donna Daniela Viscardi, who sat heavily upon a cushioned chair at the other end of the ornate walnut table coughed, and raised a linen napkin to her mouth. Nervous azure eyes darted across the diners before she lowered her head to the subservient posture she was expected to assume. Her face was properly caked with white powder, save for rouged cheeks, and the blonde braided updo she boasted was in reality an expensive wig, as years of bleaching had destroyed her own hair. Their daughter, the comely Agnese, also remained quiet as a proper lady should when dining with men. Niccolo, the son Benetto took pride in, was away at the University of Bologna studying business and law.

"Occasion?" Benetto asked after swallowing his wine. "Let me propose a toast to good, loyal Luigi for the profits his latest invention will bring our House."

"Here, here," added Benetto's younger brother Stefano as he raised his glass, a signal for all to follow suit. Stout and muscular with short coal hair brushed with ash at his temples, Stefano was dutiful to his brother, forgoing the frequent in-house wars. He realized he wasn't smart enough to run the business with Benetto's level of success.

Luigi's cheeks reddened above his unruly beard. "My lord, you are too kind. Why, the exploding shells I am developing are not even ready for use. Perhaps within the year," he gestured nonchalantly.

"Precisely the point." There was a sudden harshness to Benetto's tone that exploded through the air darkening the mood.

Agnese, who was but in her teen years, inclined her head to her mother. "Mother, may I be excused?" she timidly uttered.

The patriarch shot a glare toward the women's end of the table. "You may both be excused," he commanded rather than allowed. Mother and daughter hastily withdrew from the eloquent dining hall. To one side of the lace-covered table was a grand fireplace adorned with intricate carvings and topped by an inviting fresco of a wine bottle, glasses, and bread; the opposing wall was covered in windows, the glass open because of the summer heat. A set of oak double doors stood at both ends of the hall, the ones to the study closed and those to the sitting room providentially open for the women to skitter through. The surrounding plaster walls were all hand painted by one of Milan's many talented artists as was fitting the station of the head of a prestigious House.

Benetto returned his attention to Luigi whose former blush had now turned to pallor. "I had a generous buyer who greatly desired those exploding shells to give him the advantage over his enemies in the ever-ongoing wars from which I derive my profit, hence your income as well." He paused to blot his lips with a linen cloth. "Unfortunately for us both, you did not deliver in time and he has removed his order and placed it with one of my competitors." Luigi's blank stare prompted his host to continue. "I have just lost a fortune because of your ineptitude."

"But my lord," Luigi addressed in earnest, "No other inventor has developed a successful exploding shell. Your customer is being taken advantage of! Once he is on the field of combat and the shells fail, he will return to you and I can promise with more time and tinkering I shall provide reports that will fire as intended. You see, there is a precarious balance to be struck with the detonation device–too thin and the slightest rocking of the ammunition wagon will set it off; too thick and it will not explode on impact. It requires much trial and error, and we do not want those errors to cost the lives of our customers."

The explanation sounded reasonable enough, just as it had six months ago. No. It was clear to Benetto that he needed a new inventor. Luigi had cost him dearly, and he would have to pay. "That may all be correct, de Bossi, yet the fortune I was to make is now forfeit because of your delays. Is it true that you have no son to carry on your work after you are departed?"

A puzzled expression crossed the artisan's face. "I have no son, my lord; only a daughter." Benetto watched as a grimace pained his guest who grabbed his stomach. "My lord, I should retire. I am not feeling well."

A satisfied half grin grew across the aristocrat's lips. "Stefano, brother, will you see our guest gets home safely?" With a crisp nod of his head, Stefano rose and assisted Luigi up from his chair. In obvious distress, Luigi doubled over, slapping a hand onto the table to hold himself upright.

"There now, de Bossi," said Stefano as he steadied him with a strong arm. "I will see you home. It is too bad you weren't able to deliver on the goods you were contracted to produce."

Then Benetto saw the recognition in Luigi's eyes, the moment he knew his life was ended. He raised a regal chin, a blaze of power in his air. He was Benetto Viscardi, patriarch of one of the most–no, *the* most important merchant House of Milan. No one crossed him, no one disappointed him without paying the ultimate price. And since Luigi had no son to avenge his death, and the constables would never inquire of him anyway, there was nothing to fear. This would be the end of it. Besides, the poison he utilized was very difficult to detect and created a perfect imitation of a heart attack. What difference would it make if a mere daughter suspected anything was amiss? He expelled a breath of contentment as he watched his brother carry the dying man out.

CHAPTER 1

hree months later

Florentina de Bossi stood tall and confident in the grand entryway of the Casa de Torelli. The wealth of Milan was evident in the quality of fabric and design afforded to one as humble as an artisan's daughter; the simple V-neck forest green dress with long, straight white sleeves and full skirting, while not being as fine as society garb, suited her well. It was not position nor wealth that construed the young woman with assurance, but rather a vast store of knowledge and skills with which she was certain of a future. While she had appealed to the master of the House, Don Alessandro Torelli, to take pity on an unmarried female who had recently lost her father and her home, she had in fact engaged in rigorous research to select the right House to tie herself to in service. Though she was the applicant having sent her documents and qualifications seeking a post, she considered herself to be in control of the whole process. The Torelli's were the Viscardi's most formidable rivals for dominance in the city, and while the Torelli family's primary trade was in silk rather than arms, both Houses diversified their assets to ensure their wealth would not suffer in the event of a slow market in one commodity or another. No, she chose this family, this House specifically because it suited her to do so. Perhaps Alessandro would turn her away, but she had read about his sister's recent loss of her husband who was killed under questionable circumstances. Rumors abounded, but it was Florentina's deduction that the same vicious man who had poisoned her father did away with Donna Madelena's husband. They were allies now, even though Alessandro didn't know it yet.

It was not expected for an important merchant to rush to meet a potential servant for an interview, so Florentina was content to wait. She stood upon a colorful woven carpet surrounded by pastel plastered walls outlined by intricately carved moldings and a columned staircase. The décor included a small cushioned bench, brass wall lamps, a large mirror, and several paintings, but her eye was drawn to a clock that rested on the mantle of the entryway's hearth. She stepped closer to examine the piece. The brass housing was fashioned of two circles, the larger one on top of the smaller, and was supported by a stand carved from black walnut featuring two rearing winged horses facing away from each other which cradled the rounded bottom of the brass. The clock face sported a circle of Roman numerals with two brass hands, one longer than the other. Crowning the casing was a pair of lovebirds huddled close together in an intimate posture fashioned from polished brass. She reached out her hand and gently stroked the masterfully constructed time piece, savoring the feel of the polished wood and smooth metal, a bittersweet smile gracing her lips.

"Splendid, is it not?" sounded a musical female voice. Florentina was so engrossed in admiring the clock that she had not heard anyone enter. Turning curiously to see who had spoken with such fluid intonation, she was taken aback by the beautiful woman stepping toward her. Flame hair braided with a gold ribbon and coiled around her head contrasted her alabaster complexion. She had a high hairline as was fashionable, but only wore a small amount of rouge as her heart-shaped face needed no powder to achieve the desirable skin tone. Deep forest eyes shone like jewels beneath airy brows. While clearly older than herself, the woman maintained a youthful figure poured into an embroidered silk gown with a low square-cut neck drawing the eye to her ripe breasts, taut in the middle to emphasize her tiny waistline, then flared at the hips to complete the image.

Florentina surmised by her attire that this was no servant and must either be Alessandro's wife or sister. Immediately, she became self-conscious of her own eccentricities. Her skin was olive and her hair brown, her figure not so curved, her feet not so delicately petite. She was an oaf, a misfit, a socially awkward flounder. The confidence she displayed only a moment ago evaporated in an instant, replaced by a shroud of inadequacy. But that wasn't all. Something tugged at her from the inside. She had certainly appreciated beauty in women for as long as she could remember, but the feeling stirring in her core was beyond appreciation. Unfamiliar and indescribable it leapt in her heart with anticipation, though she had no idea for what. She was so dumbfounded she could not utter a sound.

* * *

"EVERYONE WHO VISITS our home comments that we have the finest clock in all the city, and I believe it to be true." Madelena Torelli Carcano stopped as she reached the hearth and stood close to Florentina and the clock. "Besides being an exquisite piece of art, it is even more accurate than the one at City Hall. That's because it is a da Vinci design, you see, with springs instead of weights, and it displays the minutes as well as the hours, chiming on the hour and the half hour."

Madelena cocked her head as she studied the potential employee; she was not at all what she had expected. This woman did not display the posture or bearing of the servant class. Her downy, wavy brunette hair extended past her shoulders signaling her single status. She had an interesting face–not unattractive, not beautiful–her nose a little too large, no plastering of powder for whitening, thicker than fashionable brows, and a scattering of indiscriminate freckles. However, her deep-set amber eyes shone with intelligence and her full lips were pulled into a half-smile, as if she was amused by secret thoughts. Tall, athletic, confident, old enough to be a wife yet not, the raw potential for beauty without the desire to pursue it... yes, interesting indeed. But why the sudden onset of nerves? It must be because she is anxious about the interview. "I am Donna Madelena Carcano, Don Alessandro's sister, and you, Florentina, have an eye for fine craftsmanship."

Florentina dipped her head in deference as was expected, then met Madelena's eyes. "My father made this clock," she said wistfully.

"Oh, I should have made the connection," Madelena replied in sudden realization. "I saw the name de Bossi on the papers you sent but didn't think. Certainly, and that explains much." Madelena recalled meeting Master da Vinci's assistant whom her brother had contracted to craft a one of a kind clock for his entry hall, though she was unaware he had a daughter. "I was saddened to hear of your father's passing," she said gently.

"And I was sorry to hear of the untimely loss of your husband," Florentina responded in kind. "You must have loved him very much."

"He was a good husband who did not deserve to die so young," she said, but pondered Florentina's comment. Had she truly loved Vergilio? Though the marriage was arranged, she considered that she had fared well. He was a competent businessman, a good father, and treated her with respect. They were friends, partners even; but, something had been missing. The poets' verses and minstrels' songs spoke of passion and longing of the heart, things she had never experienced with her late husband. But love was not all passion and thrills; it was hard work, standing by one's side, even standing by his grave. Perhaps she loved him in the same way he had loved her—just enough to not be unhappy with each other.

"Will you be conducting my interview?" Florentina's question shook her from her thoughts. "Or shall we wait for Don Alessandro?"

"Come with me to the study," Madelena motioned. "My brother will join us soon."

As the women proceeded into the grand mansion, two children raced around a corner, deftly dodging to miss running into their mother. "Matteo, stop chasing your sister this instant!" Madelena scolded. "Oh, where is Livia, and why can she not perform her duties?" she moaned as much in embarrassment as frustration.

"We're sorry, Mama," replied a blonde haired five-year-old girl with enormous blue eyes in the sweetest, most contrite voice she could muster.

The little boy two years her elder halted beside her. "But Mama, chasing Betta is my most fun thing to do!" Loose light brown curls flopped over his head like noodles framing a fair face lighted by laughing brown eyes.

"You know you are not allowed to run in the house," Madelena reiterated in a stern authoritative timbre. "And where is Livia?"

Matteo rolled his eyes and groaned. Betta obediently answered. "She is in the water closet with Luca. I don't understand why she needs help in there when I can go all by myself." Betta folded her hands in front of her waist and beamed up at her mother and the guest.

Madelena raised a hand to her brow in an effort to ward off a headache. This was not the impression of the household she wished to make on a potential employee. What if Alessandro decided against her? Rumors of unruly children and lascivious servants would spread all over the city tarnishing their reputation.

"My, what lovely children you have," praised Florentina with a genuinely warm smile. She bent down bracing her hands on her thighs so as not to tower over the pair. "Such energy and enthusiasm, so observant and competitive. You two could make great scientists some day!"

The children's joy with the stranger's accolades was apparent on their round little faces. Matteo put his shoulders back and stretched as tall as he could, raising his chin for emphasis. "I'm going to be a rich, successful merchant like my papa," he stated with assurance, then added with scrunched brows, "or a pirate."

Betta reached out and tugged on Florentina's sleeve. "What's a sy-tist?"

Madelena marveled to herself at the ease with which Florentina dealt with the children and toyed with the idea of dismissing Livia and hiring her as a governess. She warmed to the sound of the singular woman's laugh and listened with delight as she explained what a "sy-tist" was to her beloved daughter. Maddie determined that her brother must employ Florentina in some capacity; the woman would undoubtedly be an asset to the household. With the decision made and Florentina's lesson concluded, she ordered, "Now, out to the courtyard with you both. You may run all you please outside."

"Yes, Mama," they chimed in unison. With a mischievous gleam in his eyes, Matteo tapped Betta's shoulder and bolted away toward the archway out to the Roman style courtyard. The little girl started to race too, then stopped herself, glanced over her shoulder with a coy smile at her mother, and walked as fast as possible without running after her brother.

Madelena blushed and shook her head. "They are good children, but as you so tactfully observed, quite energetic."

"They are delightful!" Florentina exclaimed with such sincerity that Madelena dared to believe she meant it.

* * *

Florentina gazed about the elegant study in awe. An interior room, the windows looked out into the courtyard and were surrounded by row after row of leather-bound books stretching from floor to crown molding. Above the bookshelves and on every side, painted arches inhabited by suns, moons, and stars curved up to the plastered ceiling. The other walls were paneled in rich wood planks arranged in large rectangles, carved with leaf designs around the edges. A few paintings hung, but the wall opposite the windows teemed with an impressive weapon's collection. An artistically carved cherry curio cabinet housed precious vases and sculptures behind glass. A new addition was the huge globe sitting in its cradle with a representation of the continents, as well as they were known. Europe, the Mediterranean region, North Africa, the Near East and Far East had some degree of detail, while the Americas were vaguely shaped with no details; the vastness of the unexplored Pacific Ocean was a dark half of the sphere opposite the side displaying the known world. To one side of the room rested a huge desk and chair positioned near a dormant fireplace with other sitting chairs arranged near a trunk and small lamp table. Another lamp sat atop the desk with more attached to the wall.

As Florentina gazed up she spied the splendor of the ceiling art, a colored fresco framed by carved wooden molding encompassing the whole dome. Her mouth fell agape as she struggled to take it all in. Having grown up under the tutelage of a legend in his own time, she was no stranger to fine art; however, she was unaccustomed to being surrounded by so much of it outside a cathedral.

"Please have a seat," Madelena motioned toward the grouping of cushioned chairs. Florentina tingled all over with excitement. *Just think! I will have access to all these books, all this knowledge! And those children are so adorable! Add a beautiful donna to gaze upon each day. This will be an even better arrangement than I had imagined.*

"Grazie," she replied and settled herself in a comfortable arm chair. "You have such a beautiful home." When Madelena took the seat beside her, Florentina felt a new wave of excitement course through her body. These feelings were completely unreasonable. Madelena may not technically be nobility, but in practicality she was its equivalent. While some people in the Italian city-states still held titles of duke or prince or whatnot, power had already shifted to the wealthy merchant class. Theirs were also various positions of political power, and many a titled noble had become the puppet of a dominant merchant. She, on the other hand, was a commoner–middle-class, but not aristocratic. She was well versed in the classics, could read, write, and speak three languages, and even play the harpsichord, but in the eyes of society she was not, and never would be, the equal of one such as a member of the Torelli family. Even if Madelena shared her peculiar inclinations, such a relationship would be out of the question. No, Florentina would have to be content to admire this alluring woman in secret.

"It belongs to the Torelli family and has since before I was born. Alessandro and I grew up in this residence. We all lived here with our families under Papa's authority until he passed two years ago, and now Alessandro is head of the House. Vergilio didn't mind; it was advantageous for him to be in such close association with my father and brother. And I get along well with his wife Portia and their children. It's a shame they are so much older than mine, but at least Bernardo–he's Alessandro's youngest–sometimes plays with Matteo." She paused for a moment. "I'm sorry, I don't know what has gotten into me today. I am not usually so forthcoming with such a new acquaintance and do not mean to bore you with so many personal details."

"Oh, do not apologize," Florentina insisted. "I want to learn as much as possible about the House I will be serving in." *And the woman whom I shall serve,* she thought.

Just then the door flew open and an unusually tall, distinguished, broad-shouldered man entered, shadowed by his ashen, spindly butler. Madelena rose, the glow of her joy evident. "Alessandro!"

CHAPTER 2

$\mathcal{T}$he man who stood in the doorway boasted the body of an Olympian and the face of Adonis, with chin-length wood brown hair and bangs hanging above keen umber eyes. He was markedly taller than most men with a commanding air of authority swirling around him. Alessandro was as masculine as his sister was feminine; Florentina barely noticed.

"Good afternoon," he greeted while retaining his regal stance of hands clasped behind his back.

Florentina sprang to her feet beside Madelena and returned the greeting. "I am honored to meet you, Don Alessandro." She attempted an awkward curtsey, never knowing what to do in these situations.

"Ally, this is Florentina de Bossi," Madelena introduced. "I didn't think of it at first, but she is the inventor's daughter–you know, Leonardo da Vinci's assistant, the one who made the exquisite clock in the entry hall."

His eyes brightened as he crossed the room to stand with them, shadowed by his attending specter. "Yes, yes," he said in recognition. "So exactly what position are you applying for?"

"Whatever is available," she replied, trying to appear humble. Florentina was not accustomed to behaving subserviently, but she determined to play the role as best she could.

Alessandro laughed and shook his head. "We don't frequently keep domestics long; they tend to come and go, and I am looking for someone who will be with us for a while. I fear you are far over-qualified for cleaning house and washing linens. One with your educational background would become easily bored and we would have to replace you in no time. Tell me, why are you not maintaining your father's shop?"

"My lord, I did try, but the patrons fell away like leaves in autumn when word of my father's death was spread. No one wanted to commission a woman to make their clock, repair their equipment, install their locks, or develop a new gadget for their use," she explained in honest frustration. "They simply assumed a woman had not the brains for it."

"Drivel!" Madelena declared. "A woman's mind is every bit as keen as a man's; she just seldom is afforded the opportunity to use it. My question, my dear," she began turning toward Florentina, "is why you are here instead of joining a salon of intellectuals? The forward thinking humanists have begun to include women in their gatherings."

"That is true, Donna Madelena," Florentina agreed, first meeting the woman's eyes, then dropping her gaze. "However, only women of means, nobility, and those not obliged to work for a living possess that luxury." Returning her eyes to Madelena she continued. "Surely you have heard of one of my contemporaries, the Duchess Isabella d'Este, who is far more brilliant and accomplished than I. What a privilege it would be to discuss art and philosophy with her, but I am not independently wealthy; in fact, I am completely without funds." She turned back to the lord of the House. "My father was a kind, talented, ingenious man, and a fine artisan, but he never developed any skill in financial matters. Therefore, the only options that I can see are marriage or domestic service. Since I have no arrangement and no potential suitors, I have come to you, Don Alessandro, and you," she added, casting her gaze on the red-haired widow, "in hopes of finding a position."

Alessandro nodded and stroked his chin thoughtfully. "Your papers say that you are fluent in French, Latin, and Greek, accomplished in music, knowledgeable in history and the classics, philosophy, mathematics, and engineering, and the sciences; knowing you grew up under the watchful eye of Master da Vinci I have no doubt this is all true."

"Ally," Madelena said with a note of inspiration. "Matteo is certainly old enough to begin his formal education and Betta is not much younger, and very bright... Livia is not equipped to give them educational instruction. She can scarcely see to their physical needs," she added in an aggravated tone under her breath. "May I suggest we employ Florentina as a tutor for the children? In their brief interaction earlier, she established a good rapport with them. I know most parents have male tutors for their children, but a woman would be acceptable in our circles until Matteo is older."

Florentina turned an expectant gaze from Madelena to Alessandro. "I was actually thinking along other unconventional lines. Can you repair machinery found in a wool or silk factory?"

Her eyes brightened. "I have never encountered a machine or mechanism that I could not repair. I am familiar with all varieties of looms currently in use, and when I come upon any device with which I am unfamiliar, I simply take it apart, study how it works, replace or repair the offending part, and put it back together again." She smiled in triumph, honey eyes glistening with pride.

For the first time the gaunt, ashen butler inched from behind his towering master to express his disapproval. "My lord," he uttered in censure. "You cannot be considering employing a female tinker. It simply isn't done." He glowered at Florentina with a downward drooping mouth.

Alessandro raised his brow and glanced down at his chief servant. "Is that right, Iseppo? Is it written somewhere?"

"But, My lord!" Iseppo shook his head. "What will the other great Houses think of us?"

To Florentina's estimation, Alessandro was unabashedly confident and completely unconcerned with the opinions of others. "A good businessman knows how to utilize every asset to his advantage, does he not? Do you know what I see, Iseppo?" He gestured to the young woman standing before him. "An asset. Why should I spend good money employing a tinker to repair equipment when we have a better one in-house, one who will be loyal to us because this would be her home and we become her family? An outside employee may spy on us for another House, spread rumors about us, or overcharge for their services. Then, you may say, why not hire a full-time engineer? I would reply, why waste the money when we can acquire two specialists for the price of one. That is what a good businessman would do!"

Florentina could feel her heart race. This is exactly what she had hoped for! Alessandro turned back to her and said, "Suppose, I offer you the full-time position of tutor for Madelena's children, with the stipulation that you also act as our House's tinker, to repair or even improve on the efficiency of any appliance or apparatus that requires attention? The servants' quarters are on the upper floor with the kitchen; it will be often hot and you would need to share a room with Angela, the new maid from the countryside, but-"

"Oh, I don't mind; that would be wonderful!" Florentina was brimming with excitement. She had intended to be lodged on the third floor (fourth if one counted the basement); that had been part of her research in choosing this House as well. The top floor granted her easier access to the roof and Casa de Torelli was situated in the right part of town. The roommate could pose a problem to her scheme, but she would figure out something where that was concerned. All plots aside, she beamed with genuine joy at being accepted. She thought the children were adorable and being their tutor would ensure daily contact with their beautiful mother. She knew nothing would come of it, but she would like to get to know the woman, and she could always dream.

* * *

MADELENA'S SMILE lit her eyes as she hugged her brother enthusiastically. "Oh, Alessandro, I have a good feeling about this decision," she gushed. "I think Florentina is precisely the right tutor for my children and you can obtain some use from her too, just like you said!" A warm sentiment filled her heart as she considered the intelligent young woman who had won her over in less than an hour. She recalled an incident that occurred before she married Vergilio and her father still ran the House. She had been infatuated with a comely maid only a few years her elder who was not unwilling to engage in a tryst. Never had she felt so stimulated, so alive! But it was an ill-fated romance for so many reasons. For an instant Madelena thought longingly, *perhaps Florentina would be inclined to such a relationship. But no; I shan't ruin what can be a very good arrangement. I don't want Florentina to feel obligated to me in that way. No, I am her employer, although I do also wish to be her friend.*

Alessandro caught his sister's infectious smile and placed an arm around her shoulders giving her an affectionate squeeze. "Iseppo, call for Luca to come and help Florentina get her things moved in."

"Yes, milord," he replied dourly and turned to leave, but was almost bowled over by a stout man wearing a watchman's uniform and hat.

"Don Alessandro," the watchman addressed as he pulled the red cap from his head. "I am sorry to disturb you, but you will want to hear this news."

Madelena knew Salvador Sfondrati, one of Milan's city watchmen. Her father granted him an important favor, and he had remained grateful and loyal to the family all these years. She quickly noted the concern etched on his aging face as he wiped a hand across graying hair cut short to obscure a receding and increasingly thin hairline.

"What has happened, Salvador?" All revelry faded from Alessandro's countenance and voice.

"Last night Don Benetto Viscardi's shipment of weapons was attacked!"

Alessandro frowned; while Madelena said nothing, inwardly she was glad. *The unscrupulous fiend should be robbed*, she thought.

"By whom?" Alessandro asked. "What did they take? Should I be concerned?"

"No one knows who, my lord, but the matter is being investigated. The strange thing is, they didn't steal anything; the whole shipment was destroyed," Salvador explained.

"Destroyed?" Alessandro's expression turned to bewilderment. "Tell me everything."

"Well, Viscardi's people were bringing in three wagons full of weapons from one of his suppliers to the north. They were slated to be sold to one of his biggest buyers, but the caravan was attacked. Witnesses could not identify how many there were because of all the smoke everywhere. Then they heard booms, and the cargo went up in flames. When they got the fires out, there was nothing but mangled metal and charred wood. Several of Viscardi's men were injured, though none were killed." Salvador paused for a moment, worry etching deeper into his expression.

"And? What else?" Alessandro prodded.

"My lord, I fear–it's been discussed–that Viscardi will blame you, being his chief rival and all. I assured the magistrate that surely you had nothing to do with the attack," he added quickly.

"Indeed," Alessandro confirmed. "Tell the magistrate that if I had attacked one of Viscardi's shipments, he could rest assured the cargo would be safe in one of my warehouses with all the proper manifest papers in order. Why would anyone *destroy* perfectly good merchandise? You see, that makes no sense, and that is why Viscardi should know I had nothing to do with it."

Salvador nodded in agreement. "Yes, that is precisely what I thought. Therefore, I must warn you that there is a new gang of miscreants causing trouble. I suggest you double the guard on all of your shipments until they are caught and brought to justice."

"Yes, yes, I shall," Alessandro considered thoughtfully. "Come now, Salvador, let me offer you some refreshment."

As he walked out with the watchman, Iseppo returned escorting a lanky, well-muscled young man with a charming air about him. "Luca will help the new tutor with her things," he uttered with an expression of disdain. Madelena paid the butler no mind. She was fixated on the half-smile adorning Florentina's face and the capricious sparkle in her amber eyes. *What secret inspires that look of knowing amusement?*

CHAPTER 3

*D*on Benetto Viscardi stormed through the main hall of Casa de Viscardi bellowing powerfully enough to rattle the windows and shake the chandeliers. "Zuane, Stefano, how could this happen!' He shook off his calf-length brocade pleated overcoat and a nervous servant scrambled to scoop it up. He yanked the black beret from his salt and pepper hair and threw it at his wife who stood quivering near an interior door. Daniella managed to catch the cap before dashing out of sight.

Benetto spun on his heel, scanning for his men just in time to see them rush to his summons. Stefano was still chewing his brunch and held a pear in his hand. "What is the matter?"

But Zuane knew, Benetto thought as he focused piercing gray eyes on his man-at-arms. *Look at him,* he thought contemptuously. *In the prime of his life, strong and broad shouldered, experienced with sword and arquebus, yet he lets the vandals get away!* "How did this happen!" Benetto was too angry to wait for an explanation. He felt as if he may explode. "Hellfire and damnation! That shipment of weapons was for Gian Giacomo Trivulzio, King Louis XII's captain who is engaged–even as we speak–in warfare with the Spanish! He counts on *me* to supply his weapons, Don Benetto, the greatest arms merchant of Milan, no in all the city-states. What will I tell him? The king depends on me. In fact, one reason the Viscardi House holds sway in Milan is because I sided with the French king against the Sforzas; I played a major role in his victory over the Duchy, and so now that Milan is in French control, I have the king's favor. But if I can no longer deliver weapons to his armies, how long will that favor last?" Benetto realized he was physically quaking with rage and stopped his rant to take a deep breath.

"That is not good," Stefano stated the obvious and shook his head. "Zuane, what went wrong?"

The man-at-arms stood at attention, an unreadable expression on his ruggedly handsome face. Benetto dismissed the breech in fashion of his choice to wear a beard; at least he kept it neatly trimmed and his hickory brown hair hung right above his shoulders as it should. Dressed in a leather jerkin and pantaloons over stocking clad calves, Zuane's military bearing fostered confidence. So how had a small band of thugs outwitted and out maneuvered his stalwart men?

"True, I was there," Zuane began in a measured timbre. "We had the usual number of guards, two in front, two in the rear, and two on each wagon, but to be honest it has been years since any bandits dared attack our caravans. The last one's who tried never saw judge nor jailhouse."

Benetto nodded and tried to calm his pounding heart. "So, why last night? How many were there? How many did you kill?"

"Well, you see," he began, and relaxed his attitude of attention in favor of one of humility. "It was twilight, and we were nearing the inn where we always spend the night. But as autumn approaches, the days get shorter, so it was getting dark earlier than we had anticipated. Then the mayhem started. Suddenly there was smoke everywhere–under the wagons, in front of us on the road, in the trees. We became confused, and I circled about on horseback trying to find the fire. All the guards were on high alert and formed a circle around the cargo, but then there was an explosion, and the first wagon was blown to pieces. The driver was thrown clear and suffered a broken arm. Then the second and third wagons were struck and caught fire. That is when I ordered the men to spread out and search for the cannon. It had to have been a cannon–you know there is a war on. I suspected a Spanish patrol, except… why would a patrol be dragging about cannons?"

"Did you find the cannons?" Benetto demanded.

"No, there were none, and no horse prints or retreating army at all. I ordered three of the guards to put out the fires while I took the rest on an exhaustive search. I can only conclude that either someone set traps in the road, or those who attacked the caravan were as silent and swift as deer in their getaway. Naturally, I rode ahead and informed the authorities straightaway, only now arriving back at the mansion. I'm sorry to confirm the cargo was a total loss."

"Word travels as fast as our enemies it would seem," Benetto sighed in dismay. "You mean you never saw the villains?"

Zuane shook his head as his gaze fell to the floor.

Stefano, who was swallowing a bite of pear, inquired, "Do you think it was Torelli?"

"Doubtful," Benetto replied scrunching his brow. "That calculating goat would never destroy merchandise when he had a chance to turn a profit. No, if he attacked us—and I wouldn't put it past him—he would have stolen the shipment, not blown it up. I don't understand..." A confounded bewilderment consumed his features as he looked from his brother to Zuane. "Anyone would have. Unless... mayhap it was the Spanish, or a trap set in the road to inflict random destruction upon whomever passed. Miscreants, rebels, or some malcontent aligned with Sforza who simply wants to thwart King Louis's efforts," Benetto speculated, racking his brain. But it didn't make sense. *Who would destroy three wagons full of perfectly usable weapons that were especially valuable in the current climate?* Then he sighed a deep sigh and lifted steely eyes to his man-at-arms. "Post extra watches at the factory and around the residence. Stefano, I want you to go out and hire more men—good, experienced mercenaries, not drunkards from the tavern. Tell them they will be paid well. We do not know that our business was targeted specifically yet, but we cannot let this happen again."

"Truly, Benetto," Stefano confirmed. "I'll hire good fighting men with sober, watchful eyes."

"And I shall distribute them to all the necessary venues to protect our goods," Zuane added snapping back to attention.

"We've had setbacks before," Benetto recalled. "Hopefully there will not be a next time, but if there is we shall be ready."

* * *

"Good Madonna, woman, what have you in your trunks?" Luca pleaded as he followed Florentina up the stairs with one large ornately carved wooden chest on his shoulder and another more plain variety being dragged behind by his other hand. "I never knew a woman's belongings could possibly weigh more than a full grown hog!"

"Drivel! Only women's things, tinker tools, and books," she said stifling a giggle. Florentina had a leather bag slung over her own shoulder and an armful of volumes as she climbed up to the top floor. "Books in a wooden trunk are indeed heavy, but a strapping young man such as yourself should have no problem with the load."

"I say here, Luca, boy, pick up that chest and do not scuff the stairs!" scolded Iseppo most disapprovingly. "If as much as a single plank is gouged I will take it out of your hide!"

That butler is going to be trouble, Florentina considered as she led the way into the third-floor hallway. "Which room again?"

"Third on the right," Luca panted as he lifted the second trunk off the step.

Florentina opened the door into a small, Spartan chamber with two single beds on either side of a little lamp table. The other furnishings consisted of two common oak Dante chairs and a vanity on which set a wash basin, water pitcher, and short stack of hand towels with a plain mirror affixed above. *The bed with a trunk at its foot and dresses hanging on pegs across from it must be my roommate's,* she thought. *Praise Heavens there's a window!*

Luca staggered in behind her. "Just put them there," Florentina said pointing to the end of the unused looking single bed. The linens were clean and beds neatly made, but these quarters boasted nothing of expense.

"There you are," Luca said as he rid himself of the cumbersome trunks. "You can push them where you want them to go." He straighten his back and rolled his shoulders, then rubbed one as if it ached. "Angela has an afternoon break as she cleans up after dinner, so she should be around soon. Servants eat in the kitchen after the family's meal has been served. We all prepare our own breakfast and lunch, but better ask Bianca–she's the head cook–what you're allowed to have. All the fancy foods are reserved for the Torellis."

"Grazie, Luca," Florentina said in honest appreciation. She was well aware of the contents of her trunks and why they were so weighty.

The young man left and Florentina strode to the window to inspect her view. Looking out she could tell it was the back of the house, not the majestic front nor the quaint, Roman-style courtyard. Below was a narrow side street rather than the main thoroughfare, but that would be better anyway. She noted the sparse number of pedestrians, mostly laborers and servants she supposed by their attire. *I'll have to find the roof access*, she thought as she turned back to set her books on the lamp table and drop her bag beside the bed. She pushed the ornamentally carved oak chest square with the end of her bed and drug the plain one into the nearest corner. Then she returned to the masterful chest and brushed her fingers over its hand-crafted surface.

Papa made this for me for my sixteenth birthday, she recalled wistfully. *He thought I may wed soon and would need something suitable to pack and take to my new home. That never happened.* She felt along the edges near the bottom and across a raised carved plank. The brass fittings were more than corner braces and the exquisite workmanship more than decoration. *Papa thought of everything.* Florentina's smile warmed at remembrances of her father... and of her plan to avenge his death.

The Italian vendetta was more than simple vengeance. For centuries it had been society's way of punishing criminals, particularly when murder was involved. While there were watchmen whose job was to keep the streets safe and judges and magistrates who ordinarily heard civil cases of citizens' grievances with one another, in 1502 Milan had no professional to discover who had perpetrated a crime when no witnesses were available, no one to use logic and the powers of observation to uncover the criminal's identity, and no one to dispense justice upon them. That was considered to be the obligation of the wronged family, primarily of the closest male relative. But her father had no son, so by Florentina's reasoning that cast the responsibility to her. The authorities enacted no investigation at all regarding her father's death; they declared natural causes, and that was that. But Florentina knew better. Luigi had lived long enough to tell her what had happened. Now she was going to make Benetto Viscardi pay.

Her adept, nimble fingers worked over the carving and she was just starting to apply pressure when the sound of footsteps coming from the still open doorway startled her. She jerked her hands away and shot her head up, wide eyes searching, hoping it wasn't that scarecrow of a butler. Relief washed over her and a little tingle as well when she spied the lovely face of Madelena.

"I didn't mean to startle you," she commented pleasantly. "I only wanted to make sure Luca got all your things brought up. I know it's small, but-"

"Oh, no, the room is more than adequate, Donna Madelena," she jumped to confirm.

"At the moment these are the best accommodations we have available. I'm glad they will be sufficient. So," she brightened. "Are you ready to start the children's lessons tomorrow?"

"Yes!" Florentina rose from her squat by the chest and rushed to pick up a leather bound children's reader. "This is the book I first started to read with," she said holding it out to Madelena. "I also have secured two small chalk boards and chalk for them to practice their letters. To keep them from getting bored, we will go out into the courtyard to study nature and atmospheric conditions, and from time to time I may want to take them on outings to observe the majestic art and architecture of this fabulous city! I do need to ask where you wish the lessons to primarily take place."

Florentina gazed expectantly at her dazzling employer. She noted approval in the expression with which she was met. "They share a large chamber that was Alessandro's room when he was a youth. It is equipped with a study area near a set of windows onto the courtyard, with which you will undoubtedly be pleased."

"Indeed! We shall begin as soon as they clean up after breakfast." Florentina could not control the glow that she knew blossomed across her face. Then something unexpected sent her heart racing.

"You should call me Maddie; it's what friends and family call me, and all the time you will be spending with the children makes you like family," she explained, rushing to add, "Unless it makes you feel uncomfortable."

"Oh, no, not at all," Florentina confirmed. "It makes me feel… privileged. Leonardo used to call me Fiore, little flower. He got Papa to calling me that too, but no one else ever has; I mean, I had an unusual upbringing and didn't play much with other children, so…" *Stop babbling! She doesn't want to call you her little flower!*

"Fiore it is." Maddie's smile was definitely amiable, but was it affectionate? *I know what I'll be dreaming about tonight, when I'm not dreaming of flying or taking Viscardi apart piece by rotten piece!*

CHAPTER 4

Florentina's first week at Casa de Torelli flew by, but much had been accomplished in that short time. Matteo and Betta could recite, read, and write all 26 letters of the alphabet as well as numbers one to one hundred. They had also begun common phrases in French. Maddie had been so surprised when they asked her, "comment allez-vous, Mere?" On other fronts, Florentina had learned her way around the estate as well as the schedules of every person residing in it. She knew two ways to the roof—one through the kitchen ascending a narrow outside stairway, and another on the far side of the building through a storage room window and up a drainpipe. The roof was hipped and low-pitched, covered in in reddish clay tiles. Important rooms, such as Alessandro's and Madelena's chambers, boasted balconies, some which faced the courtyard and others the street. The residence along with its neighboring offices, warehouses, and production buildings, comprised a whole city block. While some great Houses located their living quarters away from their merchandise, Alessandro followed his father's practice of keeping everything in one place; it was easier to protect that way.

Alessandro had taken Florentina on a tour of the production facilities and shown her the equipment she would be responsible for maintaining. She had examined the silk looms, and the wool looms, noting the differences and similarities and even began considering possible ways to improve upon their quality and efficiency. But mostly she was committing to memory the layout, noticing where offices with their ledgers and documents were, where privately hired watchmen were stationed, and whether or not upper windows designed for airflow were equipped with locks. She had no intention of robbing her benefactors, but supposed that Viscardi's buildings would be arranged similarly. *Before my next move, I will need to don my costume and spy out the Viscardi warehouses to be sure. I know many of his weapons are actually assembled in his holdings north of the city, just as the Torellis' wool comes from flocks on their land in the countryside, but he keeps stockpiles in town along with the records and books. I wonder how much cash he holds on hand in a personal safe and how much he places on deposit with the bank? And does he use the Medici Bank or another? I cannot endanger Torelli money while seeking to abscond with Viscardi funds. There is so much to discover!*

In 1502 Milan was a thriving golden trading metropolis of over one hundred thousand residents, not counting those in the country-side of the northern Italian city-state. Though ruled by a Duke for generations, it had recently come under the auspice of the French crown and was being administered by French representatives while the wars over its eventual future raged on. Fortunately, none of the fighting actually occurred near the urban center and business continued as usual. Trade brought wealth to Milan and wealth gave rise to art, architecture, education, and the eye of the Church as well as political intrigue. Prosperous merchants such as the Viscardi and Torelli families were not nobility–and likely never would be–therefore, did not directly hold ruling authority. However, their money equaled power, and they wielded vast influence as well as enjoying lifestyles more opulent than many a rural lord. They had witnessed a break with tradition in Florence where the Medicis gained direct control over political authority regardless of having no noble ancestry, and despite the fact that Lorenzo de Medici's incompetent son Piero had managed to lose the reins of power at the moment, the banking superiority established by the family throughout Europe ensured their sustained success.

* * *

IN THE WEE hours past midnight only a week after the attack on Viscardi's weapons shipment, Florentina crept out of bed. She had paid close attention to each floorboard in the room, determining which would creek even when too dark to see them. She crouched at the chest at the foot of her bed and felt the secret buttons carved into the decorations that when pressed in the proper sequence would open the hidden compartment comprising the bottom third of the storage space. There was just enough moonlight shining through the window for her to see its contents.

She glanced up at the sleeping Angela. *Don't worry; she won't wake up. That tea I made for her will keep her out until morning,* she thought and pulled out the drawer beneath the false bottom of the trunk her father had designed. She lifted out a black silk blouse with long, fitted sleeves and a pair of black leather leggings and supple black lace-up boots. Next she retrieved the matching coif and facemask that completed the ensemble. Underneath them in the compartment were safely tucked away the tools and weapons she had devised to carry out her vendetta. She spied a half dozen iron spheres about the size of small caliber cannonballs only fitted with wicks. Some were explosives while others were merely smoke bombs. These were what she had used on the caravan, both to create confusion and to destroy the cargo. *I won't need these tonight.* Beside them was a curious device about as long as her forearm with a cylinder in the middle and a crossbow configuration at one end with a handle and trigger mechanism at the other. She pulled it out dragging behind it a cord with which she could strap it to her waist or hang it over her shoulder. *Better have this just in case.*

Leonardo da Vinci invented or improved upon hundreds of weapons, many of them during his years in Milan, years when Florentina had observed and even helped with experiments. She recalled his schematics for a rapid-fire cannon with twelve barrels set in a kind of wheel which was turned by a large crank. He had explained to Duke Sforza how the artilleryman would load all twelve then light the variable length fuses and turn the crank. They would fire one after the other with no reloading in between each shot. Sforza had turned down the design complaining that to be feasible the barrels would be too small and range would be lost. He was also concerned the contraption would be too heavy to move, especially if the ground was muddy. Florentina took the design and modified it for a lightweight miniature crossbow, only with eight slots instead of Leonardo's twelve. She had tested several prototypes before being satisfied with this one. True, it did not have great range, but it was accurate and could fire the shots as quickly as she operated the trigger. It gave her an advantage over foes armed with a conventional crossbow or arabesque which could only fire one shot at a time.

Next she removed a black leather belt and short scabbard that held an eighteen-inch carbon steel arming dagger. Also attached to the belt was a length of cord tied to a small grappling hook. *Definitely need these*, she decided. Last, she ran her hands over a black leather pack bag with two shoulder straps instead of one and two hooks at the bottom that clipped onto steel rings in her belt. It was the largest item in the chest. She hesitated, then lifted it out, taking one more glance at the sleeping woman. *Always be prepared*, she confirmed, and proceeded to peal out of her nightgown and slip into attire as dark as pitch.

Once completely transformed, she looked at herself in the mirror. No hair showed, her physique was obscured, and her face was unrecognizable. One would not know she was a woman with her height and slender build. She was a phantom, a highwayman, an obscure shadow in the night. Satisfied, she slipped on thin black leather gloves and tiptoed out toward the storage room where she could take the drainpipe to street level. From there it was about a fifteen minute jog to Viscardi's warehouses. This was planned as a spying mission, but she needed the outfit of a thief in the event she was spotted. She patted one of the pouches sewn into her belt and felt the familiar lock-pick tools and she sensed the buzz of excitement, the thrill of the hunt, and the rush of danger. No, Florentina knew she was not a typical female, but she really didn't care. She was her father's avenging angel and nothing would get in her way.

* * *

BENETTO WAS SLEEPING RESTFULLY in his great, feathered, four-poster bed with crisp linen sheets, under a woolen coverlet beside his saggy, unattractive wife when he was roused by a loud pounding on his chamber door. "Don Benetto!" sounded a fretful cry. "My Lord, come quick!"

He rolled out of bed and fought to clear his head while reaching for a robe which hung on a nearby hook. *Why is Zuane bothering me at this hour? Why doesn't he wake Stefano?* "Is the house on fire?" Benetto called back angrily. "Because it better be for you disturbing my sleep!" He slid bare feet into his slippers and opened the door.

Stefano was with the man-at-arms and grabbed Benetto by the shoulder. "Sorry, brother, but an intruder has been spotted at the warehouse offices. After the attack-"

"Yes, yes," he replied curtly, shocked into total awareness. "I want to be informed. Have they caught him?" Lengthening his stride, Benetto struck out into the lead with his two muscular aides on either side.

"Not yet," Zuane said, "but the extra guard you ordered has paid off. They shall likely have apprehended him by the time we arrive."

"Are they sure there is only one? A thief or a spy, no doubt, sent ahead of another potential attack. I swear by the devil, I will know who is behind this and finish them!"

A servant busily lit lamps as the three descended the staircase. He bowed his head as his master and escort rushed past.

"Where is the burglar?" Stefano shouted toward the warehouses which were across the street from the grand dwelling.

"On the roof!" sounded a fevered reply.

The three men lifted their heads scanning the opposite rooftop for movement. The warehouse was a large, rectangular edifice taller than the surrounding buildings. "Over here!" barked another at the sound of feet rushing over clay tiles.

"Zuane, get to the bottom of the fire ladder around the corner in that alley," Benetto pointed. "If he tries to climb down, you'll have him." Zuane gave a quick nod and jogged off, his right hand on the hilt of his sword.

Stefano pulled aside one of the watchmen who was racing past. "Report," he ordered brusquely.

Wide-eyed the smaller man replied, "I don't know much. The alarm was sounded signaling a break in. We all raced to our posts and then Giorgio—I think it was Giorgio—spotted the intruder. Everyone has been trying to chase him down. I was sent to go fetch a constable."

"On your way now," Benetto gave him leave, and Stefano released the man's arm.

Suddenly a report sounded from an arabesque followed by another. Benetto and his brother looked up to witness a tall, slim figure nimbly, even gracefully, glide over the peak of the roof and down the side toward the street in front of them. It was impossible to make out details, as the interloper dressed entirely in black was barely visible at all. Squinting and straining with his head tilted to one side, a pensive expression overtaking his face, Benetto detected the figure half turn, an object in his hands catching a sliver of light. One of the two pursuers stumbled, grasping his leg, and the other dropped to the rooftop and lay flat. The intrepid prowler turned back and continued running toward the far edge.

"What?" Benetto stood dumbfounded, fixed on the surreal scene. What happened next he would never have believed if he had not seen it with his own eyes; he was still not certain he believed it even then. The figure in black unfurled huge wings and soared from atop the warehouse across the alley and neighboring houses and out of sight into the night.

CHAPTER 5

For once you have tasted flight you will walk the earth with your eyes turned skywards, for there you have been and there you will long to return.
-Leonardo da Vinci

Florentina had been twelve years old the first time she flew. Leonardo had constructed a model of one of his early designs, a pair of human-sized wings with canvas stretched over an ash wood frame. He needed a small, lightweight adventurous young person who he said "won't break as readily as an old man like me," and Florentina had volunteered. Leonardo and Luigi had fitted the wings over her arms and sent her running off the edge of a hill into an updraft. She would never forget the exhilaration and ultimate freedom that burst forth within her youthful heart that first time her feet left the ground and the wind carried her... a whole twenty yards before contraption and all, she was defeated by gravity.

Two years later she tested another prototype, this one a glider with wings more akin to a bat's than a bird's. By age fourteen Florentina was taller with a longer reach but still a mere twig of a girl who the master inventor chuckled, "could just as easily be carried away by a kite." This flying machine was a definite improvement over the first and she stayed aloft for several minutes while her father and mentor chased behind on the ground. However, the fatal flaw of this model was its lack of a steering mechanism and she was at the mercy of the wind and physics. A few hundred yards from the take-off point she landed in a tree. It did mark a development, but clearly more innovation was required.

Leonardo was fascinated by the idea of flight and was convinced human ingenuity would solve the enigma; however, his time was always being demanded for other projects—art for the church and his patrons, weapons for the Duke—and then there were his many other undertakings, such as generating accurate diagrams of the internal organs and systems of the human body as well as explanations as to how each functioned. Medical schools were overjoyed by the textbooks he produced. He was also an accomplished musician who performed his own compositions on the lyre and flute for his noble patrons. When he wasn't painting, inventing, or playing music, he was creating codes and codices, writing jokes and witty sayings, and contemplating the great mysteries of life, such as why the sky was blue and how old the earth really was. Therefore, during his years in Milan, the great Renaissance man had not perfected his flying machine.

Florentina, who jumped at every opportunity to learn from the master, not only remembered all he taught her, but had kept old drawings of his models and in her spare time speculated on how they may be improved, even making sketches of her own. But after Luigi died, she devoted day and night to engineering a design that would work, at least for a person her size and to fit her purposes. She incorporated Leonardo's parachute into her design, utilizing the strength and light weight of silk for her wings and the pack idea to fold them into. For a frame, she used hollow bronze piping jointed for folding and unfolding. When open, her gliding wings were about eight feet long and three feet wide, tapering at the extremities. The frame was connected to the pack itself, which was strapped to her back and belt leaving her hands free to operate pulley handles attached to flaps in the rear of the wings which helped bring her down earlier than gravity if needed and to help with steering. Additional experimentation had shown that she could also steer by simply pushing on a hand-grip and leaning in the direction she wished to move. It was not a precise system, but thus far it had kept her from landing in trees.

The most difficult part to perfect was a deployment device that would pop the wings out of their pack and into position in a matter of seconds. That was crucial. Florentina did not kid herself to believe she would surpass her mentor by creating the initial fully functional flying machine; she just needed a quick getaway... and produce a shock and awe effect. In order to defeat an enemy, you must first cause him to fear you. What better way to make him fear you than to show him you can do something that no one believes possible? So she spent weeks perfecting a series of levers and string pulls along with strong, precise hinges that would allow the packed wings to burst forth into place with a single catalyst.

In the end her "wings" were actually one expanse of a kite-like glider that would allow her to soar over short distances when starting from a height, such as a hill or rooftop. Her invention did not realize Leonardo's dream of flight. But to the uniformed observer it would appear that she had sprouted wings like a tremendous albatross and flown away into the night.

* * *

FLORENTINA WAS DREAMING that someone was shaking her and calling her name. "Florentina, wake up; the children will be done with their breakfast soon and the Donna will be very cross with you if you aren't ready to begin their lessons." This was an odd, silly dream! She decided to ignore it, but then there were those hands shaking her shoulder again. Still in a groggy, not quite conscious state, Florentina opened one eye. Through a haze she spied a youthful face framed by golden hair. Dressed in a maid's day dress and apron, Angela stood over her impatiently badgering her to wake up. *What time is it anyway?* she thought.

But when Florentina opened her other eye, she saw the room was flooded with daylight from the window and panic shot her into awareness. She threw off the cover and sat straight up, which made her head spin. "Don't worry, you aren't late yet," Angela soothed. "But you need to hurry. I don't know why you slept so late; did you not sleep well? The tea you made put me under right away. Why, I can't remember having such a good night's rest in ages! You aren't ill, are you? Shall I tell Donna Madelena-"

"No, no, I am well," Florentina interrupted, else she would have never secured a turn to speak. She had only been in bed for a couple of hours, and those were spent recovering from her adrenaline high. She had almost been caught, men had shot at her, but she accomplished her goals for the night. Her alter-ego had gotten a good look at Viscardi's shipping schedule for the next few weeks; she knew where and when weapons and other commodities would be coming from and going to, allowing her to carefully plan her next move. Secondly, at least half a dozen of his men had seen her fly! She didn't know if Don Viscardi himself had witnessed her escape, nor if he would believe the reports when he received them, but rumors would surely be spread. *Make him afraid.* Florentina winced as she rose to her feet, but a smile crept across her lips despite her discomfort. Her plan was not simply to kill Benetto–she would destroy him!

"If you say so," Angela replied, placated for the moment. "I have to get back downstairs to clear the table after breakfast. Don't dally, now. I like you, and would hate to see you dismissed from your post."

Little chance of that, she thought, but hurried to dress and brush her hair.

* * *

ALESSANDRO SAT at the head of his large mahogany dining table in a brocade cushioned chair formed to accent the heavy table. To his right was his petite wife, Portia, her glossy, buff strands gracefully arranged on her head and dressed for the day in the latest Milan fashion. Beside her was their younger son, Bernardo who did his best to imitate his father in every way, and to Alessandro's left sat his oldest son, Antonio, who favored his father's appearance yet was in all ways determined to be his own man. To Antonio's left was their middle child and only daughter, Pollonia. Her burnished locks and ivory skin more closely resembled Madelena's natural coloring. She had almost reached a marrying age, but Alessandro was in no hurry to rid himself of her loving attention. Madelena was posted at the opposite end of the great table with her two youngsters on either side of her. The family of eight was a perfect fit.

"Antonio, I should like you to accompany me to the guild meeting this afternoon. You are old enough to be more involved in our family business and you should make the acquaintance of the other merchants as well as observe the meeting," Alessandro stated. "Do you have a preference between the Bologna or Naples Universities? You could begin your studies after the new year."

Antonio shifted uneasily in his chair. "As you wish, Father," he replied, then hesitated. "Suppose I don't desire to be a merchant? I have other interests, you know. I enjoy painting and many people say I am quite good at it."

Alessandro sighed and shook his head. "Art is fine to pursue as a side interest, but you cannot earn a living at it–not in the lifestyle to which you are accustomed. And one day you will wish to marry; how will you provide for a wife and family? You are heir to one of the greatest fortunes in Milan, but only if you remain part of the business."

"So you are using money to coerce me?" Antonio blurted angrily. His smoky eyes seethed beneath dark brown bangs. His handsome features reddened, and he set his jaw. "So, if I chose another profession I will be disinherited?"

"No, son, that is not what I am saying," his father chided. "Did you hear the word 'disinherit'? No, you did not. But the fortune itself is tied to the business. Do what you want, just don't come crying to me later."

"Don't bother about him," Bernardo chimed in perkily, a smile brandished across his smooth, pre-pubescent face. "I want to be your business partner! I'll be good at it, you'll see. Let me go to the guild meeting with you."

Alessandro smiled fondly at his youngest son. "And a fine partner you'll be one day–whey you're older. You must be in school today, but perhaps another time."

From the other end of the table Matteo piped up. "Why does Bernardo go away to school but I have to stay home with a tutor?"

Madelena stroked his hair. "Because Bernardo is older; he attends the *Studium Generale*. When you are older you will too, but there is much to learn here from Florentina first." Madelena smiled at the thought of the intelligent slim woman with her exotically attractive Mediterranean aspect. She was so enthralled with the image in her mind that she didn't even notice Angela come in.

"Shall I take away those empty plates?" she asked politely.

"You may, grazie." While Angela cleared the plates, Madelena's thoughts turned to concern over the growing rift between Antonio and her brother. She hated to see them quarrel, but it hadn't been that different between Alessandro and their father. *It's just his coming of age*, she thought, trying to push worry aside.

Iseppo materialized in the dining room doorway. "My lord, a messenger has arrived with urgent news. Shall I have him wait in the hall or show him to the sitting room?"

A furrow crossed Alessandro's brow. "If it is urgent, show him in," and he gestured to where they sat. Madelena felt unease rise into her throat as she watched Portia turn an anxious gaze to her husband and reach for his hand. He smiled at her reassuringly. *Nothing rattles Ally*, she thought. *It is good he is head of the House. I have never known a calmer, more in control man in my life.* Having her brother in charge made her feel safe.

Iseppo reappeared with one of Alessandro's employees who stood with hat in hand. "Don Alessandro," he greeted and bowed his head.

"Yes, Carlo, what is the pressing report?"

He swallowed. "Two things, actually my lord. One is very bad, and the other is just... bizarre."

"Then start with the bad news and get it out of the way." Alessandro sat up straight with his hands folded on the table in front of him, cool as a snowy peak.

"You recall the armor order that you arranged with Gian Giacomo Trivulzio, for the French army?" Alessandro nodded. "It seems, my lord, that Don Benetto Viscardi went to the general and undercut your bid. He stole our customer; Trivulzio has cancelled the order with you and is not buying from Viscardi."

Alessandro smirked and Madelena fumed. "Ally, he can't do that!" she protested angrily. Although not officially a partner, Madelena had assisted her brother in running the business since their father passed. There were many tasks to be accomplished, and she was a skilled book-keeper as well as a persuasive seller. "We have already paid for that armor; it is being delivered to our warehouse tomorrow. We'll be out our invest-ment. That rat's bastard!" She was sure her brother was aware of the level of hatred she felt toward the man she suspected of having her husband killed, and at that moment of further betrayal her blood boiled.

"Calm yourself, Maddie," he said placidly. "We can always find a buyer for fine armor." While the family's main trade was in cloth and textiles and Alessandro detested the idea of selling sharp objects that men used to kill each other with, he had no such moral qualms about trading in armor plating that protected men from the sharp objects. He undoubtedly expected no less of Viscardi. "And the other news?"

"Well, it's about Viscardi also, but Don Alessandro, you won't believe it," Carlo said, his eyes widening.

"Still, I would hear the report."

"You know Viscardi's caravan was attacked last week, and did you ever think he may suspect you, and perhaps that is why he stole your contract? Anyway," Carlo continued after shaking his head. "They had an intruder last night, a burglar who—get this—sprouted big, black wings and flew off the roof of his warehouse! I know, right?" he questioned his own report. "It's all over town this morning, so who knows how much is exaggeration. People are calling him the "Night Flyer". Do you believe it?"

Madelena's eyes moved from the incredulous Carlo back to her brother whose mouth had dropped open most uncharacteristically. He blinked, then started to smile. "That is very interesting indeed. I suppose we must be on more careful watch lest he break into our warehouses." Then he burst into laughter, followed by his wife and children. "Spread his wings and flew away, you say?"

"That is all the talk, my lord."

Madelena sat back in her chair. "I hope he made off with a fortune of Viscardi's cash."

"I don't know what was stolen, but what a tale!" Carlo declared.

She watched Alessandro's expression change to one of intrigue. "What a tale indeed," he echoed.

CHAPTER 6

*A*s the day's lessons came to a close, Matteo sat in a child-sized wooden chair beside the student desk while Betta snuggled cozily on Florentina's lap gripping a small chalkboard where she had correctly written her name five times in a row. Matteo turned a page in the large print primer. "The dog ran after the cat. The cat ran after the rat. The rat ran into a hole. The dog and the cat sat." He grinned up at Florentina with two permanent teeth looking much too large for the rest of his mouth.

Florentina smiled, honey eyes sparkling with delight. She had only been with them for two weeks, but already she found their progress to be remarkable. "What brilliant children you are; what exceptionally bright students I have!" Betta gleamed up at her, bubbling over with joy while Matteo sat up a little straighter and raised his chin proudly. "As a reward, I have made a present for you both; however, you must share. Can you do that like good siblings?"

"Yes, we can!" Matteo blurted out excitedly while Betta nodded and batted her lashes above incredibly wide, blue eyes.

Florentina reached into the leather bag beside her grownup-sized chair and withdrew a carved wooden box. "This is a puzzle box," she explained. Betta quickly laid her writing board aside and grasped for it, an expression of awe on her rosy, round face. "Right now it is all put together." Matteo stretched over and opened the lid revealing its empty interior. "But it comes apart into 10 pieces and there is only one way to fit them back correctly."

"Let me see," Matteo said. "I'll bet I can figure it out."

"I'm the littlest," declared Betta. "I get to try first."

Patiently, Florentina lifted the box from the children's hands and disassembled the pieces on the desk, mixing them around several times. "I know you are both very smart, but are you also very wise?" she asked.

Betta scrunched her face peering up at her tutor. "What do you mean?"

"Anyone can be smart," Florentina shrugged nonchalantly. "Given enough time anyone could put the puzzle together. But," she changed intonation, drawing in their attention, "wisdom is a rare thing indeed. Do Betta and Matteo want to be smart and wise?"

"Yes, yes!" they both chanted in excitement.

"It is wise to work together. Ecclesiastes 4:9 in the Bible teaches us that two are better than one. To be both smart and wise, rather than compete with each other over who can solve it first, you should work in harmony with one another. That way not only will you solve it faster, but you can both be proud of your accomplishment." Hearing a faint noise from the doorway, Florentina turned her head to spot Maddie watching and listening, a radiant glow on her face. "Here," she said getting up and setting Betta on the seat. "Play together and solve the puzzle." She and Maddie met in the center of the room.

"It is such a joy to see you with my children," Madelena confessed. "They both simply adore you, and they are learning so quickly, why I can scarcely believe it!"

"They are quite bright and very well mannered," Florentina replied, her breath catching in her throat at the expression and words coming from the beautiful donna whom she dreamt about. "It is impossible not to love them. But there is so much for them to learn."

"So much you can teach them." Madelena peered over at her young-sters discussing quietly and trying to fit pieces together. "Where ever did you find that charming puzzle box?"

"I made it," she acknowledged blithely with a shrug of her shoulder. She wished to spend more time with Maddie, to get to know her better, to form a relationship–any relationship other than merely that of employer-staff. But who was she kidding? How could there be more, and what more could there be? Still, her heart raced whenever Maddie entered the room, whenever her melodic voice sung in her ears. And she felt warmth emanate from the red-haired widow. Was that her imagination?

"You made it!" Madelena exclaimed and rushed to stand over the children and inspect it.

"Look, Mama," Betta gushed. "Florentina gave us a present!"

"I'm about to," Matteo started to say, then corrected himself. "We're about to solve it."

"How clever you both are!" their mother praised and turned astonished eyes to Florentina. "And how clever you are, Fiore." Her tone sounded suddenly sensual and her lush green eyes darkened. Florentina's heart skipped a beat, and she forgot to breathe. Her mouth fell agape, and she found she could not produce a sound. Maddie crossed back to her and asked, "Could you make one of those for me? Perhaps a bit more challenging? It would be a wonderful diversion for my guests at parties, not to mention a good mental exercise for me as well."

"Certainly." Mouth dry and palms sweating, Florentina at least found her voice. "I would be pleased to." She lowered her gaze lest Maddie read the desire that smoldered in her eyes. Then an idea popped into her mind. "Next week I plan to take the children on an outing to the monastery of Santa Maria delle Grazie to see Master Leonardo's painting of the Last Supper. I thought it would be polite to ask if you wish to join us."

She was relieved to read the pleasure in Madelena's expression. "I would be delighted to join you for the outing. Do you have a particular day in mind?"

"Weather will be a factor, now that autumn winds and rains have arrived. I don't want to inconvenience you."

"There will be no inconvenience," Madelena stated. "I shall simply arrange the rest of my schedule to accommodate the trip. I shall have a carriage drive us all there on the fairest day of the week. Actually I have only seen the masterpiece once, and should love to experience it in the light of your personal expertise."

Florentina bowed her head once more. "You honor me," she replied, almost trembling.

"I believe it is you who have honored me," Maddie echoed before turning to glide out.

* * *

FLORENTINA WAS STILL FLYING on an emotional high as she got into bed that night, her mind ablaze with imaginings about her upcoming excursion with Maddie and the children, which threatened to replace strategizing the next move of the Night Flyer as upper most in priority. *The Night Flyer,* she pondered. *So my avenging persona has been given a name.* A soft rain fell carving patterns and streaks on the windowpane. Angela was not in yet, so she took out a book to read while she waited keeping the lamp lit for her. She did more staring at the page deep in other thoughts than actually reading the popular romantic adventure novel, *Orlando Innamorato.*

Just as she was about to nod off, Angela scurried in, head down, and quickly locked the door. Florentina thought she heard a sniffle, but she absolutely felt an abrupt change in the atmosphere of the small chamber. Setting the book aside, she pushed herself up in bed, focusing her attention on the young blonde maid. "What's wrong?"

"Nothing," Angela lied, wiping her nose with the back of her hand. She proceeded to pull off her uniform and toss it on top of her trunk. She slipped a robe over her undergarments, and went to the basin to wash her face. Florentina watched her in silence, assessing the situation.

"I understand if you don't want to talk about it; I certainly shan't attempt to coerce you," she said in a soothing, compassionate manner. "But it is quite evident that you are upset, likely due to an unpleasant occurrence that happened this evening." She paused but Angela shook her head. Florentina continued. "I am also aware that you haven't known me long, but truly, Angela, you can talk to me. It may help–I may can help. Honestly, who else is there aside from your family who are far away?"

Angela put down the wash cloth, and slowly turned toward Florentina, but refused to raise her damp, red eyes. "There's nothing you can do; there's nothing anyone can do. I'll just have to get used to it I suppose."

That sparked a whole different line of suspicion than Florentina had been previously considering. "Come, sit on your bed and tell me what happened. I am not too much older that I can't be your friend. I'm twenty. How old are you?

Angela gingerly made her way around to sit on her bed before answering in a dull, listless tone. "Fifteen."

"Well, you see," Florentina responded amiably. "That might have been a lot when I was five and you were an infant, but now it is nothing at all.

We are both single young women forging our futures together in the service of one of Milan's great Houses."

The younger woman expelled a sigh. "I suppose." Then she looked up at Florentina and cocked her head curiously. "Has anyone ever, or has anyone tried to... no," she answered before asking her question. "I should think not. Look at you and look at me!"

At first Florentina was baffled. "Si, you're beautiful with your light skin and blond hair, youthful figure, cute little nose, sweet laugh, while I'm so ordinary and undesirable." Something clicked within her sharp mind.

"Oh, no, that's not what I meant at all!" Angela rushed to say, an aspect of embarrassed panic covering the previous distress. "I don't think you are ordinary or unattractive. You are tall and strong and smart and confident, while I'm... none of those things."

"Angela, did someone hurt you? Did one of the men," she hesitated trying to figure how to draw it out of her. "Was it Don Alessandro?"

That elicited an immediate and dramatic response as she had hoped it would. "Oh, no, not Don Alessandro! He is a perfect gentleman, he would never-"

"But someone did," Florentina stated with assurance. She slid her feet over the edge of her bed to face the frightened young woman directly and gentled her voice. "Who was it? We can go to Don Alessandro and-"

"No, no!" she replied with a horrified expression. "You must promise to never tell anyone! He is too important, has too much authority. It would be my word against his–and who am I? A little girl from the countryside? The lowest maid in the pecking order. I can't tell anyone; I would be dismissed without references! Then where would I go, what would I do?"

It was Florentina's turn to sigh. "Alright, Angela, we won't tell Alessandro. Perhaps we could take the matter to the chief butler, that scarecrow Iseppo?" Angela covered her face with her hands and laughed a ridiculous, humorless laugh. Florentina's eyes widened in shock and her mouth fell agape. "Iseppo?" she asked incredulously. "But, he's so old, and practically half dead already!"

The laughter was snuffed out and Angela's eyes burned. "He is boney, old and disgusting, but he is still a man–the man who runs the staff, who is in charge of everybody. A word from him and I'd be out on the street. 'Men have needs,' he said, and 'it would be in your best interests to be nice to me.' I told him no, that I was a virgin, but he just grinned and backed me into a closet."

Florentina could feel her blood boil. She had disliked him from the start, and now she comprehended why. "I would have stomped his foot, thrust my knee into his groin, smacked him across the face with my elbow, and run. He'd have been too embarrassed to tell anyone about the encounter."

That brought a fleeting smile to Angela's lips, but then her shoulders slumped. "That's because you're you," she gestured toward Florentina. "You're like one of those heroines in a Greek tragedy, but not me. I'm weak, small, uncertain, afraid. I don't want any trouble. I'm sure he will tire of me. At least I wasn't beaten, only..." Her head drooped again.

"Are you sure, absolutely certain that you don't want to tell Don Alessandro?"

"Without a doubt! You promised I could trust you, Florentina; please!"

She sensed that Angela was becoming distressed again, so she acquiesced with a nod. "Maybe I can rough him up for you," she suggested and winked.

One laugh lightened the mood as Angela shook her head. "Please don't. One punch may do him in and how would we explain that? I just want to forget it happened. Dirty old man! I want to take a bath and wash him off and forget the whole thing."

"Then let me accompany you down the hall to the bathing room," Florentina suggested as she rose to her feet. "I agree that a nice, hot bath will make you feel better, and I'll be there so no one will bother you." She reached a hand out to her distraught roommate.

"Now that's something I *will* let you do!" she declared leaping to her feet.

Florentina had promised not to tell anyone what happened and pummeling the little old pervert would not serve either of them. However, she determined to keep a very close eye on Iseppo from that moment forward.

CHAPTER 7

*A*lessandro and Antonio joined colorfully silk-clad merchants strolling down the walkways and through the high-arched entry to their impressive guildhall, as they, more than all, could afford the luxury. Every craft and trade in the city had a guild, a professional organization that looked out for their well-being along with setting standards and determining who would be allowed to operate within their jurisdiction. By the turn of the sixteenth century in Milan, the guilds held almost as much power as the government–in some cases more–and foremost among their number was the *Gilda dei Maestri Mercanti*, the Guild of Master Merchants. The city had guilds for weavers, dyers, metalsmiths, shippers, and every phase of the production process, but atop the pyramid of tradesmen sat the merchants. Then one had to pass stringent requirements and be approved by the council before being awarded a seat within the ranks of masters. Verily, the vast majority of Milan's wealth was represented by its membership. Master's were allowed to bring their sons as guests, but Antonio was still a mere apprentice to his father, and should he choose to dedicate himself to the occupation it would be many years before he could prove himself a master. Madelena's late husband, Vergilio, had been a journeyman employed by Alessandro, though close to achieving the coveted master status.

The fall weather was pleasant that afternoon with gusts of wind swirling harvest colored alder and elderberry leaves about. Situated in the Po River Basin in the north of the peninsula, Milan was prone to hot, humid summers and cool, rainy winters, leaving spring and autumn as the favored seasons. Snows had begun to blanket the mountains surrounding the basin presenting a spectacular panorama. None of the three major rivers that crossed the valley flowed through the city proper; that would be too unpredictable. Instead the navigli, a system of canals, was built connecting Milan to Lake Como, Lake Maggiore, to the lowest part of Switzerland, and to the Adriatic Sea, an impressive feat which began in 1179 and was not completed until 1475 when Leonardo da Vinci made improvements and added the final pieces–an innovative arrangement of locks that connected to the Alps. Therefore, while being many miles from any coastline, Milan was linked to the sea allowing goods and ideas to stream freely in and out maximizing the profits and importance of the city.

As father and son passed under the arch into the portico, Alessandro spotted Don Benetto leaning against a pillar with his arms folded across his chest. The head of House Viscardi met him with a steel glare. Alessandro was going to pass him by but Benetto stepped out in front of him and sneered. "Word is that the great man Torelli has employed a woman as a tinker," he stated loudly enough for all hear. "Just what is it you wish her to tinker with?" He raised his eyebrow, a smile edging outward as the sound of a few snickers could be heard.

Alessandro stopped and gazed down at his rival with a look of bemusement. There was no way he would allow this insect to rile him. "It is true that the tutor my sister hired for her children is as skilled as her father, an assistant to Master Leonardo. I could waste my money like some people by employing another to repair my equipment, but I chose to wisely allocate my resources. As to your innuendo, Benetto, you may recall my wife is very attractive and able to meet my needs quite satisfactorily. Is yours?" Benetto's face reddened, and he refolded his arms. "And as we are talking of word spreading around, I hear you will bottle no wine from your vineyard this year."

"Someone snuck in and salted the ground; I have lost that vineyard for the next ten years!" he shouted in angry frustration, his aspect descending into a deeper crimson. Alessandro's eyebrows rose and his lips parted. He had no idea the misfortune ran so deep. "Who would do such a thing? How could they get away with it? Rest assured I dismissed everyone in charge of the property, useless morons!" Then Benetto pushed a finger into Alessandro's chest and spoke in a low, menacing heat. "If I find you had anything to do the attacks on my House, there will be nowhere you can hide from my retaliation!"

Alessandro raised open palms out to his side. "On my oath" he said. "How would ruining your vineyard profit me? I raise sheep in the countryside, not grapes?" The heated discussion attracted attention and others began to gather around them.

"Enough of this," commanded a distinguished older man wearing eyeglasses and a red velvet beret adorned with a peacock feather. The other merchants moved aside as he strode up between them. "Don Benetto, I presume you will bring up the matter of these attacks on your shipment and the intruder at your warehouse in our meeting today. At point is the fact that we are all vulnerable to such intrusions." He shifted his gaze from one man to the other and they both nodded. "Gentlemen," he said to the assembly. "Let us gather now in the hall."

With Antonio at his side, Alessandro fell in behind the guild leader. Giovanni Sacchi, perhaps the third richest merchant in the city, was serving his two years as chairman of the guild council. While the guild was designed to be as democratic an institution as possible to prevent any one member from creating practices that unfairly favored his own House, to be efficient and well organized required some hierarchy and leadership. So long ago rules had been adopted stipulating the creation of a seven-member council comprised of the most successful master merchants. Whenever one died or retired, his position was filled by the next most worthy candidate from among the membership. It was further established that members of the council would take turns presiding over the guild as chairman with the primary responsibility of making sure meetings ran smoothly and trouble within the ranks was avoided.

In his early fifties with distinguished silver hair cut shorter than the prevailing fashion, Don Giovanni's face was long and studious, with bushy brows, and a crooked nose. The absence of a beard revealed hollow cheeks and a cleft chin while his spectacles hid dark bags sagging beneath hazel eyes that alluded to a lack of sleep. Of average height and build, he moved with the confidence and grace of a nobleman despite his common birth. Alessandro knew that unlike Benetto and himself, Giovanni had not inherited his fortune; he had earned it, along with the respect of his peers. He also supposed this was likely to be a contentious discussion and drew in a deep breath as he entered the hall.

* * *

WITH THE OFFICIAL portion of the session concluded, Antonio was restless to leave the chamber crammed with older men whose only thoughts were of money and profits day and night. His father turned to him and asked, "So what did you learn from today's meeting?"

Burying his true opinions, he replied, "First, I learned that powerful men of wealth tend to acquire enemies, but it is notable that on this occasion it would appear only Don Benetto has acquired a new enemy, a very elusive one who seems to have developed the singular ability to fly."

"Take note, Antonio," Alessandro instructed, "that while underhanded practices may bring you coins in the short term, when one aims to harm others through his business methods or otherwise, it often comes back to bite him."

Antonio flashed an agreeable grin. "With that, Father, I wholeheartedly agree." After exchanging a knowing glance, he stood a bit straighter and said, "I wish to spend time with my friends before returning home." At Alessandro's nod he relaxed and added, "I will see you at dinner or send word if I'll be dining elsewhere."

"Very well," his father approved and rapped an affectionate hand on Antonio's shoulder. "Enjoy company with your friends. I'm glad you have started coming to meetings with me. I know it hasn't convinced you to embrace the merchant profession, but I am pleased you are trying to show an interest."

"Yes, Father," he said with a nod then struck off down the street toward the fashion district. Before the meeting had commenced when everyone was milling about, he recalled hearing mention that Don Benetto's daughter was shopping for a new dress. A warm glow filled his heart as he thought of the fair, demure Agnese. He remembered that as a child she had dark hair, but now it was as golden as wheat. Her soft sky-blue eyes had not changed, yet too often he noted sorrow in them. He would solve that problem–as soon as he could arrange to marry her. The only obstacle was that their parents hated each other, and he admitted that was one momentous complication.

Anticipation swelled in the young man's heart as his light feet skipped along the cobblestones and eagle-eyes scanned for the object of his affection. He smiled and nodded politely to people he knew on the street and occasionally paused to peer into the window of a dress shop. "Have you seen Agnese Viscardi?" he asked to a few passersby. It seemed an eternity before he spied her exiting the front of Tomisina's Fashion Boutique. With a spring in his step, he trotted over, a bedazzled grin on his smooth face. "Good afternoon," he greeted and extended a violet rhododendron blossom he had plucked from one of the decorative shrubs.

Immediately her anxious eyes began darting left and right, up and down, and even over her shoulder. He could tell her breathing grew quick and color drained from her cheeks as if she had seen a ghost. "Antonio," she articulated, "how nice to see you. What a pleasant surprise. I hope you have been well." His brows drew together in consternation at the formality of her words and tone and he slowly withdrew his outstretched fist of flowers. Then she whispered, "Meet me behind that shop across the street in ten minutes."

Though he wasn't sure what she was about, he played along. "It is good to see you looking as lovely as the weather," he declared in a resounding voice. "Have a pleasant afternoon. Mayhap I'll see you at Mass."

"I should hope to see you then," she replied ceremoniously and then continued on her way into the seamstress's shop across the boulevard. Antonio possessed a sharp wit and deducted that she did want to see him, but that she didn't wish anyone to know about it, so he proceeded down the street into a men's establishment and then out the rear to circle back. Ten minutes later she emerged into the deserted alleyway. Antonio stepped out of the shadows with more trepidation than enthusiasm, no longer harboring the makeshift floral bouquet.

"What is wrong, Agnese?" He came to her and reached for her hands. Instead she wrapped her arms around his neck in a trembling embrace.

"Oh, Antonio!" She buried her face in his shoulder and he hugged her close, a flood of emotion swirling through him like a tornado. When she pulled back, he detected tears welling in her eyes. "Father saw us together at the Friuli's ball and became very angry. He forbade me to even so much as speak to you again!" Now the tears came and Antonio's spirits fell with them.

"There now," he consoled as best he knew how. "We'll just have to be more careful and only meet in secret."

She shook her head violently and dabbed at her eyes. "You don't understand; he has spies everywhere, probably watching me all the time. He threatened to marry me off to some old fat man if I ever... if we..." Her bottom lip began to tremble and she dropped her gaze remorsefully.

"I'll not have that!" Antonio declared. "I want to marry you myself, I just need time to get established."

She answered him with an incredulous stare. "Are you mad? That will never happen. He would never allow me to wed a Torelli."

Antonio swallowed, holding panic at bay, and gripped Agnese's hands firmly. "Then we shall run away together," he proposed. "I have money saved from my allowances and more that my father doesn't even know about. I am skilled at gaming and often win substantial funds. I may not be able to keep you in finery, but neither will we live in squalor. We could go to Venice or Florence, even as far as Sicily. I can apprentice with an artist there–I do have talent; everyone says so."

Agnese sighed leaning her head to one side as her shoulders slumped and pinned him with damp sky-blue eyes. "That may be, but it would never work. My father would send out as many men as necessary to hunt us down. He would drag me back in shame and humiliation, and you he would have murdered!" Her eyes widened in a mask of desperation. "He's killed men before, or had them killed, for lesser offenses than absconding with his daughter."

"But–" he tried to protest, but she placed two fingers to his lips.

"You are the best thing in my life; I shan't let him destroy you. That is why we must never see each other again. If we pass on the street, we must force ourselves to look the other way. Don't you see?"

Gradually her words and the passion behind them began to register in his mind and in his gut. She meant it. He knew Don Benetto was unscrupulous as a businessman and wouldn't hesitate to place his thumb on the scale if he could get away with it, but murder? Then everything he had ever observed about the man and his daughter whom he loved began to slide into place–her timidity, apprehension, sadness. What kind of hell must it be to live in her household, to be in constant fear from the one who is supposed to protect her? He may have arguments with his father, but he was secure in his place. Alessandro loved him, even if he didn't always understand him. In that instant he coveted nothing more than to scoop Agnese up and carry her far away to somewhere safe and start a life with her!

"I'm not afraid of Don Benetto," he uttered quietly.

With a sound of stone resolve she replied, "You should be." The next moment her arms were around his neck and her lips pressed to his in a frenzied, impassioned kiss. He responded in kind, with the hunger of a condemned man lapping up his last meal, even as he felt his heart breaking. The fever gave way to tenderness as he caressed her back and she stroked his cheek. When lungs demanded breath, they eased apart. "I do wish to thank you," she began. "Your attention and affection has made my life bearable. You have given me moments, memories, and feelings that I can draw upon, remember, and relive for the rest of my days. Many women never even have that. I do love you, Antonio. But Father will arrange my marriage to the man of his choosing. You should move on. Why, any young woman in Milan would be giddy to gain your eye! You have everything a woman desires in a man—a handsome face, a gentle touch, and a true heart. Be happy."

She started to turn away but Antonio caught her. "Agnese, because I love you too, I will do as you ask, except…" He waited for her eyes to return to his before continuing. "You are young, barely of an age to wed. It could be a year or two, perhaps three before your father makes his decision and much can occur in that time. So I will stay away, hard as that is for me, but I shall not give up on us, not yet. You are kind and generous. I have seen you pass coins to beggars when you thought no one was watching. I have even stayed behind at church to listen to you pray. You deserve so much better." He raised a hand to her face and wiped aside a stray tear with his thumb. "You deserve to be happy too." He lifted her fingers to his lips and kissed them tenderly before letting them slip from his grip. Then he lowered his head, so he didn't have to witness her pass through the back door of the shop and out of his life—at least for now.

CHAPTER 8

*A*fter two days of rain and drizzle the weather turned fair and sunny. Madelena had arranged a carriage to convey Florentina, the children, and herself to the monastery of Santa Maria delle Grazie to view the celebrated masterpiece of Leonardo da Vinci. Maddie enjoyed listening to Florentina whet the children's appetite with stories designed to heighten their anticipation of studying the painting. "So who can tell me the story of the Last Supper Jesus shared with his disciples?"

"That's when he poured the wine and broke the bread and why we have the Eucharist today," Matteo answered matter-of-factly. "Everyone knows that story."

"Do we really?" Florentina questioned in a sly, knowing manner. "Were you there?"

Betta and Matteo giggled. "Of course not," Betta replied, an infectious grin across her round face. Florentina flicked her eyes from the girl to her mother who sat beside her and Maddie returned her gaze, stifling a chuckle of her own. "That's silly," she continued. "It was a long time ago."

"Yes it was," their tutor agreed. "So we don't know everything that happened that night, only what the four Gospels record, and they didn't write down everything that was said, or where each person sat, or what clothes they were wearing. That is why the artist, Leonardo, had to use his imagination. When we get there, I want you to notice as much as you can about the painting. Play like it is a hidden objects puzzle and see what all you can find. Can you do that?"

They both nodded enthusiastically. Matteo, who sat beside Florentina, gripped the edge of his carriage seat as if he strained to hold himself still. Madelena draped an arm around her daughter to keep her from bouncing right off her cushion. *She truly has a way with my children,* she thought, her eyes on the dark haired beauty. She had decided that although she was not fashionable, she found Florentina to be quite beautiful indeed. Maybe it was not her look, she considered, but her manner, her mind, her aura. Something inexplicable drew her to the singular woman increasingly each day. It was as though a wave of some unseen substance washed over her whenever Florentina was near. She knew she shouldn't feel like this about an employee of the House, but it was beyond her control. All she could do was to refrain from acting on her feelings, for she could sooner dam up the Po than prevent their flow.

When they arrived at the monastery Madelena instructed the driver to wait for them, but that he could take a break as they would be a few hours. Then holding her children's hands, she followed Florentina through the main entrance. They spoke with one of the monks explaining the reason for their visit and he motioned them toward the refectory. "This way. It is in the dining hall, but there is already a young artist in there making a copy of the work, so please do not disturb him."

After entering through an arch, Madelena was immediately struck by the impending size of the painting that dominated the room, filling an entire thirty-foot wall. She had to stop momentarily to catch her breath and orient herself. She didn't even notice the artist until he spoke.

"Fiore!" exclaimed a gangly young man about Florentina's height. His long, flowing acorn hair was tied back from an amiable, blocky face lit by luminescent olive eyes. He appeared to be only a few years older than Florentina, although the errant facial hair that was trying to decide if it was a beard or not could have influenced that estimate.

"Cesare!" she exclaimed, an aspect of nostalgic affection flooding her features as she skipped across the room to where the painter had set up the tools of his trade. He met her halfway and lifted her off her feet, spinning her around laughing. Madelena was struck with mixed emotions. *Who was is man, and why is he so free with my tutor?*

By the time he set her down, Madelena and her progeny had crossed the room, now paying more attention to this upstart than the masterpiece on the wall. "Cesare, how have you been?"

"Good," he grinned and motioned to the canvas on his easel. "I've been commissioned to create an exact replica of the masterpiece. The powers that be decided that since I was Leonardo's student, I could do it justice."

"Oh, forgive me," Florentina flushed as she turned to Madelena. "This is Cesare da Sesto. We practically grew up together. Cesare, this is Donna Madelena Carcano of the House Torelli, and her children Matteo and Betta. I am currently their tutor and we are here to study the painting."

The eager young man bowed to Madelena. "I am pleased to meet you, Donna, children. There is much I can tell you about it, but no more than Florentina can. We both spent many days in this room playing, studying, and assisting Master Leonardo while he worked on it."

Madelena did want to learn about the great masterpiece, but at that moment she was far more focused on the exuberant artist whose hand still held Fiore's. "I am honored to meet a student of Master Leonardo's," she replied as Matteo and Betta wandered over to observe his collection of paints and brushes. "Don't touch anything," the mother in her absently instructed. Focus returned, she had to ask. "So, you and my Florentina seem to be quite close though she has failed to mention you. May I inquire, were you two perhaps young lovers at one time?"

Cesare burst into laughter letting go of Florentina's hand to wave that idea away. "Oh, goodness no! You could say we are like siblings, but lovers? No. She prefers women and I prefer men." Florentina kicked him in the shin, an embarrassed scowl darkening her face. "Ouch!" He lifted his sore leg and gave her a disbelieving stare. "What's that for? Was it a secret?"

Seething, she crossed her arms and uttered in a low voice, "Just consider everything I ever said to you a secret."

Relief and unbridled joy rushed through Madelena at the revelation that spilled from Cesare's lips. *So she does prefer women! I have a chance! This is so wonderful! I should close my mouth from gaping now and say something to reassure Florentina.* "You should not be self-conscious, Fiore," she stated calmly and took a step closer. "After all, we live in the modern age of Humanism, the revival of the ancient wisdom set down by the great Greek and Roman civilizations. They found nothing wrong with having a lover of the same sex; why should we?"

"But the Church—" Florentina began.

"Drivel!" Maddie exclaimed with a disapproving frown. "The Church has no moral authority to speak to such matters, not while we have a Pope who openly keeps a mistress and has fathered children with her despite his supposed vows of celibacy. The Church can mind its own business and keep its hypocritical nose out of ours."

Florentina's eyes met hers and Madelena registered the relief in them, but was it enough? No, she needed to offer more. "I tell you the truth, before I married my late husband I engaged in such an affair and it was quite exhilarating. People should be free to love whoever they wish, isn't that right Cesare?"

He grinned and raised his chin. "Indeed. Fiore, as always you only surround yourself with the best sort." Madelena watched Florentina's stance relax and noted a new smoky glint in her tawny eyes. Anticipation seared through her veins and she was suddenly very grateful to the lanky artist with the too long hair and scraggly chin whiskers for making a social blunder.

"I do try," Florentina answered him with a wry smile. "I suppose you will do as well. Now, enough of this personal blather. We are here to observe one of the greatest works of art known to man, past or present." She looked over her shoulder to the children who clearly were too busy poking and prodding art utensils to have even been aware of the awkward exchange. "Matteo, Betta, come stand here," she instructed, and they dutifully obeyed.

She put her hands on each child's shoulders and arranged them in turn to stand precisely in the center of the room, then motioned for Madelena to join her behind them. "What do you see?" she asked.

Betta's big eyes rounded. "It looks like we're in the room with them!" Madelena's curiosity sated, she could now appreciate the nuances of the painting and began to feel the awe it inspired.

"That's called perspective," Cesare explained. "Leonardo gave the painting depth so that it looks more three-dimensional than flat."

"Remember when he was setting it up?" Florentina asked him nostalgically. "He hammered a nail into the wall right there," she pointed, "to the spot where Jesus's right eye is depicted. He tied strings to the nail and ran them from there to where every other point in the painting would be–the table ends, floor lines, and edges of the columns. Then he drew lines and diagonals to create the illusion of depth in the room."

"That's what we artists call one point perspective," Cesare expounded. "That way everything in the picture converges on this one place, the vanishing point, which in this case is Jesus's face, or his right eye to be specific."

"The technique does draw my attention to the central figure of Christ," Madelena noted.

"I just think it looks really big," Betta said. "I can't even see it all at once!"

"Then look at the pieces individually," Florentina suggested.

"Why is the fresco's paint peeling off?" Madelena was suddenly alarmed as she noticed flakes and fading colors.

"Actually, it's not a fresco," Florentina corrected. "Leonardo was always experimenting. He said that art wasn't worth doing unless he could do something new."

Cesare added, "In a fresco the paint is mixed with the plaster and applied to a wet wall. The master experimented with an oil-tempura on a sealed dry plaster. His hope was to capture the appearance of an oil painting on the wall."

"Unfortunately, it didn't work so well," Florentina continued. "It took him a few years to complete the project and no sooner than it was done, paint began to flake away. But he always taught us that we learn as much from our failures and from our successes."

"I think it was more," Cesare gently amended. "If I remember it was that we learn more from our failures."

"The technique may have not worked, but everything else about this piece is certainly a success," Madelena observed. "See the expressions on each face?"

"Hey, there's six disciples on each side of Jesus," Matteo noted.

"Good," Florentina praised and patted his shoulder. "That's symmetry."

"Look," Betta pointed. "They are having dinner and the painting is in a dining room. Isn't that funny?" Madelena smiled and glanced at Florentina who was beaming down at her little girl.

"What food do you spot on the table?" Florentina asked.

"I see bread and fruit," began Matteo.

"And fish!" Betta exclaimed.

"That makes sense," Matteo announced. "Most of the disciples were fishermen."

"And Leonardo doesn't eat meat," Cesare added. "Maybe fish, but not meat like pork, lamb, or beef."

"He's a vegetarian?" Madelena asked in curiosity. Florentina nodded. "What is your take on that?"

"Leonardo is a very gentle soul. He doesn't approve of the raising and slaughtering of animals and would from time to time quote one of the Greek philosophers on the topic of a healthy diet. I cannot speak to the morality of killing livestock for food as I can't ascertain if they possess a soul or not. I suppose it would be prudent to err on the side of compassion, but I mostly abide by the teaching of Aristotle on the subject–all things in moderation."

Betta turned and looked up at her teacher. "What does that mean?"

Florentina smiled at her and laid a hand on her shoulder. "It means it may not be bad to eat some meat, cakes, and other rich food, but eating too much of those things would be bad for us. Like it's not harmful to drink a little wine, but if you drink too much, you become drunk and it makes you sick. Some sunshine is good for you, but too much burns your skin... things like that."

"Oh," she replied. "I understand."

"Look at that!" Matteo exclaimed. "That man spilled the salt."

Madelena raised smiling eyes to Florentina who returned the amused gaze before being overtaken by a new pink flush. Cesare answered the boy. "That is Judas tipping over the salt container. The moment the painting captures is that when Jesus announced that one of those at the table would betray him. Judas was nervous because he knew it was him, so he knocked over the salt. See, he is also holding a money bag with his thirty pieces of silver inside."

Matteo's studious face turned to an angry frown. "Judas was bad. It is wrong to betray your friends, especially Jesus." Then he spotted something else. "Hey, that man has a knife," he said pointing.

It was Florentina's turn to teach. "That is Peter, one of Jesus's closest friends. I think he feels the same way as you, Matteo. He's like, 'I won't let someone betray you, Jesus. Show me who it is and I'll stab him'."

"Did he?" Betta asked breathlessly.

"No," her mother answered with a smile. "Later he did try to protect Jesus and drew his sword, but Jesus told him to put it away and not to hurt anyone."

"Even the bad people?" Matteo asked. "Even the people who killed Papa?"

Madelena drew in a deep breath and looked to Florentina for help. She nodded and obliged. "Sometimes bad people break the law and then those in authority ensure they are punished. But in this particular case Jesus knew he had to die in order to save us from our sins, so he didn't want Peter to stop the bad people. Besides, Jesus knew he would rise from the dead so it wasn't like with your Papa. One day the bad people who hurt him will get caught and be punished, unless they change and become good."

Satisfied for the moment, Matteo turned his face back to the Last Supper. Then Betta pointed. "Is that one a girl?"

"That's the Apostle John," Cesare said. "He was the youngest, probably in his teen years, and didn't have a beard like the older men."

"The disciple that Jesus loved," Florentina added with a smile. "Although some people want to claim it is Mary Magdalene."

"Don't you remember?" Cesare asked her. "He stood there talking to himself for weeks about whether or not to include her in the painting."

"And did you ever hear him make a decision?" Florentina replied. "I think he painted an androgynous character so that the viewer could decide for himself who he thinks it is."

Cesare shook his head and made a dismissive expression. "It has to be John or there's an apostle missing. Besides, Mary was probably serving the meal."

"So, that is all you think women are good for, eh? Serving the meal?" Florentina winked at him and he elbowed her in the side. Madelena wished she could be on the same easy footing with her as Cesare was, but mayhap in time.

CHAPTER 9

*A*fter the children went to bed, Florentina found herself seated on a walnut carved settee complete with a rose velvet cushion in Madelena's private bedchamber. She suspected the request to come and view a Madonna and child painting by an unremarkable local artist was simply an excuse to be alone; excitement and apprehension vied for dominance within her breast as she speculated on what may be the real reason for the invitation.

She was still exhilarated from the perfectly wonderful day the four of them had enjoyed. After viewing the Last Supper, Maddie had taken everyone for lunch at a popular café with outdoor seating. It was a simple fare–minestrone soup and a green salad with sugared figs for dessert. Then the carriage drove them to the spacious Piazza del Duomo in the shadow of the majestic signature cathedral of Milan, its Gothic spires pointing Heavenward. There Madelena purchased a paper kite from a street vendor for the children to play with while Florentina sat with her on a bench near one of the piazza's fountains. They had each recounted tales from their youth and childhood getting to know each other better. Florentina was not surprised by how different their upbringing had been with the notable exception of both losing their mother at an early age. They laughed at stories of how their fathers had dealt with a young woman's arrival at puberty. Maddie had an older brother and Florentina had Cesare. The daughter of House Torelli had been raised under a strict regimen while for the inventor's child each day had been a new, often spontaneous adventure. The sun had sunk low in the sky and the evening's chill whipped through the air before they could bring themselves to take the carriage home.

Florentina made a polite comment about the painting without mentioning the partial nudity of the subject which was rather common at the time, and now she waited in a breathless state of vibration wondering just what would happen next. Madelena sat beside her on the cozy bench for two. "I can't recall when I have enjoyed a day quite as much as I have this one," she said in her dulcet voice. "You must have experienced many such exhilarating times."

Not daring to meet her eyes, Florentina replied, "None like today." She wasn't certain what Maddie was planning to do; she hoped for the moon, but was also just a little terrified. There was one thing, however, that she truly believed she should be privy to before anything further transpired between them. "Maddie," she began tentatively. "What did happen to your husband?" She sensed the atmosphere in the room dampen in an instant and almost wished she hadn't asked; but the Night Flyer needed to know.

Madelena folded her hands in her lap and expelled a breath. "I don't talk about it, but I think I should like to tell you. It's silly, I know, but I cannot recall anyone with whom I have felt more at ease or more stimulated. You make me feel alive, Fiore; you make me feel real. Vergilio was a good enough husband, but we were not close in the way I feel close to you. After all, his world was that of a man, the domain of business and mercantile. I was only his wife." She pivoted on the settee to face Florentina who looked on her with honest compassion.

"One evening he was late getting home. He had formed a partnership with my father upon our engagement and was in charge of the wool division; Ally's primary expertise is silk. Anyway, he had traveled to our pastures in the countryside to oversee the spring sheering and inspect the quality of the wool. It is only an hour's ride at a canter and he was an accomplished equestrian. That is how I recognized something was amiss. There are several spirited steeds in our stables, but he purposefully chose a docile gelding for the trip as it was for business."

Florentina detected the signs of distress in Maddie as she relived the event and reflexively reached over to take her hand. Madelena flicked appreciative eyes at her, took a breath, and continued. "It was well after dark and he still was not home, which was very unusual. Then there was pounding on the door and Iseppo opened it. I was worried so Ally and I rushed to see. Two men whom I had never met were holding Vergilio, who appeared to be unconscious, and dragged him inside. They laid him on a fainting couch, said they found him along the road thrown from his horse. Then they left, and I never saw them again. We didn't even catch their names. Ally sent for a physician, but…" she lowered her gaze to their intertwined fingers. "He was already dead. I think he was dead when they brought him in."

"Maddie, I am so sorry that you had to experience that," Florentina comforted. "It must have been awful to see your husband like that. I know it was to watch my father die."

Madelena raised dew-moistened forest leaf eyes to her in a moment of solidarity. "But I am convinced he didn't simply fall from his horse," she declared with vigor. "He was a damned good rider on a gentle mount in fair weather. I even traveled out to the sheep pasture, and they said he never arrived–gone all day and he never even got there! The whole episode was bizarre. I tell you the truth, Fiore, someone killed him. Naturally I suspect Don Benetto, but I can't prove it." Her voice trailed off, and she lowered her head.

"But why would Viscardi want to kill your husband?" Florentina asked gently.

Madelena sighed. "Who knows? Because he's a mean rat's bastard, Vergilio looked at him wrong or some other perceived slight, he's petty and jealous, it was a Tuesday." At that her voice cracked, and she lifted one hand to push her hair aside. She had removed pins and ribbons and untwined the braids leaving a flow of flaming silk to drape her shoulders. Florentina gave the hand she held a little squeeze and stroked her other across Maddie's back in solace. "Truly though, Vergilio was too outspoken on his political views, which were in direct opposition to the Viscardi's."

"Oh?"

"You see, my husband was a stanch supporter of the Sforzas. It made sense," she explained. "The Sforza family dukes did much to bring our city-state to prominence. Their policies stimulated the economy, they patroned the arts, they commissioned grand architectural and engineering projects." Then she turned her eyes to Florentina's. "They brought Leonardo da Vinci to Milan. But then larger neighboring nations wanted to lay claim to Lombardy, and Benetto saw gold. He shifted his support to the French king, knowing that wars fought over our land would send coins streaming into an arms dealer's coffers. It did pay off for him politically when the French King Louis defeated Ludovico il Moro and he was sent into exile. Vergilio never liked that foreigners rule our Duchy instead of Milanese and said so publicly far too often. I suppose the French could have had him killed to silence his rebellious speech. But you suspect Benetto murdered your father?"

"I know he did," Florentina affirmed. "He told me as much just before... No one would believe a grieving daughter who surely was mistaken. The physician wrote that his heart gave out as there were no signs of injury to the body, but Viscardi poisoned him and that is a fact; it is also a fact that no judge will ever hold him to account for it, or anything else he may have done."

In the next instant Maddie placed a caressing hand to her face, leaned in, and kissed her. Although she had been anticipating this very possibility for hours, it came on her as swift and unforeseen as a summer storm. The sensual heat of those urgent lips melded to hers ignited something deep within Florentina's core that sprung to life for the very first time and exploded throughout her being, a sensation so phenomenal, so novel that she had no context in which to place it. Breathless, her mind went totally blank, and she simply savored the moment.

When Madelena withdrew she whispered, "I'm sorry, I didn't mean to overstep."

"Sorry?" Florentina's heart sank and her head spun. *How could she be sorry?* "Why? I'm not."

"You're not?" Maybe Maddie was as uncertain as she, as overcome with raw emotion and not knowing how to express it. "It's just that–and I have contemplated this–with me being your employer and all, I don't want you to expect you must do something you aren't comfortable with. I would never pressure you–"

It was Florentina's turn to be impulsive. She silenced Maddie by repeating the gesture, tasting again those full, cherry lips that flooded her mind, body, and soul with sensations. When it broke, they gazed into each other's eyes looking for confirmation. "I understand I am only a servant in your household."

"Don't say that!" Maddie replied firmly. "That is not how I view you. Please, Fiore. How can I explain?"

The earlier butterflies began to settle in Florentina's stomach and the fog of trepidation evaporate. She could perceive that the beautiful wealthy widow *did* regard her with esteem, *did* have feelings for her. This was not a mere dalliance she realized. "I care for you also," she spoke softly and stroked Maddie's luxurious strands. "Do not think you press me to do something I have not wanted to do since the moment I first saw you."

Relief engulfed Madelena's expression, and she brushed her cheek to Florentina's then nuzzled her neck with moist, eager lips. A euphoric sigh escaped Fiore's mouth at the intimate touch and she pulled Maddie closer. When their lips found each other's again she opened to the honey-sweet tongue that was impatient to delve into it. Without willing them to do so, she realized her fingers were wound in those silky red strands while her other hand slid down Madelena's back as far as the bench would allow. She could perceive her heartbeat against her own heated breast. This is what she had dreamt of and it surpassed her expectations. All she wanted to do was touch, caress, explore, and please this singular woman. Even as she was rendered breathless from the physical passion, her heart was telling her head that what she felt was far more, endlessly deeper. It was a very dangerous cavern, a bottomless pit that could spell her doom; she was falling in love.

* * *

Madelena realized she was making a mistake. She had acquired a good tutor for her children and a new friend to share meaningful experiences with, but a romantic affair? Where could that possibly lead? What would her brother think or do when he found out, and she knew he would, eventually. Hadn't she lived a well-disciplined life? Could she not control her desires for more than a few weeks?

As her mind was blaring at her all the reasons to say no, her heart had been pleading an opposing case. Yes, she had found a teacher and a friend, but in Florentina she had discovered abundantly more. She was interesting, witty, talented, intuitive, and compassionate. She opened whole new worlds to the widow whose entire education was meant only to prepare her to be a merchant's wife. For the past six months she had felt lost, as if she had no place and no purpose. She had helped Alessandro with the bookkeeping and personal relations with customers, but she had also spent her nights alone speculating on what the future may hold for her. She still could not answer that question, but she had spoken honestly when she said that Fiore made her feel real and alive. Since growing closer to the dark-haired inventor's daughter she had begun to experience so many things. And today–today had likely been the best day of her twenty-eight years on this earth! Then the emotion of sharing her story, it was just all too much to expect her to maintain self-control. But now that she had initiated this passionate encounter, what would she do next?

Presently, she drew back from those sultry lips trying to regain some restraint. "Have you ever been with a woman before?" she asked to fill the silence.

Florentina shook her head. "If you mean sexually, I am quite inexperienced with anyone, male or female. Years ago when Cesare told me he was attracted to men, I mentioned that I was more drawn to women. I didn't think he'd ever say anything; it's not like we talked about it much, but now," she paused casting starry eyes at Maddie, "I'm glad he did."

She smiled and stroked Florentina's cheek. "So am I."

"I know you have experience," she noted. "So, what do we do next?"

What indeed! Madelena considered. "Take one step at a time. May I suggest we try to get some sleep and take a night to process it all? I'm feeling a bit overwhelmed at the moment."

"You're overwhelmed?" Fiore laughed. "I'm not certain my legs will carry me upstairs!"

Maddie hesitated to move, as the tug of an invisible cord was drawing her back to her newfound treasure. Neither was Florentina moving away. *One more kiss and you must move. Give both of us time to think.* She touched her lips to Fiore's and closed her eyes. *What makes one kiss a sloppy flop and another a driving, sensuous pleasure? Is it one's mental perception or a physical current that connects two individuals who are similarly charged? I can feel the energy pass between her and I unlike any other before.*

"I shall see you in the morning." She released Florentina and pushed herself to her feet with a sheer force of will. Florentina followed saying her good-nights and Madelena closed the bedroom door behind her as she left. Alone once more, she glanced around her empty chamber and wished her lover could have stayed all night.

CHAPTER 10

*A*fter a long restless night, Madelena made a decision; embarking down a path of passion with a member of the staff was a categorical mistake. Despite how she felt about Fiore–particularly *because* of her feelings for the remarkable woman–she could not entangle them both in an affair with the potential to ruin everything. Florentina had become the single greatest asset to their household and she would not engage in behavior that may cause them to lose her. The best solution was to find her at once to discuss the matter. Maddie encouraged herself with the notion that one as intelligent as Florentina was likely to reach the same conclusion herself.

Madelena dressed quickly and struck out upstairs to catch her before she ventured out of her room. Being a Saturday with no lessons for the children, Florentina was free to go anywhere. She first knocked on the door, then turning the knob found it open. She peeked inside and frowned at the empty, made bed. A sleepy Angela looked across to her mistress. "Did you require something, Donna?" she asked groggily and started to push back her covers.

"No, it is early yet. Where is Florentina?"

Angela blinked. "I don't know."

"Very well. There's no rush, Angela. Just follow your regular weekend schedule." Madelena closed the door and wore a frustrated expression while descending the stairs. She had resumed her formal air of aloof power by the time she reached the front hall in search of the head butler. He would know where she was.

Upon spotting him she called, "Iseppo?"

He turned, took a few steps toward her, and stood at attention, hands clasped behind his back. "Yes, Donna Madelena; what can I do for you?"

"Where is Florentina?" The demand that cut through in her tone was sharper than indented.

"Your children's teacher exited the residence at dawn with a large shoulder bag. She said there were tools and materials she had to hunt down and purchase to repair one of the silk looms that is malfunctioning at our production house. She informed me that between the shopping and repair work she may well be away all day." His speech was monotone, void of any emotion or concern in the matter.

Maddie sighed. "Grazie. That is all I needed to know."

"Today is Saturday," he noted. "My schedule shows that yours and Donna Portia's ladies circle will be gathering here for brunch at 11:00. Shall I be expecting their arrival?"

"Yes. I will coordinate with Portia and Bianca for the menu." *I completely forgot about the ladies meeting. I suppose I'll have to wait until evening to discuss this matter with Fiore.* She departed toward the kitchen in search of the cook.

* * *

FLORENTINA WAS DISCOVERING that keeping up with the Night Flyer's activities while living in a dwelling filled with other individuals was not an easy task; neither was planning a daytime strike, but this was her best opportunity to land a substantial blow. According to the calendar she had studied during her midnight break in at Viscardi's warehouse, this day his people would be returning home from a major delivery of weapons with full coin bags from the sale. Fortunately, the tools and materials required to make the simple repair to the loom were already in a box at the production house; the workers there had no clue what was needed so she could buy plenty of time with an unnecessary "shopping" trip.

There were pitfalls, however. She would have to leave town in her everyday clothes, walk a good distance along the appropriate road without drawing suspicion being a woman walking out of the city alone. Then she would have to disappear from the highway into the woods to change into her black costume, venture through the trees and underbrush parallel to the main road until she spied Viscardi's wagons and undoubtedly doubled guard returning. Most difficult of all would be making the strike to extract the money during daylight hours and getting away without injury. This had required the most precise planning. Once she had the coin box, which would be quite hefty, she would need repeat the process. She had selected a charity house near the edge of town to drop off the box so she wouldn't have to carry it any farther than necessary.

Every colorful leaf, every bird's song, every puff and swirl of cloud made her joyful heart sing! She had scarcely slept for replaying last evening's words and sensations over and over again. Maddie was beautiful, but she was so much more—a caring mother, a progressive woman, a tough exterior with a tender heart. But to keep Don Alessandro's sister safe, she must never discover the identity of the avenging bandit out to destroy House Viscardi. If they start spending more time at night together, that might become a very difficult balancing act indeed.

* * *

MADELENA and her sister-in-law Portia greeted their guests as they arrived. Their circle of youngish upper-crust, non-noble ladies had been meeting weekly for years alternating between the members' homes or a local café as a venue. Viewed as society's second tier, they played an important economic role in the city as well as carrying influence with their husbands, but mostly they just wanted an opportunity to socialize with their peers. The group included four other women between twenty-five and forty years of age, all merchants' wives. Julia Sacchi was the much younger second wife of guild leader Giovanni Sacchi. She paraded in led by her immense breasts that threatened to burst forth from her gold and white gown at any moment. Next was Isabella della Gazzada, a plump woman who waddled through the threshold with a hand fluffing her light brown updo. Then Tomasina Luino strode into the ladies' parlor as tall as a tree and thin as a twig, her curly dark hair elaborately braided about her head. The last to arrive was the moon-lit blonde Rose Bombello who glided into their midst with the temperament of a fawn.

The petite Portia started off the conversation by standing in the center of the room and swirling about in her new wine colored silk and velvet dress. "What do you think of master fashion designer Rocco Astolfi's latest masterpiece?" Her presentation was met with a flurry of "oohs" and "aahs". "Isn't it the pinnacle?"

"Fabulous, Portia dearest," agreed Julia whose face shone as if she had just seen God. "That color would be perfect for my new set of jewels, don't you think?" She brushed a delicate hand below her neck to draw all eyes to the dazzling colorful rocks dangling from a gold chain above her ample bosom.

"And look at Rose's exquisite hair style," Portia said directing attention toward the shy woman. "How ever did you achieve so light a shade? Why there's barely a hint of color at all!"

Isabella piped up, "I had a fitting with Rocco yesterday and he said my new gown will be ready before All Saints' Day. It is similar to yours, Portia, but two-toned with a cut he said would accentuate my particular figure."

"I'm sure it will be absolutely stunning!" predicted the towering Tomasina. Then she thrust out a hand baring a sparkling diamond. "Look what my husband picked up for me while he was in Venice." More "oohs" and "aahs".

At last, quiet Rose spoke. "What about you, Madelena?"

She didn't have any new clothes or jewelry and had only recently given up wearing black. But she did have something fresh to relay to her friends. "I went to the monastery of Santa Maria delle Grazie with my children and their new tutor to view the painting of the Last Supper. We met a young student of Master Leonardo's who was making a copy. It was quite exhilarating."

"Leonardo," Julia mused scrunching up her brow to think. "Isn't he that eccentric fellow from Vinci with the wild, scraggly beard who was Ludovico Sforza's pet artist?"

Tomasina added with a wave of her long-fingered hand, "My governess takes my children on outings so I don't have to."

"I heard that painting is a disaster," Isabella stated shaking her head. "Peeling off the wall like bark off a tree."

"Ludovico Sforza had some sense of style," Portia noted, "but Giovanni is the dreamiest man in the family."

"Dreamy doesn't even begin to describe him!" gushed Rose. Tomasina began to giggle, a high pitched sound akin to clinking a spoon on glass.

They continued to talk incessantly about men's good looks, clothes, and gossip–who was doing what with whom, all to the tune of Tomasina's tickling laugh. *Drivel*, Maddie thought. She felt as if she was fading from the room, an act of self-preservation. She tuned out all their meaningless words and initiated a deep self-examination. *It's nothing but drivel. Was this me? Has this been my life?* She could recall when the routine lunch with this circle of women had been the highlight of her week, a chance to get out of the house and socialize with others of her age and station. But now she perceived the gathering as a foolish waste of time and energy. Were these other merchants' wives even true friends? Could she confide in them? Certainly not. Were they interested in her life, her children? No, that much was clear. Her sister-in-law frequently played the role of friend, but her interests centered on fashion and social events. She didn't want to appear rude, but Madelena had to take a step back with her head throbbing as if it might explode at any moment.

The day the intriguing, dusky intellectual walked through their front door, her world began to change. Maybe that transformation had already started. Dealing with the death of a spouse at a young age may have given her a more serious mind, and unlike many of the upper-class, she took a hands-on interest in raising her precious children. She had intelligence, and she yearned to use it, not just go through the paces of a meaningless existence seeking nothing more than comfort and finery. She wanted to learn, to feel, to experience life at its fullest, and until now she had only stepped her toe in the water. In that moment she longed to dive in and swim!

Florentina and I discuss art, music, philosophy, and religion. She listens attentively when I speak, and with genuine interest. She has given my life meaning, brought me out of this prattle and opened my mind to countless more important topics. How could I possibly consider turning back our relationship? I wish to spend a lifetime with her! I have fulfilled my duty to family and society; I was married and have borne children. Now I should be able to live the life I want. Many a well-to-do widow has remained so quite successfully, continuing to run their late husband's business affairs. In these modern times marriage is not a requirement, and a second marriage even less so. I can do it! I could continue to assist Ally with the business, raise my children, and keep Florentina as a legitimate member of the household. When Matteo starts at the Studium Generale and Betta at girls' school, we will still need her to fill other roles. It may work; I will make it work!

CHAPTER 11

*D*ressed completely in black, coif and mask in place, the Night Flyer sprinted through the cover of trees along the westward road from Milan to the Duchy of Savoy. It was a number of miles to the bridge over the Ticino River, a tributary of the Po. That was too far a distance to travel on foot and the span was in clear ground, not a suitable site for an ambush. She would need a remote and wooded area; Florentina remembered such a spot. Much of the land near the city was open grazing pastures or farming fields and she had been obliged to walk that portion of the route in her skirts toting her oversized bag, but now she was safe in the forest's protection.

Florentina came to a bend in the road as it followed the landscape with dense old-growth trees lining both sides. Listening and hearing none approach, she laid her trap, hoping no other caravans would arrive first. She spotted the fallen branch of an ash tree that was too thick to run a wagon over and decided it would create a good barrier to cause them to stop. She took out her grappling hook and length of rope with gloved hands and draped it around the chest-high limb of a poplar on the other side of the road, then wedged the alloyed hook into a fork of the large ash log. Wrapping the free end of the rope around her back, she stepped backwards across the road toward the timber she was hauling. The make-shift pulley system allowed her to drag an object much too heavy for her to have moved otherwise. Soon the barricade was in place.

Next she chose a gnarled live oak with huge low-hanging branches and climbed onto one overhanging the trail. She checked her supplies and rehearsed the plan in her mind again. Speed was essential as she possessed no ability to engage a troop in broad daylight. After an hour's wait she heard the clomp of hooves and the rattle of wagon wheels. Then came the sound of voices as several of the guards conversed as they rode. Her heart raced, and she felt a trickle of sweat roll down her back but her hands were steady.

Crouching on the branch and obscured by its year-round foliage, she studied the approaching band. *There it is, Viscardi's House symbol; this is it!* Peering intently, she counted four men on horseback, two in each of three empty wagons, and a coach driver of a covered carriage. *There'll be a few more inside and that is where the gold will be,* she deduced. *Between twelve and fourteen men.*

"Wait," called one of the horsemen in the lead. "We'll need to stop and move this log for the wagons to get by." She hovered above the last of the three carts but the coach she needed to infiltrate was still several yards behind. She determined not to chide herself; who could calculate the exact span the caravan would make, especially since she had not known the number of wagons? She could work around that distance. "Joseph, Teodor, get your lazy asses out of those saddles and come help me," the guard demanded.

All four riders were now on foot trudging toward the log in the road; it was time. Using a sulfur match, the Night Flyer lit a croquet ball sized smoke bomb and tossed it at the group of guards. Immediately she lit a string of firecrackers that was wound about one of her bolts and fired it into the forest across from her. She did not use her unique invention of the rapid-fire crossbow this time, as the bolts had to be loaded into chambers, but instead utilized a smaller version of a traditional crossbow that could be operated with one hand. The pops sounded at a distance in quick succession.

"He has an arabesque!" shouted the driver of one of the wagons. All attention was focused in the direction of the "shots."

"There must be more than one," called another. "I count five reports." The hired soldiers crouched in the smoke and readied their weapons. That is when Florentina saw Stefano lean out of the carriage window.

"You sardin' cowards!" Stefano bellowed. "Get that wind-fucker!"

She shot off a second array of firecrackers just beyond the front of the caravan. "Over here," called another. Everyone save those in Stefano's coach were running about through the smoke in disarray, shouting and firing their weapons into the forest when she swung from the branch by her grappling rope onto the top of the carriage and tossed a glass bottle through the window. It shattered on the hard floor and a chemical vapor bloomed in their midst that set the men inside coughing and squeezing, their stinging eyes shut. She whacked the driver on the head and he slumped in his seat. The Night Flyer dropped in beside him and pushed his limp body to the ground while behind her Stefano and his companions stumbled out of the cab onto their hands and knees gagging and gasping for air.

Florentina turned the team of horses away from the soldiers, smoke, and chaos and popped the reins calling for a gallop. She didn't travel long in the opposite direction, but far sufficient to have time to collect the money box, free one horse from the carriage tongue, and trot off with the spoils into the woods. She only kept the horse long enough to circle around and pass parallel to the road to the spot she had left her bag and other clothes. In the distance she could hear men's shouts, the discharge of gunpowder, and Stefano's furious roar of curses. Sliding from the lathered draft gelding, she pointed him back toward his troop and slapped his rear. Then she lay down in the thicket, her lungs burning and blood pumping until she could catch her breath and be certain they wouldn't find her.

* * *

Two hours later the deflated Viscardi party passed her on the road into Milan. Florentina kept her face ahead, totally disinterested in the wagons and guards with glum expressions and slumped shoulders. She pretended the leather bag hanging from a wide strap across her shoulder was not overburdened with heavy coins as she stood erect ambling along at a leisurely pace. She was simply a traveler with her overnight bag walking from some villa in the countryside to the city, mayhap to celebrate mass in the Duomo on the morrow. They paid her no more attention than they would an insect. Once through the western gate she sought out the charity house, withdrew sack after sack of coins, placed them on the doorstep shaded by the arched entry portico, and knocked. No sooner than she heard the sister start to undo the latch, she turned and scurried away to the sound of a surprised gasp and a shout of "Praise Jesus!" She smiled to herself as once around the corner she slowed her gait. It felt good to give Viscardi's hoard to a worthy cause. She knew there were unfortunates whose lives had not been as secure and comfortable as hers had been, those plagued with poor health or injuries from war, children with no parents and elders with no sons to care for them. *They need this gold far more than Benetto,* she thought as she strolled on a cushion of air toward House Torelli's district of town.

Florentina strode into the textile production house and set her significantly lighter bag near the loom needing repair. As it was already late afternoon, only a few members of the cleaning crew were present in the large, open facility where weavers would sit at their looms crafting fabric from the raw silk which arrived on Torelli ships from the Orient. With the swift and effortless ease of a hungry friar saying Grace, the equipment was repaired and in proper working order. Just to be effectual, she checked over each of the other looms, seeking any worn parts or loose wheels that may need attention. *I am part of House Torelli now,* she figured, *so it's like these are my machines too. I will take excellent care of them for Don Alessandro.* Upon determining all was well for the evening, Florentina positioned her bag filled with secret treasures over her shoulder and glided out humming a merry tune to herself. It had been a good day!

* * *

THE SUN HAD SUNK below the rooftops and its fading glow mingled with rising moonlight in the dusk sky when Florentina passed through the servant's entrance to House Torelli. Madelena had been pacing the floor, nervously wondering what had been keeping her. "There you are!" she declared and had to purpose her feet not to run to Fiore. "Where ever have you been? What took you so long?"

Florentina met her with a puzzled expression. "I was busy at the production house repairing equipment for Alessandro," she replied in an innocent tone.

Maddie let out a frustrated sigh. "All day?" she questioned and cocked her head to one side trying to determine if she was telling the truth. *What are you suspicious of?* she asked herself. *What else would she be doing?*

"I am sorry," Florentina answered. "Was there something I was needed for here? I don't recall-"

Madelena shook her head. "No, but it's so late. Have you even eaten today?"

Realization lit in Florentina's eyes and she let out a little laugh. "No, I suppose I haven't. I was really busy and forgot."

A smile of relief crept across Madelena's lips and her expression softened. "Let's see what is in the kitchen, shall we? Dinner is over but I am certain Bianca will have something."

"Maddie," Florentina said in a hush as she placed a hand on her arm. "Do you often go into the kitchen to eat with the help?"

Madelena flushed and her mouth dropped open. "I didn't even think," she began. "I just want to be sure you are taken care of, and I have been waiting to talk to you all day." She kept her voice low as well, scanning the hall for anyone who may walk by.

Fiore smiled at her, a warm, knowing grin with eyes as bright as stars. "Where shall I meet you later?"

Joy washed over Maddie from her head to her toes and sloshed around within her as though she was a vessel created specifically to house the emotion. She met Fiore's smile with one of her own. "I would like that very much. I can secure the door to the ladies' parlor from inside and no one will be using that room tonight."

Florentina slid her hand down Maddie's arm, gave her hand a quick squeeze, and nodded with a wink. "I'll be there shortly."

Just then two rambunctious youngsters burst down the hall. "I'm going to catch you and eat you up! Grrrrr!" sounded a little boy's voice followed by a giddy squeal in a higher pitch.

"Florentina!" exclaimed Betta as she skidded to a halt. "Matteo is a bear, and he wants to eat me!"

Seeing his mother and tutor standing in the hall, Matteo slowed his pace, lowered his arms and stood up straight. "We were just playing," he explained.

"We didn't break anything," Betta added batting impossibly blue eyes up at the adults.

"Very well," Maddie said, "but it is time to prepare for bed now. Have you had your baths? Where is Livia?"

"She said Luca hurt himself and she had to make it better, but that she would get us to the bath when she was done," Matteo explained, oblivious to any untoward implications.

Madelena and Florentina exchanged a knowing glance and Maddie shuffled them off. "Why don't I help you with your baths tonight? I do believe the two of you are getting too big for a governess, anyway." At that compliment the children beamed up at her filled with pride.

Maddie turned her head over her shoulder and mouthed to Florentina, "One hour."

* * *

FLORENTINA WAS RELIEVED that she would have a chance to put away her Night Flyer disguise and gear before anyone questioned the contents of her bag. She considered that could be a problem should someone demand to search her. And what of coming home late in the evening in her costume if Maddie was awake waiting up for her? It would be quite the balancing act to achieve but she felt it was worth the risk to develop her new budding relationship.

* * *

MADELENA OPENED the door to the ladies' parlor to find Florentina seated on a carved walnut Savonarola style loveseat fitted with a spring green cushion. There was a twin love seat across from it and flanking each were three matching chairs arranged symmetrically of either side of a neat fire-place. Between each loveseat and its armchairs was positioned a small round table for setting tea cups or other items. Tonight they each displayed vases of flowers that had been set out for the occasion of the ladies' brunch. A finely woven decorative rug spanned the center of the pinewood floor. The seating ensemble comprised all the furnishings in the room. Their style was light and delicate to appeal to feminine tastes, each piece a work of art bearing architectonic elements from the Classical World such as columns, pediments, and cornices. Coordinating drapes hung around windows that looked out to the central courtyard. Often the entertaining would take place out doors in the temperate peninsular clime, therefore more quality and less quantity was the rule for interior furnishings.

Aside from the seats and small tables, the parlor was fitted with an overhead chandelier, currently not lit, and several wall sconces, of which only one bore a flame casting the room in a muted amber and green hue. Classical paintings framed in gold leaf matching the light fixtures hung along the wall opposite the windows. The air was cool as no fire glowed in the hearth, but Maddie was warmed by the fire that blazed in her own heart.

Madelena closed the door behind her, turned the latch, and stood for a moment gazing at Florentina bathed in pale incandescence, anticipation blossoming within her. Leisurely she sashayed across the room. Florentina, whose eyes were fixed on hers, spoke first. "Alone at last," came the husky phrase. "I did not mean you any distress by my absence."

"You are here now," Maddie replied and settled down beside her. She caressed Fiore's face and touched generous lips to hers. She could feel the ardent response from her partner and laid her other hand on Florentina's thigh. "About last night." Although she had practiced a dozen versions of what she wished to say, none seemed perfect in this moment.

"I enjoyed it," Florentina replied with a note of apprehension in her voice.

"As did I," Maddie assured her. "But there is one concern I have." She steadied herself and gazed seriously into Florentina's eyes. "You are the single most important asset to this household and the children love you; I simply cannot afford to lose you, Fiore, and if this were to not work out, if something went wrong or feelings changed..."

Florentina's hand closed over hers. "I have dedicated myself to House Torelli, and no matter what comes of our relationship, I will not abandon Matteo and Betta, nor Alessandro. The only thing that would ever cause me to leave is if you ordered me to do so. Maddie, I do have feelings for you along with a hopeless attraction, but if our romance should fade or something come between us, I would do whatever is required to remain faithful to this House and your family, even if you were to toss me aside for another. I am not a young school girl who would run home to her mother. Truly, I have nowhere else to go."

Madelena breathed a sigh of relief. "Good, thank you. I certainly have no intentions toward another, it's just that who knows what unforeseen circumstances may lurk around the corner? You have brought breath back into my lungs, opened my eyes to worlds I wish to explore. Now that I have found you, I cannot imagine ever returning to how my life was before. You inspire me."

Florentina blushed, a pleased smile broadening across her face. "You inspire *me*," she echoed lustily, "in more ways than one." Maddie knew the gleam she saw in those tawny eyes. They moved in tandem, lips parting as they pressed together. She wrapped her arms around Florentina and held on as one clinging to a small boat without a rudder being plunged down river rapids. Where ever this ride was going to take her, she would bask in the glory of the adventure!

CHAPTER 12

Several blocks away situated between Casa de Torelli and Casa de Viscardi lay another wealthy merchant's domicile. Casa de Sacchi was equivalent in size and grandeur to the other Great Houses as only the absence of an inherited head-start placed him third in line. Their fine estate encompassed a Roman style central courtyard also, as was common in Milanese mansions and palaces. Julia sat in front of a mirror at her dressing table wearing her a chemise and petticoats carefully applying her various powders and enhancements before the family went to Mass.

Madelena has been different since her husband died; in truth, she considered, *should it matter all that much? Her brother holds the riches and power, not that unfortunate Vergilio.* She blotted white powder over her not quite alabaster enough face. *But she was acting odder than usual yesterday. I must discover her secret.*

Julia was not the featherhead she presented to the world; in fact, she successfully ran her own private enterprise in the information business. She loved nothing more than to collect juicy tidbits of gossip-worthy news on those in society and proceed to charge a fee to keep them to herself. She was so crafty an extortionist that her friends–at least those who were not on her list–had no idea what she was about, and that clueless husband of hers? Please! It wasn't that she needed the money; she enjoyed the power.

As she was applying the last bit of her eye make-up, Giovanni entered their master suite. "I will be unable to accompany you to the cathedral this morning," he announced as he strode in. "I have an important consultation in Venice and am obliged embark straight away."

"Oh," she said pushing out her bottom lip into a pout. "You can't leave later?"

"No, Dear. I just received word that our planned meeting has been moved up and it is vital that I don't miss it, so must go now. You can manage a few days without me." He stepped up behind her and placed a kiss to the top of her head.

Julia stood up and spun to him with a gleam lighting her face. "While you are there, will you buy something for me?"

He let out a slight laugh and replied, "Certainly."

"I was looking in a magazine and there is a lovely little seaside villa for sale in Genoa that we simply must own! Summers are too hot and sticky in the city and the article says the seaside is cool and refreshing. Oh, it is darling; you will simply love to take our summers there!" She beamed into his lined face.

"Julia, I am traveling to Venice; that's the opposite direction from Genoa. I won't be shopping for any villas on this trip," he answered humorously.

The pout returned to her lips, and she thrust her bulging breasts toward him. "Isn't Venice by a seashore? Couldn't you buy me a villa there?"

He laughed shaking his head and placed a light kiss on her lips–the only part of her face not caked with powder. "We'll see. Now, behave while I'm away and try not to spend all our money. Pietro will accompany you to Mass in my absence."

Pietro, Julia mused to herself dreamily. *How I would love to get my hands on that body! He is the pinnacle! Strong, handsome, rugged. How a man that spectacular came from frumpy bespectacled Giovanni I have no idea. And I've seen him look at me, oh yes he has, but... I do not find it worth the risk. If Giovanni were to find out about us, I'm sure I would be the one to meet with an unfortunate accident like Vergilio did. I wonder if that's what happened? Madelena caught him in adultery and had him killed?* She shook off the notion. *If every wife took such action there would be no husbands left.*

* * *

Don Benetto hadn't slept all night. He wasn't going to Mass this morning, why should he? To see and be seen? That was over. God wasn't protecting him so why should he waste his time. Daniella tried to get him to eat, but he waved her away. When he saw Stefano venture into the main hall, he called to him. "Stefano, in my office, now."

"Should I call for Zuane?" his brother asked. "He was there too."

"No," Benetto growled. "I don't trust anyone at this point."

Once inside the study with the door locked, Benetto took a seat at his desk and motioned to a nearby chair. "So tell me again," he began, biting back his temper. "How many were there?"

Stefano sighed. "I'm not sure; no one actually saw anyone except that character in black who drove off with the carriage. But there must have been more of them because of all the shots fired."

Benetto rubbed his chin and furrowed his brows. "Did the bandit do any flying this time?"

"No," Stefano answered firmly. "I can't even be sure it was the same thief as before. Maybe the whole gang wears masks."

"And you say he used a chemical, some sort of choking gas on you?"

"Yes, it was the most afraid I have ever been, Benetto." Stefano leaned forward with an elbow on his knee. "I couldn't fight it, couldn't breathe, couldn't see. Do you know how helpless I felt? Me?" he questioned motioning to his broad chest and muscled biceps. "I can pick people up and throw them, bash heads together, wrestle a bull, but against this potion," he shook his head in shame. "I'm sorry if I let you down. I know it was a large sum that was taken, but honestly, that gas knocked me out."

"Potions, flying bandits, invisible cannons, arabesques firing with no shooters," Benetto mused thoughtfully. "We are not dealing with any ordinary criminals here."

"Exactly!" Stefano returned to leaning back in his chair and rubbed a hand over his close-cropped dark hair.

"I ran across some interesting reading material," Benetto said placing his hand on a plain leather-bound volume. "A diary with notes about a secret society operating an underground enterprise. At first I thought it fantasy, but now I am not so certain. It's all mysterious and full of symbols and suspicions, no hard evidence, no names or places or other real facts, only what sounds like the ravings of a madman. It speaks of a horse and a dark specter. Could this Night Flyer be that dark specter? I want us to study this matter quietly, Stefano, not a word to anyone–even

Zuane. We don't know who may be a spy. It might be nonsense, but if such an underground organization exists, it would be extremely powerful and dangerous. Who is the most powerful, dangerous man you know?"

Stefano considered, then answered, "You are."

"Precisely," Benetto quantified, "and yet I was not invited into their number." He looked at his brother with the first hit of fear in his eyes. "That speaks volumes."

* * *

SUNDAY NIGHT WAS a quiet in Milan. Businesses were closed, families returned to their homes from Mass, and most people enjoying a relaxing evening at home playing cards or music, reading books or telling stories. The streets were empty - a perfect time for the Night Flyer.

Her black silhouette faded into shadows as Florentina made her way stealthily toward the Viscardi warehouses. She ventured that he would not expect another strike so soon. She hadn't planned a large heist for this evening, merely a mayhem mission to destroy his books and records. But as she slinked through the back alleys of Milan, she observed misery and want that in her world of academia and middle-class comfort were only ghosts of the past. She stepped over a man lying drunk in the street, the odor of alcohol so strong as to almost topple her over with him. She saw a young woman in a ragged dress, barely out of puberty, beckon to her, then an older woman with stringy hair and sores around her lips push in front of her and smile invitingly revealing a missing tooth. "Looking for a good time?" she called.

Florentina swallowed the revulsion that rose from her gut and kept moving. *These poor people!* she thought even as feelings of sympathy swirled in her heart. *But it is their own fault they live like this, isn't it? They could do better if they applied themselves, couldn't they?* She lowered her head and jogged on.

The next block was no better. An old woman coughing from consumption wrapped in a blanket rocked herself as she sat on a rickety barrel in the alleyway. She held a rag to her mouth as another series of coughs seized her. Florentina's feet slowed without her even thinking about it. "You shouldn't be out in the damp night air," she said to the hunched figure. She hadn't thought about how the Night Flyer should sound, as she had never intended him to speak, but she was inspired to form a deep voice, ambiguous to gender, and flavored it with a Venetian accent.

Sunken eyes stared up at her masked face. "I haven't anything for you to steal," came the scratchy, dry voice.

"I'm not going to rob you," she insisted. "I am concerned for your welfare."

"Got no home," she wheezed. "Couldn't pay the rent."

Another cough sounded farther down the narrow passage followed by the sound of people stirring. There were more of them! Why had she never known there was this refuse of humanity that the city ignored? "Why don't you go to an alms house?" she asked. "Why isn't the Church looking out for you all?"

A few snickers and assorted sneers of disgust arose. The grizzled voice from a sliver of a man replied, "Not enough room at the alms house, and they have rules there. Can't bring your wine, can't bring your dog."

"I'm too ill," the tubercular woman added sullenly. "They say I'll infect everyone else." *This is where Viscardi's money is needed,* Florentina thought as she felt her heart soften even more. *This is where my money is needed.*

"Something should be done to help you all," declared the Night Flyer.

That brought even more laughs. "A masked criminal who stalks the night wishes to help us?" she heard one incredulous voice declare.

"Yes," she replied resolutely, but with no clear notion of how. "I'll be back another time," she said and trotted on to the sound of laughter, coughing, and one disbelieving, "sure you will."

Several blocks later she encountered a robbery taking place. The thug pointed a short sword at a well-dressed man as he thrust out his other hand. "Hand it over or I'll cut you," he demanded in a menacing tone.

Neither of them had seen Florentina and she flattened herself against the side of a building as she continued to creep nearer.

"I need this money for medicine for my sick child," the man pleaded. "I'm on my way to wake the apothecary and beseech him to rise from his bed and help me."

"You're lyin', and I don't care about your ailin' kid no how," he answered poking the man's coat with the tip of his sword.

Before either man was aware what was happening, the Night Flyer burst out of the shadows with a length of rope in her hands that she looped around the thief and pulled tight. His sword clamored to the cobblestones as the unwitting bandit cried out in surprise. "Hey, what's this? Who are you?"

Florentina yanked him back, his arms pinned at his sides, and pressed the tip of her own dagger to this throat. The would-be victim's eyes widened, and he took a step away. "You're that arch criminal, the Night Flyer!" Fear drained all the blood from his face that turned as pale as death. "Don't kill me! I'll give you the money."

"No," she said in a firm low tone. "But tell me the truth, for I will know if you do not; is your child ill and in need of medicine?"

"Yes, yes!" he cried, as he leaned against the wall for support.

"And you," she said shifting the dagger along the thief's neck, "were going to take his coins and leave his child to die."

She sensed him quivering in her arms and knew when the strength in his legs began to fail. "I, I have a child too!" she felt his terrified tears fall on her hands as she had not yet donned her gloves. *Why is everything so complicated?* She wondered. *I used to believe there was right and there was wrong, but since I started this vendetta, I see the world with different eyes. They are so afraid of me!* She marveled at the thought.

"You," she said pointing her dagger at the shaking victim. "Go buy medicine for your child." When he didn't move she added darkly, "Now!" He scampered off, stumbling a few times as he steadied himself against the wall. "And as for you," she mused returning her blade to the robber's throat. "Find an honest profession with which to care for your family!" In a sudden swoop, she spun him out of her rope's coil. As he fell dizzily to the ground, she sped away.

After the confusing and somewhat harrowing journey to Viscardi's warehouse, the mission went off without a hitch. Using her grappling hook, she climbed up a rear wall, entered through a top-floor window, and crept to the office. A guard had been posted, but being a Sunday night, he was leaned back in a chair snoring. She thought of rapping him over the head, but that would make noise, so she craftily picked the lock. Next, she drew a small can of machine oil used in Alessandro's production house and squeezed a few drops onto the door hinges before opening it. Once inside, she collected the ledgers and papers and soundlessly placed them in a barrel that seemed to contain the trash. She took out a tin of sulfur matches and lit fire to the papers. She waited long enough to be sure it wouldn't go out, then crept out of the room, past the sleeping guard, and back to the window where her grappling hook and rope would speed her descent to street level. No sense wasting the display of her flight with no one there to witness it. By the time her feet hit the pavement she heard the alarm sound as men rushed to put out the fire. She had to smile to herself as she dashed away. Having been disturbed in her spirit by what she witnessed earlier, Florentina decided to take a different route home and rose to the rooftops skimming her way undetected from any below.

* * *

MADELENA COULDN'T SLEEP. All she could do was think of Fiore, of their sweet and passionate kisses, of how she would devise a plan to move to the next level of intimacy. She was toying with the idea of telling her brother before he found out on his own. She thought that would receive a much better reception, however she worried about the possibility that he would forbid the relationship. But why would he? He was not an overly religious man. Weren't their thoughts on the subject bound to be similar?

She decided fresh air was the cure and stepped out onto her balcony which faced the courtyard. Even the chill in the breeze felt revitalizing to her skin. She walked to the railing and cast her gaze up to the stars. There were some lights burning in the city all night, but it was dark enough to enjoy the twinkling constellations of the Milky Way. She thought about the newest discoveries and how Florentina was sure to have read all about them. *They are now saying that the earth isn't flat after all, but round,* she mused. *If that is so, what keeps us from falling off of it?*

Maddie closed her eyes and breathed deeply of the clean, cool air, letting it fill her lungs and wash over her like the breath of God. It was then that she heard a sound resembling one of the roof tiles slipping to break on the courtyard walkway. She opened her eyes in the direction of the crash only to be arrested with the shock of what she beheld. She missed the landing, but there on her rooftop was the Night Flyer folding in wings as he nimbly danced in her direction. Her gasp was audible a hand rising involuntarily to her throat. But the thrilling tingles that cascaded through her body were not those of terror, she decided, but of fascination.

The dark figure stopped in its tracks and stared at her from behind a mask. It finished tucking in its wings without taking its eyes off of her and began to make slow, unintimidating steps in her direction with open hands held outward. Once closer, a voice spoke. "I am not here to rob you; I am not going to hurt you."

She tilted her head in curiosity as the enigmatic character edged near enough to speak softly and still be heard, then stopped and crouched down on the roof above and to the left of where she stood. The vocal timber was neither deep nor high, maybe a tenor or contralto, and the accent, yes, Venetian, she recognized it. "Then why have you come?" she asked.

"I have been patrolling the city and your rooftop was convenient. I did not mean to disturb you and will be on my way."

Standing so close to the infamous outlaw made her heart flutter. He was being blamed for every crime in the Milan, but as far as Maddie knew he had only attacked her enemy. "Patrolling?" she asked, not wanting him to leave. "Choosing targets, like crooked merchants and bloodthirsty men of power?"

She could have sworn she saw the Night Flyer's mouth turn up in a smile. "House Torelli has nothing to fear from me, Good Donna. But if I may suggest, there are unfortunates dwelling in misery down the alleys off Slues Street. Your charity may mean another week of life for them."

What an odd thing for a thief to say! she thought and was suddenly stricken as he started to scamper away. "Wait!" she called out, then covered her mouth, regretting the volume she had used. The Night Flyer looked over his shoulder to glance back at her from the pitch of the roof. "Will I ever see you again?"

"Time will tell," came the response, and he disappeared from view.

* * *

Florentina was in a panic! She whirled down the access stairs and through the kitchen's back door like one fleeing a burning building. *How am I going to get back in my bed by the time Maddie bursts in to tell me about meeting the Night Flyer?* Luckily, she had planned for such as this by hiding old clothing in several discrete places around the mansion, one being the bathing room. She knew it would be unoccupied at this time of night, so she rushed on tiptoe down the hall, around a corner, and into the small space locking the door behind her. Now she could breathe, but only for an instant. Next she was stripping off her black, stuffing her equipment into a linen chest, and throwing on the sleeping gown and robe she had stashed in here. Her heart was pounding so hard it seemed it would burst from her chest. There was water in the basin, so she splashed it on her face and dampened her hair. As she did so, she focused on her breathing. *Slow down*, she told herself. *Slow, steady, deep breaths, that's it. Calm. Just taking a bath. Odd time? No, I always bathe at midnight on a Sunday—God that sounds so ludicrous!*

With her breathing under control, Florentina slipped from the bathing room and strolled toward her bed chamber. Sure enough, Madelena was standing outside her door with her hand raised to knock. "Looking for me?"

Maddie initially jumped at her voice, then turned around with a beaming expression. "You'll never guess who I just met!" she gushed in subdued excitement.

Florentina put on a curious face. "Who?"

"The Night Flyer!" she couldn't stand still from the exhilaration and threw her arms around Fiore's neck so she could whisper in her ear. "He was here, on our roof!"

"And you aren't afraid?"

"Oh, no, he doesn't want to hurt us! He's not a bandit at all, Fiore—he's a vigilante!"

CHAPTER 13

$\mathcal{T}$he habitually unflappable Alessandro paced his front hall in an exceptional state of agitation, his strong shoulders bent and elegant face drawn up in consternation on Tuesday afternoon. The preceding night's frost had compelled the last of the autumn leaves to be unfettered from their twigs and branches, drifting in finality to the damp earth and paving stones beneath. However, it was not the initial precursor of winter that filled his heart with trepidation.

He played the news over and over in his mind. *There must be some mistake,* he told himself. Whether he had been this way for minutes or hours he could not tell, but eventually Antonio returned home. Alessandro halted his disconcerted march, knowing the sound of his son's footsteps and the scent of his bathwater. He turned searching eyes to Antonio. "Is it true?"

"May we speak in private?" he asked, meeting his father's gaze with some trepidation.

Alessandro nodded, swearing to himself as this was all but an affirmation of the worst. "In the study," he consented, and led the way. With the door to his private domain, his seat of power closed, Alessandro resumed his air of authority, standing straight with arms crossed over his tight chest. "What is this I hear about you joining the army?"

He eyed his son as the young man tried to decide upon a stance to strike. At first, he seemed apologetic, slouched with his head down. Then Alessandro witnessed a transformation, as with a deep breath he stretched tall, lifted his chin, and spoke with determination. "It is true, Father. I enlisted in the armed services of France in the Milanese division as an entry level artilleryman."

Alessandro dropped his arms and his mouth as he stared at his first born in disbelief. "Why would you do such a foolish thing? Just a few weeks ago you were telling me you wanted to become an artist; a soldier is the farthest extreme in the world from an artist!" He didn't even realize he had begun to shout. The self-possessed head of House Torelli never shouted.

"Si, well, I have my reasons," Antonio retorted, his own temper sounding in his voice.

"Then tell me what they are," he demanded. "What could possibly compel you to completely throw your life away?" Despite his desire to address his son's faulty reasoning, Ally found he could not hold back the tide of fatherly lecture that gushed out of his mouth. "The army? Really?" He began to pace again. "I forbid it, simply forbid it! You have a life, a future, a good future to among the most important men in the Duchy, and perhaps pursue your art or other interests, but certainly to head one of the Great Houses when I pass. You possess an inheritance, hundreds of employees, this mansion, more wealth than God and the power to use it how you see fit. Don't you know who you are, Antonio? And you would throw it all away, go off and get yourself killed in a war that has nothing to do with us or our security? That is fool-hearted folly! That is irrational! Didn't you learn anything from your teachers? This is the age of reason—use your mind, son!"

By then Alessandro's face was red, his blood pressure was elevated, and he shook all over. He stopped pacing and looked back at his son with pleading eyes. Antonio spoke more calmly. "Are you finished, Father?"

"No," he muttered in dismay, rubbing a hand to the back of his neck. "But I would hear your reasons now."

"Thank you," he answered respectfully. "It would appear you have my life all planned out for me—what I will do, where I shall live, how I must present myself to the world. Have you chosen a bride for me as well? Will I come home one day to meet a stranger who is the daughter of some Great House and be expected to take her as my wife?"

Alessandro frowned. "I've not chosen a wife for you, and I would always consider your input to be of primary import in a decision such as that."

Antonio let out a little laugh and shook his head. "Yet you admit you have all other parameters of my future selected for me. The fact is that I need to be in charge of my own life. I must make decisions for myself. I am of age, father, a man. It is time I stopped being Alessandro's heir and started being my own man."

"Independence is fine and good son, but not in the army. Do you possess any idea of the needless waste, the death and debilitation that await you?"

"I know it is dangerous, but I will acquire the essential skills. I have no intention of a permanent career as a soldier, although the Condottieri have gained much notoriety and power of late. Still," he continued, "I am only in need of the experience. I want to learn to handle myself, to fight, to be able to stand up to any foe, whether foreign or across the street."

Alessandro sighed and sank into one of the chairs. "You studied fencing and did well. Perhaps we can find you a more advanced course."

"No, you don't understand." Antonio took the seat beside him. "There is no actual danger in such a setting, no chance anyone will be injured. I want to cultivate courage through real life trials. If I can stand up to the charge of a Spanish cavalry bearing down on my position and not flinch, just hold my ground, then I can stand up to anything and anyone. I promise you I would return a man you could be proud of."

Alessandro looked into the eyes of his son wanting desperately to talk him out of this tremendous mistake while admiring his daring at the same time. "Antonio," he said with a hitch in his voice, "I am proud of you already. I do not see you as lacking in courage or any other attribute–a bit headstrong, but when turned the right way can be a positive trait. You don't need to impress me, or any man for that matter. You are bright, strong, handsome, talented, and at this moment possibly a bit mad, but any woman would want you, any father pleased to secure an arrangement for his daughter with you."

Antonio shook his head and cast despondent eyes to the floor between his feet. "Not any father; not Don Benetto."

All at once Alessandro was struck to the heart with the arrow that had pierced his son's. "Ah, son," he moaned in empathy placing a hand on Antonio's knee. "Why of all the girls it would be Agnese?"

The young man lifted his gaze to his father's. "I love her, I can't help it but I do. And Don Benetto is so cruel, to her and everyone else. She said he would never approve of us and if we run away, he would hunt us down and kill me." Of that, Ally had no doubt.

"Life doesn't always work out the way we want it to, and sometimes that is a good thing. Agnese is a lovely young lady, but there are many others. Perhaps what you feel for her is an infatuation, but even if it is love, there is enough love in you to share it with another. Mayhap one you admire as much or more is just over the horizon waiting to meet you."

Antonio shook his head. "Even if that's true, I believe I must test myself, prove to *me* what I am made of. I can do that in the army. The commitment is for two years–that is all, just two years. By then who knows? I may have determined you were right and I was crazy and I'll be eager to dive into the family business. But I need to find myself, discover what is right for my life without being told. You probably don't understand," he added lowering his gaze once more.

Alessandro understood all too well. There had been a time when he had felt lost and ineffectual. He had found a calling during that time, one which led him on a journey of sorts, but not one that had daily threatened his life. Nevertheless, he had found himself and grown into the assured man of quiet strength he was today. Still waters ran deep in him, but his son wore his heart on his sleeve, reacting rather than responding to the circumstances in his life. Some people couldn't be told; some can only learn through experience.

He patted Antonio's knee and then pulled his hand back, straightening his posture. "You know I do not approve of this potentially deadly decision of yours, but at least allow me speak with the captain. You have enough education and standing to be commissioned an officer. That will give you even more experience as you will be in charge of others rather than simply following the orders dispatched to you." *And make you less likely to be killed,* he reasoned.

Antonio raised a questioning gaze. "But how can I be in charge of others when I have no experience? I've never fired a cannon or even an arabesque. I'm decent with a sword, but–"

"Let us just talk with the captain and hear what he has to say about it. You are a fast learner and they will teach you what you need to know before giving you a squad to command." He still could not believe this was the direction his son, the son of a pacifist who despised war and all its waste, was taking. *There comes a time when a father must relinquish his role as authority figure and assume one of supportive friend, else his son remains a child forever.* "But you must tell your mother of your decision."

For the first time he read unrestrained terror in Antonio's expression. He gulped and stiffened. "Will you go with me?"

Alessandro laughed. "So, you are ready to face down the Spanish cavalry and stand up to Don Benetto and his assassins, but are too afraid to deal with your mother?"

Antonio blinked, wiping damp palms on his leggings. "That's different; she will cry."

"Yes," Ally assured him, "she will. Come; this is as good a time as any."

* * *

MADDIE WAS RETURNING from a meeting with a client when she saw her brother sitting alone in the men's parlor to the left off the main hall. The chamber was neither lighted nor did fire burn in the hearth. Noticing a distinct deviation from his regular mood, she ventured in and lit one of the lamps.

"Ally," she began in an apprehensive tone. "What is wrong?"

When he lifted his head, she noticed he held a half empty wine glass and a copy of Petrarch's *Secretum meum* lay open in his lap. His eyes were rimmed with red and conveyed a hopeless expression.

"Are you experiencing a crisis of faith?" She glanced at the famous work that had practically launched the Renaissance a hundred and fifty years earlier. *He looks so tired,* she noted and took a seat across from him.

"It's Antonio," he said sullenly and finished off his wine. She waited while he swallowed and set the empty glass aside. "He has joined the army."

"What?" Madelena couldn't believe what she was hearing. "Oh, Ally, I am so sorry." She reached her hand over and gave his a squeeze. "If you need anything, I am here for you."

He tilted his head and offered her a soft smile hinting at the myriad of emotions he held inside. "You are, aren't you?"

"Yes," she assured him. "Always."

"Do you believe in God, I mean actually believe that He is real?"

She sat back contemplatively. "Politics of the Church aside, yes, I do believe someone or something greater than man created all that is, and that he, she, or it watches over us and holds everything together. It is only rational."

"Precisely what Petrarch says," Alessandro replied. "God gave man vast intellectual and creative potential to be used to their fullest, to benefit both mankind and the earth, God's creation. I hate war," he sighed.

"I know," Maddie consoled.

"What I don't understand is that if God is so all powerful, why doesn't he prevent it?"

"This is one of the mysteries pondered by monks and saints, one we can scarcely comprehend, but..." She paused for a moment while she gathered her thoughts. "Maybe God is a little like you." At that Alessandro's eyes popped wide, and he gave her his complete attention. "Maybe he loves us so much that he lets us do what we want in hopes that one day we will return to Him wiser and more appreciative than we were in our reckless, willful pride."

Ally regarded her in wonder as he clasped his hand around hers. "Sometimes, Maddie, you amaze me." They sat in silence for a time just being together. No words were needed to feel the love and support between brother and sister. Presently, Alessandro said, "Portia is devastated. She will need your shoulder to cry on—you should go up to our rooms and sit with her."

"I will," Maddie promised.

Then he added, "I think the most difficult thing at first will be to see his seat empty at the table. It will be a constant reminder that he is far away and in mortal danger."

Madelena considered. She slid her hand away and pushed back a stray hair which had slipped from its formal arrangement. "Mayhap I could suggest..." she began tentatively.

"Yes, go on."

"Suppose Florentina was to occupy Antonio's place at our table." She waited breathlessly, the implication hanging in the air between them.

Her brother relaxed and radiated a bit more of himself than this sullen imposter she had been consoling. "I thought I noticed a spark between you two," he noted with a wink. "You know I have no objection to whom you spend your private time with, but I will issue a strong word of caution; this cannot leave the house. Furthermore, the rest of the staff must not be made aware of anything of a personal nature between you. I don't trust them. They talk, they gossip, and I strongly suspect a spy among them. How is it that Don Benetto knows our business almost before I do?"

His warning shot into Madelena' consciousness like a command from the Almighty. "Yes, I agree. I wholeheartedly understand and agree such rumors would be damaging to our reputation, and you know I would never-"

"Yes, I know," he said, a twinkle in his eye. "I like her; I think you have chosen well."

CHAPTER 14

Florentina sat on a bench in the fresh, cool air of the courtyard under the watchful boughs of an olive tree. Being an evergreen, its silvery-green oblong leaves, and those of its twin a short distance away, still adorned its branches, but all its fruit had been picked for the season to add to the bounty of the Torellis' table and be pressed into their household oil. She studied the ancient, gnarled trunk and limbs of the squat bushes and wondered how old they were. Olive trees had been prized since the days of the Roman Empire and the ancient city of Mediolanum, now Milan, with its Celtic roots from around six hundred B.C. and its subsequent prominence as a capital of the Western Empire. It was entirely possible that Casa de Torelli had been constructed around these trees to purposefully preserve them. She had read of such an ancient one in Athens named "Plato's Olive Tree" that grew in what had once been the grove where Plato's Academy had been situated almost two millenniums ago. Florentina marveled at their endurance before the march of time, as nature's perfect food producing year after year, and the symbiosis of man and the earth in general.

She gazed about the part garden, part lawn with its late blooming chrysanthemums bursting forth in a colorful array of white, yellow, red, and purple and its ornamental cherry laurels, forever green. The children, who had been scampering about expending energy after a day of study, raced to the fountain–a stone sculpture of two cherubs pouring water from a vessel that trickled down into a round basin on a pedestal–to quench their thirst in the clean, pumped water. She smiled, musing to herself how Matteo and Betta's round, smiling faces resembled those of the little angels.

Then Florentina closed her eyes to the gathering twilight, lay back her head, and drew in a deep, cleansing breath and listened to the song of a humble snow finch and the shout of the great spotted cuckoo. A flock of swallows passed over steering southward followed by the trumpets of a "V" of purple herons. It was a busy time for migratory and resident birds, especially after that first frost. As she took in her next deep breath, she noted a new fragrance in the air and smiled opening her eyes to savor the vision of a beauty with sunburst red hair and dazzling verdant eyes sashaying toward her. Now she knew she was in Heaven!

"Mama!" Betta shouted and ran over for a hug. Madelena lifted her daughter for an affectionate embrace and a kiss on the cheek before setting her feet back on the ground in front of Florentina. "Want to know what we learned today?" she asked, beaming with enthusiasm.

"I do," Maddie replied. "Why don't you tell us all at dinner?"

By that time Matteo had arrived for his hug. "Good," he declared. "I'm hungry!"

She smiled, eyes laughing. "You are always hungry! Now, you two go wash up and change to clean clothes. It is almost time to eat," she instructed.

"Yes, Mama," they both acknowledged and raced away.

Florentina stood to meet Maddie's gaze, a warm glow emanating from the center of her chest. Then she caught a hint of sorrow in her lover's expression and her smile faded. "What is wrong?"

"Antonio has committed himself to the army," she returned with the sound of dismay. "I have spent all afternoon consoling Ally and his wife and I just can't talk about it anymore."

"That's alright," Florentina responded in empathy. "There is no need." She could easily enough imagine the heartbreak. She started to reach for Maddie's hand, then stopped herself to scan the courtyard, porticos, and archways.

"Two things," Maddie said as she began to stroll. Florentina fell in step beside her. They passed an opening where one of the maids leisurely swept dust out the open doorway. "Portia is overwrought at the idea of Antonio's chair at the dining table laying empty," she said in a robust volume. "Ally fears it will constantly remind her that her boy is in harm's way, and he requested that I ask you to assume that seat for our family meals." Florentina noted Madelena's eyes drifting about catching the presence of staff members in the vicinity. "He said, 'Why waste learning opportunities? Must Florentina wait until after breakfast to initiate a lesson? Why must her instruction end at four o'clock? It would be in all of our best interests if next week when Antonio has left for training that she be present to occupy the chair'."

Florentina nodded in understanding. "I would be honored to be of service to Don Alessandro in any way possible. I can only imagine a mother's heartache at such a turn of events."

As they continued to stroll, Maddie turned a corner leading them away from the servants and back toward the olive trees. This time her voice was almost a whisper. "We spoke about you. He already suspected, and he likes you, has no problem with us being us." She paused again, her eyes once more surveying the area. "But he requires complete discretion."

Florentina nodded. "That is wise, Maddie. I wish that I could kiss you in the beauty of this garden, right now in the fading light of day, or at midnight under a blanket of stars. If only I could stroke your skin and hair with no concern for who was about, but I am fully aware that is not an option."

"I long for that freedom as well, and Ally would accept you into the family, save the scandal it could create," she explained. "He believes there is a spy, a traitor in the household who runs to our enemies with every morsel of information he or she can collect."

"What lovely mums your garden produces!" Florentina exclaimed as they paused by one of the flowering shrubs. "Such vibrant colors," she observed as she spotted Angela pass by a portico with an armful of folded linens. Then she added, "That is a strong possibility."

Then Madelena stopped and turned to Florentina with a markedly changed expression. "Have you ever been to Slues Street?"

Florentina knew what this was about, but she feigned surprise. "No," she replied as if the question had come out of the blue. "But I hear it is a bad part of town, one to be avoided."

"Then I should like to go there," Maddie pronounced. "My whole life has been sheltered. I have lived twenty-eight years in this house, frequenting the piazzas, cathedrals, the shopping district, fine cafes, and the mansions of other merchants and their wives—all safe, clean, affluent venues—to the point that I had convinced myself none other existed in our cultured, artistic, wealthy Milan. But the Night Flyer spoke of poor people living in misery in that part of town." Sympathy consumed her features, and she looked away toward the rising moon. "I suppose somewhere in the back of my mind I knew that the poor were there; after all, the church has a large 'poor box' in which to place our alms. I know there are more modest homes in other neighborhoods, quite like the one you said you grew up in, but they aren't *poor.*"

Florentina nodded in agreement. "I know what you mean. I have busied my mind learning about science, nature, philosophy, and faraway places, seldom taking time to think about who and what lay across town. I confess that I love beauty so much, I tend to turn away from anything that is not."

Maddie began to stroll again, this time toward the arch leading to the dining room as the aroma of fresh bread and pasta wafted out into the private piazza. "But are not acts of kindness beautiful too?" she asked and Florentina's heart was struck as with a flaming arrow. *It is official,* she said to herself. *I am most assuredly in love with this woman!*

"Yes," she confirmed. "Perhaps the most beauty a human being can create."

"Will you go with me on Saturday? I need to see for myself. I want to do something to help."

Florentina nodded. They stopped at the entry to the residence. "Antonio leaves Monday morning," Madelena said soberly. "Thank you for doing this for Ally and Portia."

"My pleasure," Fiore replied with a slight bow of her head.

Maddie silently mouthed the words, "Tonight, my chamber," then turned and entered the dining room.

* * *

It HAD BEEN *a splendid night indeed,* thought Florentina, still glowing with incomprehensible joy. She took a small sip of sunflower oil and swished it in her mouth while she dressed for the day. They had not yet "consummated" their relationship, but the flow of physical intimacy was heading in that direction. She recalled the giddy teasing and sensual exchanges and replayed them in her mind, adding to her present euphoria.

"What are you doing?" a curious Angela asked as she donned her maid's uniform. It wasn't often they rose at the same time.

Florentina held up a finger. Still swishing, she pulled a brass chamber pot out from under her bed and spit into it. "Oil pulling," she replied as if everyone should know about the practice. Stepping back to the table bearing their wash basin, she opened a jar, retrieved a mint leaf, and popped it into her mouth to chew.

"What is that?" Angela asked with a baffled expression. "And why are you eating leaves?"

Florentina laughed and pushed the chewed leaf behind her gum. "Oil pulling is an ancient way of cleaning your teeth and mouth. The Greeks wrote about the practice which originated in India. And I'm not eating a leaf—it is mint, to freshen the breath." She doubted the girl from the countryside even knew there was a place called India, but surely even she had heard of the ancient Greek civilization.

Angela gave her a sideways glance and pursed her lips. "You are a very strange woman—a nice one, but strange."

"Have a good day," Florentina called after her as Angela left for her morning duties.

Another good thing about last night was convincing Maddie I needed the day off, she thought as she brushed her long, brunette strands. She envisioned how silky and fine Maddie's hair was compared to her more coarse variety. *Nothing to do about that,* she consoled herself.

Florentina had learned that Wednesdays were Iseppo's days off and she had determined to shadow his every move in an attempt to catch him doing something he shouldn't. It was a long shot, she knew, but anyone that distasteful had to be up to no good. That is why she had risen with Angela before dawn; she couldn't take a chance that the bony butler would leave before she could follow him. Having robed herself in the most plain, unremarkable day dress she had in hopes of blending, Florentina reached for the common gray cloak hanging from a hook on the wall and picked up a navy blue women's beret appropriate to the cold drizzle of the morning.

She noted that Iseppo habitually used the servants' entrance in the rear of the house, so Florentina exited that doorway just as light began to filter through the neighborhood, casting everything in a shimmering red and golden hue reflected off the terracotta roof tiles. She made her way across the secondary back road and slipped into an alley from which she would watch the Torelli servants' door. While standing patiently for the hour it took him to appear, her stomach reminded her that she failed to feed it.

He emerged in his perpetual black attire adding a thigh length cape to guard against the unpleasant weather and strode toward the shopping district. Florentina followed at a safe distance but was careful to not lose sight of him. It was fortunate that he was not an intuitive man; he never bothered to glance behind himself.

His initial stop was the barber's shop. While it was common to see the red and white pole of a barber-surgeon in Northern Europe and the British Isles, the Milanese, Florentines, and other Italian city-states were ahead of the times with educated physicians and apothecaries, and while some local barbers still performed tooth extractions, they mostly stuck with cutting hair and giving shaves, both to the relief of their customers and themselves.

Barbers of Milan transacted important services for their high-class clientele as to the Italian fashion was everything. They had their own guild, and to run a shop such as this one, the barber must be qualified as a master. Less proficient artisans would have to practice as an apprentice and then a journeyman assisting a master until he proved himself adept and gained regulars of his own. A good haircut and a proper shave declared one's station to the world, so it did not surprise Florentina that this was the major-domo's first destination.

Afterward she followed him about to various shops where he browsed but always left empty handed. *Why does he shop and not make a purchase?* The very concept baffled her, but still she trailed him in a slow march across town. When he stopped to have brunch at a café, she determined she must do the same. Her feet were tired, and she was hungry; she could keep an eye on him from the eatery across the street.

She ate quickly to be done before her quarry and was ready to follow when he made his next move. This time he left the shopping district and hiked to the part of town where several of the Great Houses had their mansions and warehouses. *Now it gets interesting,* she thought as she took slow, quiet steps, stopping now and again to approach a doorway. The dreary drizzle had given way to cloudy gray, so at least her shoes would no longer slosh.

When he rounded the next corner, her blood began to race. *That is the way to Don Benetto's!* She quickened her pace to be sure to see if he entered the residence. Since the rain had stopped, there were other pedestrians on the sidewalks and a few carriages rolling down the street, so it was easier for Florentina to blend in until he turned down a narrow alley that led to the back of Casa de Viscardi and their servant's entrance.

She waited for him to exit the other end of the lane, then scurried through herself, disturbing a cat that yowled at her. She arrived at the far terminus just in time to see the flap of his cloak pass through Benetto's servants' door. *I've got you now, you rat's bastard!*

* * *

It was not Florentina who delivered the news to Alessandro. She decided the report must come from a source outside the household. Instead, after her evening rendezvous of tender kisses and caresses with Madelena, she donned her persona of the Night Flyer, scuttled down the drainpipe, and skulked around the house to fire a bolt with a note attached at the door post to Don Alessandro's balcony, which faced the main thoroughfare. She waited to see if he heard the sound and when he did not appear, she threw a pebble at his window. This time a light came on and a tall robed figure opened the balcony door. He looked about, and spotting the bolt and paper, retrieved it. She had written, "To discover the traitor in your midst, follow Iseppo next Wednesday. It will be worth your while." He raised his eyes searching the rooftops, but she was crouched in the shadows below. Presently he retreated inside, the shaft and note still in his hand.

At last, that dirty old man who violated Angela and filled Viscardi's ear would get his just reward!

CHAPTER 15

"Are you certain you want to do this?" Florentina asked as she and Madelena struck out for a Saturday morning walk which would lead them far from the comfort and security of Casa de Torelli. "It is cold and raining, and it may not be safe."

"Drivel," Maddie replied. "We have parasols and cloaks to keep dry." Florentina glanced up at hers. It had a straight ash wood handle that extended beyond the top of the octagon shaped gray canvass covering. The mechanism pushed open and folded closed, much as the Night Flyer's wings. Then she glanced over at Madelena's fashionable deep plum silk parasol with a maple hook handle that could be hung on a peg to dry, or looped over a lady's arm for easy carrying when not in use. She had seen Maddie shortly after they first met use a white, lacy parasol to block the sun from her delicate porcelain skin, but this one was designed to keep off the rain. While its origin dated back thousands of years, the accessory had been lost to European use during the Dark Ages and only recently returned to popularity in France and the Italian city-states–one more reason Florentina was glad to live in this modern age of learning and invention.

"What do the poor people we are going to help own to keep them dry?" she asked. Florentina didn't answer, but she knew–nothing. "Besides, should we need protecting I have no doubt your quick wit and youthful athleticism will take care of any problems we may encounter."

"I suppose." Florentina had no doubt she could fight her way out of jam, but she did not want Maddie to suspect she was a night-flying vigilante. "I think we go right at the next corner."

"Oh, Fiore, I wish you had met him!" Madelena gushed, her eyes blazing with excitement. "He was so unearthly in that black suit, swooping out of the sky onto our rooftop, nimbly floating across the tiles. I think he may be from Venice, from the way he talked," she speculated.

"If I didn't know better, I would think you are infatuated with him," Florentina mumbled, feeling oddly jealous of... herself.

She sensed Maddie's touch on her arm. "I am infatuated with *you*," signaled the sultry assurance in Madelena's voice. "I just find him fascinating, that's all. And, by targeting the Viscardis, he is providing a service to the community."

* * *

MADELENA'S MIND and emotions were prodded by Fiore's question; was she infatuated with the ingenious masked man? The notion was too silly to consider! She had no idea who he was, if he was a virtuous person, or if he had a wife and family somewhere. The whole idea was preposterous. Besides, she had an exciting romance blooming with Florentina—a real live, flesh and blood person, with a name and face, and with whom she enjoyed easy access. Why would she even *think* about this mystery man? And after the pleasures she had been experiencing at the hands and lips of this amazing woman, why fantasize about a *man*?

It isn't that, she thought. *Not really. But he stimulates my imagination, and he wants to bring down the proud and raise up the humble... he's unique and mysterious. That's it! I just want to discover his secrets, not go to bed with him.*

"I've heard he's committed all kinds of crimes and is very dangerous," Fiore said.

"Nonsense." Maddie waved the notion away with a flick of her wrist. "Lazy constables would rather blame an impossible target than do their jobs. And have any reports noted that he killed anyone? No. I don't think he's bad, just misunderstood."

The farther they walked from their neighborhood, the more neglected the buildings became. Some were constructed of materials other than brick, and many had no plaster at all. Madelena wrapped her cloak around herself a little tighter. She had expected this, but she had not expected what they found in the alleys off of Slues Street.

The smell hit her first, with a powerful rankness of smoke, urine, garbage, waste, decay, and death all mingled together into a stew of misery. She had to watch her step on the cracked and crumbling remnants of paving stones and tossing propriety to the wind, she reached for Florentina's arm to steady herself. "I didn't know an area of our city was in this dreadful condition," she whispered.

"Neither did I," Florentina concurred as she kept an even pace with Maddie.

"I think you ladies took a wrong turn," said a small grimy man who stepped out of a broken doorway.

Her heart raced, but she kept her head high; even she was a more physically intimidating figure than this poor soul, and Fiore could step on him. "We know what we are about and are not here to seek nor find trouble."

He bowed his head as they passed but a disfigured woman who appeared to be wearing a sack replied, "Nothing but trouble here on Slues Street."

She ignored the comment and tried to look away from the hideous form. One of her arms was shriveled, she bore a deep facial scar, and most of her hair had fallen out. Maddie heard a severe coughing fit emanating from the next alley up the road and was almost afraid to continue lest she contract some dread disease. Madelena retained intimate knowledge about dread diseases, and the incessant coughing sound triggered a forgotten memory–one of her earliest.

There had once been four children in their family, two other sisters born between Alessandro and herself, but they both died of whooping cough when she had been a toddler. She remembered the "whoop" sound as her sisters gasped for breath and she recollected having the symptoms as well. As her mother had relayed the story to her, she and her sisters, all under seven years of age, had gotten sick; only she had recovered. After that, she gained her brother's constant attention and affection, despite the difference in their ages. He doted on her and once he discovered her aptitude with numbers, insisted that she receive a more well-rounded education than was commonly granted to girls.

A chill ran down her back and she must have visibly shivered because Fiore was asking, "Are you all right?" with a tone of deepest concern.

She nodded, but then began to notice a small crowd gathering around them. Naturally, they stood out–they were both clean and had all their teeth. Apprehension began to needle at her chest as she counted more than a dozen of the unfortunates, some wearing curious expressions and others extending soiled, calloused hands in their direction.

"What are you going to give us, you sweet cherry blossoms?" asked a young cripple who leaned on a tree branch he had converted to a crutch. The tone in his voice was much too covetous for her liking.

Madelena stood tall, pushed her shoulders back, raised her chin, and lifted her hand from Florentina's arm. "I spoke with the Night Flyer, and-"

She paused as the crowd began murmuring among themselves taking steps of retreat. Then the old woman who suffered from consumption rose from the crate she had been sitting on and tittered toward the gathering, all of whom had no choice but to stand in the dismal rain. "That fellow in black, the one what flies sent you?" she asked followed by a shallow hack.

"Si." Florentina answered this time, taking a step in front of Maddie. "He told us that you fellow citizens of Milan have fallen on hard times and need a small measure of assistance."

A few snickers arose from the crowd, but the old woman shushed them. "Your kind don't never come here."

"I know," Madelena replied. "But we are here now."

"Let's rush them, take their coins, and have our way with them!" the lusty young lame man suggested.

"You fool!" denounced the scarred woman. "Do you wish to call the fury of the Night Flyer down upon us?"

"Indeed," agreed a hunched bald man whose clothing hung on his bones like a tent. "If you kill the goat, you may get one meal, but keep her well and you have milk for many years. I say if these fine women wish to become our benefactors, we thank them-not attack them!" The lame man hung his head at the rebuke.

"We brought some coins," Florentina said. "They will help, but only temporarily. We wish to do something more constructive."

"Are these your dwellings?" Maddie asked as she began to distribute the coins into the outreached hands of the beggars.

The sick woman laughed setting off a new coughing fit, and she lifted the stained rag to her mouth. A tall, thin man with a grizzled beard who had not spoken yet stepped forward with his hands cupped to receive his coins. "We have no houses," he replied with a dry voice drawn from between thin, chapped lips.

Madelena's heart sank. *No shelter, no medicine, and winter in almost upon them.* The mood of the crowd transformed from suspicious and malignant to appreciative and hopeful, all the while the cold, pelting rain was chilling them to the bone.

The two women exited the alley to the tunes of, "Thank you," and "God bless you," and began the walk back to Casa de Torelli. They moved in silent contemplation, not sure what to say. Madelena had encountered a higher class of beggar outside the doors to the cathedral from time to time; these sort were too dirty, too ill, and too unseemly to be allowed near "respectable" citizens.

After a few blocks, Maddie asked, "How do you suppose they came to be in such unfortunate circumstances?"

"Hard to say," Florentina replied. "Lost their jobs, maybe due to injury or illness, were evicted from their apartments, have no relatives to take them in... the possibilities are endless."

"But by the grace of God I am what I am," Maddie quoted in wonder. "The Apostle Paul said that, then added, 'and his grace toward me was not in vain.'" Back on the main thoroughfare, she stopped and took Florentina's arm again, turning to face her wearing an expression of deep revelation. "Fiore, I understand I am privileged, that I come from wealth, that my life was spared from a childhood illness, and that while I have faced tragedy, I have also been blessed... I enjoy my health, my sweet children, a brother who loves me, and now you. I don't want God's grace toward me to be in vain. If I can't use my position to do some good in the world, then I don't deserve it."

* * *

FLORENTINA PLACED her free hand over Maddie's as it rested on the arm that held her parasol. She had been blessed, too, she realized, with a keen mind and creative abilities, with physical strength as well as strength of will. She had created the Night Flyer as simply a way to carry out her vengeance on Benetto Viscardi, but what if she could use it to do so much more?

"You have such a kind heart," she said, feeling the words flow emotionally from her core. "It is one of the characteristics I love about you. You do good every day running an honest business and raising two charming children who brim with possibilities; now you can add allotting money to charitable deeds, knowing that there are those in need who can benefit from your generosity."

"I don't want anyone to know about it," she said thoughtfully. "I don't think it means anything if you just give excess coins to appear generous in front of others."

Florentina smiled, admiration for Maddie growing, burning deeper in her soul. "Speaking of others, don't you have your ladies' brunch to attend?"

"Oh, that." Madelena's voice was dismissive. "I suppose I am obligated to appear. If I stop attending meetings, they will become suspicious and spread all sorts of gossip about me."

"Nice friends you keep," Fiore said sarcastically, exchanging a glance with Maddie.

"Indeed," she chimed in cheerfully. "They are one of the reasons I decided I must keep you!"

"Oh, in that case, I love them, one and all!" Maddie's smile warmed Florentina and soon they were both laughing.

"You could not abide five minutes with them," Madelena commented as she batted her eyes flirtatiously at Fiore. "So much prattle about nothing!"

Becoming conscious of people out on the street despite the rain, Florentina removed her hand from Maddie's and looked away. "You are a singular, extraordinary woman, Madelena." She stared ahead at a passing carriage lest she lose her self-control under the spell of those seductive eyes. "You may keep me forever, if you wish."

She felt Maddie's hand lift from her arm and they continued their stroll. Florentina sensed the energy and heat between their bodies and held tight to her parasol handle. She wanted to hold her lover, to shower her with kisses, to run her hands over that satin skin, to declare her love unequivocally; instead she put one foot in front of the other, daring not to glance her way. Then she heard in melodic tones, "That sounds like a good plan to me."

CHAPTER 16

"The morning meal is lovely, Bianca," Alessandro commended the plump, full bosomed cook as she set the final touch, a bowl of succulent Barbera grapes, in the center of the table, their purple so deep it looked almost black.

"Grazie," she replied before returning to the kitchen.

The bread was fresh, the cheese aged, the porridge hot, and the fruit divine. Florentina felt incongruous her first time eating with her new family; Matteo and Betta knew no different, but the others were aware this was an unusual arrangement. Thankfully, word had spread as to the reason she was there, officially anyway, and that Matteo had decided he should be the one to sit in Antonio's chair to the left of his uncle. Florentina was especially grateful to him for that as it placed her between Pollonia, with whom she had engaged very little, and Madelena.

Matteo, beaming with importance, sat up straight, placed a cloth across his lap, and made sure to keep his elbows off the table. He started to reach for a grape then heard his mother clear her throat. "Uncle Alessandro hasn't said grace yet." He withdrew his eager hand.

Alessandro closed his eyes. "Thank you Lord for your bounty which we now do humbly receive. Amen."

Florentina gathered her courage, deciding she may as well initiate a teaching moment. "Matteo, why do people say grace before eating?"

"Because we're supposed to," he answered without concern while legally reaching for a handful of grapes.

"Betta?" Florentina turned to the proper little girl.

"Because God sees everything and He will know if we don't."

Fiore caught Maddie's repressed smile and resisted the temptation to wink at her. "Would anyone else like to offer a reason?"

She had caught Bernardo's eye thinking he may contribute to the conversation. The lad was at that in-between stage that signaled the onset of puberty. He was not a man like Antonio, nor a child like Matteo, but he was now the oldest male, save his father, at the table. She recognized he would soon be assuming new responsibilities within the family.

He cleared his throat, and she thought he was concentrating on his speech lest his changing voice squeak. "Being grateful is a virtue. Voicing thanks for our food aloud helps us to remember to be thankful for all of our blessings and good fortune."

"Well said," she praised giving him a smile and nod before turning an approving gaze to Alessandro.

"What?" he questioned innocently. "If the boy says the right thing, that is his mother's doing. I just earn the money around here."

That drew a refreshing laugh around the table.

"So," Bernardo ventured, "Tell us about Master Leonardo."

"Let's see," she pondered while buttering her bread. "He was born in Vinci, which is in Tuscany, and his parents weren't married." She was bemused by the stunned expressions of the others. "Not that scandalous," she dismissed. "It was a small village and both his father and mother were commoners. His talent was recognized at a young age and he moved to Florence where his career began. But here are a few things you may not be aware." She used her story-telling voice to hook her audience and noticed Bernardo's attention was riveted as he spooned porridge into his mouth. "Leonardo is ambidextrous. Who knows what that means?"

There was a brief silence until Pollonia's quiet voice ventured, "Doesn't that mean that he was both handed, like for writing and such?"

Florentina beamed approvingly. "Excellent! Leonardo mostly paints with his left hand, but he can use both with proficiency and I have even witnessed him using brushes in both hands simultaneously. But do you want to hear something truly amazing?"

Now she even had Portia and Alessandro hooked. "He can write forward on a piece of paper with one hand, while starting at the other side of the page and write backward with the other creating a mirror image of the line." Little mouths dropped and Alessandro shook his head, chuckling in disbelief.

"Wow!" exclaimed Betta. "I am doing good just to write normal. Do you think I could do that some day?"

"It is possible, Betta," Florentina said with speculation. "But Master Leonardo is a special kind of genius."

"He did that drawing, the Proportions of Man," Bernardo said then took a bite of his bread. "We studied that in school. You can always measure how tall someone is by their arm-spread."

"That's correct," said Florentina.

"Don't talk with food in your mouth," Portia whispered. "Manners make the man."

"Yes, Mama," he replied contritely.

"Maddie," Alessandro spoke in his usual good humor. "I think we made a wise decision asking Florentina to join us for meals. There is no telling what new directions our conversations will take."

Madelena had been quiet, but Florentina had felt her positive energy and support from her close proximity. "I concur," she said with a knowing smile to her brother. "Now children, get washed up and meet Florentina in your room for lessons."

"Yes, Mama," they responded. Matteo grabbed one more handful of grapes before hopping up from his chair and trying to beat Betta to the door.

Florentina was unaware if Alessandro had told Portia about his sister's new love interest, but she determined to act in a manner consistent with no one having knowledge of their relationship. It was safer that way. She wanted to brush a hand across Maddie's shoulder and caress her hair before leaving the room, but she restrained herself. She must to be content with stolen moments and secret rendezvous.

* * *

ALESSANDRO HAD MUCH WEIGHING on his mind early Wednesday morning. In addition to dealing with the absence of his eldest son and speculating about his military training progress, there was the revelation that his sister was engaged in a romantic liaison with a member of the staff, and then this business about the Night Flyer. Who was he and what was he about? At first he had considered the reports exaggerations, but now he wasn't so certain. One thing Alessandro had deduced was that he was most likely carrying out a vendetta against Don Benetto.

Not surprising, he thought as he shrugged into his oldest, least ornate coat. It was a long, gray, sleeveless outer garment that covered his every day wear. He hadn't worn this garment in years and judged it to be his most common, least conspicuous one. After selecting a matching beret, he carefully arranged it on his head to produce a haphazard look. Taking a glance at himself in the mirror, he sighed. *Who am I kidding? I can't disguise my unusual height, so what difference will a coat and hat make?*

"Why are you rising so early, Amore Tanto?" A sleepy Portia pushed herself up to one elbow, her long golden hair falling around her shoulders.

In her late thirties, three children, and still she takes my breath away! He turned from the mirror to his wife of twenty years. "I have a mission this morning," he answered solemnly. "Something important needs tending to."

"Dressed like that?" she queried with a timbre of dread. "Let me find you something better to wear," she offered as she slid out of bed. "No one will take you seriously dressed in those old rags."

Alessandro laughed and caught her shoulders. "It's all right, Tesoro Mio; I don't want to stand out." She stared at him for a moment and then they both burst into laughter. "I know, I always stand out." He leaned down and pressed his lips to hers. "Go back to bed and don't give a care. I shall be home for dinner if not sooner. I'm sure you can manage without me."

She frowned and fussed with the shirt beneath his coat. "It's Iseppo's day off. I'll need be in charge of the staff, and you know how they laze when he isn't lurking about."

"I have complete confidence in you," he declared and placed an affectionate kiss on her forehead.

ALESSANDRO FOLLOWED Iseppo through his rounds, attempting to be as discrete as possible. He had a great deal of experience in conducting secret undertakings himself, but sneaking about physically was another matter. His physique stood out and everyone in town could recognize his face, so he had to follow at as far a distance as he dared. A couple of times he feared he had lost his quarry, but each time he was able to spot his butler once more.

After consuming his noon meal, Iseppo's path took them into a rich district that riled Alessandro's senses. He was familiar with this neighborhood and the prominent men who lived here. *That Night Flyer was right. Have I been made a fool? How could I have not known?* But chiding himself served no purpose now. He would reserve his blame for the man who had betrayed his House.

He peeped around the corner of the lane to watch his long-time butler step through the arch of Casa de Viscardi's back door; then he crept to the door-post and peered inside. "I am here to see Don Benetto," Iseppo uttered dourly.

Tucking his head back, Alessandro listened as footsteps approached. "Ah, Iseppo." Benetto's tone was quite agreeable.

"I bring some very tasty news for you today, my lord," chimed a sound Ally had never heard from his dull major domo. It was bright, excited, and almost youthful in its exuberance. He ventured a peek. The two men stood inside the alcove ten or twelve feet away. Alessandro was patient. He wanted to discover what the treacherous bastard was going to reveal of his private affairs.

"Do tell." Benetto sounded intrigued and his voice was accompanied by the tinkle of coins in a pouch.

Alessandro stiffened as a storm of fury raged beneath the surface. *This betrayal was for money?*

"It is about Don Alessandro's son, Antonio–you know the one, his eldest."

"Yes, I know him, go on," Benetto prodded.

"The foolish lad has defied his father's wishes and joined the army; can you believe that? Don Alessandro was able to secure a commission for him, but still..." Iseppo's pitch was that of glee.

"The family must be devastated," Benetto replied in a mocking tone. Ally locked down the violent rage that sought to burst forth. He was a temperate man, well-practiced in the art of self-discipline. He would not lose control in the presence of his enemies. "Why, anything could happen to young Antonio. He'll probably end up dead and I would not have a thing to do with it." He could overhear them both laughing now.

"Have you ever heard of anything so absurd?" Iseppo cackled.

"Now Agnese will see how wise I was to forbid her to associate with that fool-hearted boy. He must possess a death wish, one I would have been more than happy to grant had he ever laid a hand on my daughter, but now I shall win. He will be killed and I will stand totally innocent in Agnese's eyes."

Alessandro, standing coolly with his shoulders back, chest raised, head high, and an expression of mild disappointment stepped through the open back archway. He saw the self-satisfied smirk on Benetto's face as he dropped the coin bag into Iseppo's hand while patting him on his treacherous, bony shoulder.

Iseppo's gaze turned to the sound of heavy footsteps and the little color his face once possessed vanished in an instant. His eyes flew round and his mouth dropped in abject terror. Seeing his distress, Don Benetto pivoted to see what had this effect on his spy.

"Well, well," Alessandro began as one might say to a child caught with his hand in the cookie jar. He planted his feet shoulder width apart and crossed his arms over his broad chest. "What have we here?"

Benetto's expression was overtaken by a wicked grin, that of a snake that had been successfully stealing eggs from the henhouse for years. Iseppo stuttered. "Ah, Don Alessandro," was all he could squeak out before having no breath at all.

"Iseppo Castillini, you have been serving House Torelli for, what, twenty years? Certainly long before my father died as I recall. You have risen to the highest level of your class and have been paid quite handsomely compared to those in other Houses. But I see you acquired another source of income," he stated, nodding to Benetto whose pride was beginning to unravel before Alessandro's intimidating presence.

"Guards!" Benetto called warily.

"Oh, please, Don Benetto, there is no need for that," Ally brushed aside carelessly then moved fists to his hips. "I only want to know for how long? And was it just for the money, or have I wronged you in some way?"

"I, I..." Iseppo still could not speak and Alessandro feared he may fall victim to a heart attack on the spot. Two guards arrived but Benetto motioned for them to hold their positions. Then he spoke for the quivering man.

"Iseppo has served me for years. I may not pay better than you," Benetto explained, "but am more persuasive in other ways. You are likely unaware, but Iseppo fathered a child by a woman in my service years ago. When I threatened to have her and the infant killed, she told me the most curious thing–that a prominent member of the Torelli household loved nothing more than to take advantage of inexperienced maids and serving girls. I knew you would not tolerate such lack of character under your roof, so I called him in, had a talk with him, and we came to an arrangement." His self-satisfied grin returned as it seemed he tried to look down his nose at a man a foot taller than he was.

The jagged twist in Alessandro's gut sent a jolt of fire through his veins, but he was determined to maintain his composure. "Touché, Don Benetto," he replied with a nod of his head. "Very clever indeed." Then he sighed. "Iseppo, you are most assuredly never allowed back in my domicile under penalty of death. I will see that your belongings are placed out on the street where you may collect them at your leisure." Then he added with a dry humorless smile, "You know Benetto, you may have kept a spy in my household, but ask yourself this–how did Alessandro find out about him? Perhaps I retain my own spies." He gave Benetto a wink out of searing eyes, turned his back deliberately, and strode out.

CHAPTER 17

*A*gnese and her mother, Daniella, had been standing near enough to catch the entire exchange and with Don Alessandro's departure, they scuttled down the hallway into the ladies' parlor. Daniella reached for her needlepoint and Agnese grabbed a news sheet that lay atop a small table and they hastened to occupy seats across from each other.

Agnese trembled as she could not help but overhear the heated exchange. "You fool! You idiot! You let him follow you?" Benetto raged.

"I didn't know," followed a mournful cry. "He has never shown the least suspicion of me. I've done all that you asked, Don Benetto."

"No, actually, you have not. I recall telling you not to be found out. It appears I no longer require your services." They heard the coin pouch fall to the floor and the scuffle of feet over the floorboards.

"But I wasn't, I haven't been, for *years* my lord. I am loyal to *you*, truly I am!"

As the panic trembled in Iseppo's voice, so it rose in Agnese's heart. She sat as still as a stone, staring with unseeing eyes at the paper in her hands. *Please, God, don't let him kill him; don't let him kill him; don't let him kill him!*

"Loyal?" Benetto laughed. "You have been spying on your own master, reporting to his enemy anything worth sharing, and you expect me to trust *you*? You are dirt! You are slime!" he railed contemptuously. "At least when I get urges I can find a willing wench or courtesan and have never felt the need to force myself upon a woman. You are almost too pitiful a specimen to bother killing," he spat in disgust.

"Oh thank you, my lord, Don Benetto," came the gushing sound of relief in Iseppo's voice. "You are as wise as you are benevolent. I can still be of service to you in other ways."

Then the steel hardness that lay at the core of Benetto's being issued forth in a biting tone. "I said *almost*."

Agnese jumped in her seat as did her mother, both too horrified to move a muscle. Agnese kept her head down and she assumed Daniella did the same, but she could perceive the cry of shocked pain, the gurgling sounds, the moans, and the body dropping to the floor. *Probably stabbed him; sounds like he stabbed him. I didn't see at least.* She swallowed, terror clawing at her soul, her breaths coming fast and shallow. *Maybe I didn't hear. That's it, I heard nothing, nothing at all. Just my imagination.*

"Get this cleaned up," her father instructed and then his footsteps were marching down the hall.

Reading. I'm only reading. "What are you staring at you fat, ugly slug?" He was in the doorway, yelling rudely at her mother. Agnese peered at the visage of a monster while Daniella cringed.

"I'm, I'm not loo-looking at anything," came Daniella's timorous reply. "You are the master of the household; I am merely embroidering a pillowcase."

"That's right, you good-for-nothing lump," he sneered. "Alessandro's wife is about your age and she still has a pleasing shape and her natural hair. What happened to you? I suppose you heard all that." He waited for a response. Agnese was frozen in place, unable to move, speak, or even breathe.

"Hear what?" Daniella's voice and hands both trembled.

"The part about the wenches and courtesans," he retorted with a laugh. "Well, you can't blame me."

Relief poured over Agnese like a waterfall as her father continued down the hallway leaving her and her poor, distraught mother alone. When she was certain he was gone, she moved to the settee and nestled in beside Daniella, closing an arm around her mother's hunched shoulders. Silent tears streamed down a face that was warped by despair.

"Pay no mind to him, Mother," Agnese consoled. "It isn't true."

"What part, Vita Mia?" Daniella buried her face in her hands and shuddered. "Didn't plan for my hair to fall out," she sobbed. "I didn't want to get fat. I never wish for…" The sobs began to flow in waves and Agnese held tight to her mother.

"I know; it doesn't matter. You've done nothing wrong, nothing to deserve the way he treats you."

"I tried to be a good wife," she sputtered. Agnese dug out a laced handkerchief and handed it to her. Daniella lifted it to her face, dabbing at her eyes and wiping beneath her nose. Then all at once, it was as if the tap ran dry. No more tears, no more sobs—only morbid resignation. "I wished to live long enough to see you wed into a good family, to see you move away from this dismal place. I wanted your fate to be a better one than mine."

"What are you talking about?" Agnese gently chided. "You will be."

Daniella lifted old, tired eyes to her daughter. "I don't think so. I have not been well for some time and am only getting worse."

"What do you mean? Have you seen a physician? Why did you not tell me sooner?" Like a raptor's claw, fear seized her heart and squeezed. *You can't die! You can't leave me alone in the house with him!*

"I didn't want to worry you, Agnese," she explained. "The physician ordered me a tonic, and it helps some, but my nerves are in shreds, and I can barely get through each day. At times I'm sick to my stomach or my bowels don't move properly. Other days I get headaches that pound so ferociously that I wish I was dead." She sighed, sniffed, and continued. "I have trouble sleeping and always feel exhausted. I become confused, lose track of what I was doing, and sometimes forget when and where I am. My chest is tight, my joints ache, and maybe I'm just getting old. Maybe this is what old feels like."

"You aren't that old, Mother," Agnese stated with concern. "Like he said, you're almost the same age as Antonio's mother and she appears to possess plenty of energy. You must be suffering from some chronic ailment. Perhaps if you keep taking your tonic and get enough rest, your health will improve."

"Antonio's mother doesn't live with the stress I am pressed beneath day after day. Did you hear Don Alessandro? He never even raised his voice. He possesses a powerful stature and could have squashed Benetto like a rat beneath his boot. I wish he had," she added in a dark whisper, then continued. "But he didn't even raise his voice." Agnese leaned on her mother and began to shed her own tears. "Now, now, child. I don't mean I'm dying right this minute. I may yet carry on for another year."

"Antonio has joined the army," she cried, "because of me. He might die, and my heart would perish with him."

This time Daniella put her arm around her daughter and hugged her close. "Why because of you?"

"I told him we must never see each other again, because Father forbid it. I was scared for him, Mother, I still am!"

"You did the right thing, child. It was not you who drove him away; it was the man that rules our lives. But," she added raising her tone to one of optimism. "It might be a good thing. He will come back a mature, fully grown man, with skills and experience in combat, with confidence and determination." Excitement grew in her voice. "He may challenge Benetto to a duel and slay the beast."

"Mother!" Agnese lifted her head and stared dumbfounded at Daniella. She couldn't recall her mother speaking so openly with animosity toward her father. The woman was usually so subservient and docile. Conceivably it was these thoughts of her imminent death that made her so bold.

Roused from the rebuke, Daniella resumed her quiet demeanor. "What were we talking about? Oh, yes, Antonio. Do you love him?"

"I do, Mother; God help me, but I do. What can I do besides pray for him?"

A shiver ran through her mother's frame and then she shook her head. "That is all that I know, Vita Mia. I had no choice in my marriage and you will likely have no say in yours. I am sorry, but that is the way of it. We are women; we don't get to make choices."

Then a thought occurred to Agnese. "There is one choice I might make, and father could not stop me." Her mother looked at her with a puzzled expression. "I could move to the convent and take the vows of a nun. I could become married to the Church."

Daniella shuddered. "That is a hard life from what I understand. No comforts, long days, taking orders from bitter old abbesses and prioresses, never being able to bear a child of your own." She shook her head. "Hold that as a last resort, Agnese, a last resort." Daniella patted the hair on her wig and handed Agnese back the handkerchief, now damp, and changed the subject abruptly. "I don't want you to dye your hair any longer."

Agnese was confused. "But Mother, you said it was the fashion, that golden hair was more desirable than my mousy brown and I should do everything possible to be attractive to men so I can entice a good match."

"I know what I told you, but I may have been wrong. I noticed that many women my age who dyed their hair in the past now are wearing wigs as I do. It may possibly be something in the dye that caused my hair to fall out, or it could have been the same malady that causes my other symptoms." Her eyes bore upon Agnese's face. "And don't use too much powder. I understand whitening your face is the thing to do, but I wonder..." She reached a hand up and stroked Agnese's cheek. "How can one improve on God's workmanship? You are beautiful just the way you are, without enhancements."

"Oh, Mother," she sighed and held her in a tight embrace. "I love you. Things will get better, you'll see. Keep taking your tonic and try not to dwell on unpleasantries." *And I shall do the same.*

* * *

MADDIE HAD NOT BEEN LOOKING FORWARD to Friday morning. She stood with Portia and Alessandro in their entry hall. Florentina was upstairs with her children and her niece and nephew were off to their respective classes.

Ally lifted his travel bag and looped the strap over his shoulder. "I will only be gone for a week," he promised with a smile. "Madelena can look after the business and you, Tesoro, can administer the household."

"But we haven't even acquired a new chief butler yet to replace Iseppo," she pouted as she secured a belt around his overcoat.

"Then promote another member of the staff, at least temporarily. You know my client in Bern is a very important one."

"But that is in the Swiss Confederation," Madelena pointed out, "and you will need to cross the Alps."

"Which is why I am leaving now, before the snows get too deep. You two women behave as if I'm a lad taking his first trip away from home," he laughed. "I'll be safe, you will behave, and all shall be well."

He hugged them both, kissed his wife, and struck out before they could put up even more of a fuss. But Maddie had reason to be apprehensive; the last time she sent a man of the house out on a journey he didn't return alive. However, she did not voice her concerns to Portia. "Oh, he'll be as safe as treasure on the moon," she said dismissively. "We women are perfectly capable of running things for a week."

"You know," Portia mused placing a hand to her narrow chin, "every year about this time he has to travel somewhere far away on business. Last year it was Napoli, and before that Vienna. Do you remember a few years ago he traveled to Paris and brought us each back such lovely parasols?"

"Yes, I remember," Maddie said with a smile. "That's what happens when you are married to the most successful merchant in the city known around the world for its merchants. I'm surprised he hasn't voyaged as far as the Orient!"

"Shush," Portia demanded as she drew in her lips. "Don't even think such a thing!"

Maddie tried not to worry. She was confident Ally could handle himself and she knew there were men she may call on in a pinch just down the street at the production house. Alessandro had asked the friendly watchman, Salvador Sfondrati, to look in on them daily. Still, unease needled the back of her mind.

CHAPTER 18

Florentina had planned Saturday's strike by the Night Flyer with precision. It was the afternoon of the city's big Calcio championship, the last game of the season. It would draw thousands of spectators to the sandy playing field surrounded by rows of seating for the audience which was fortuitously situated near the eastern gate through which Benetto's men should be entering sometime around dusk. Unless he had changed his schedule–in which case the whole mission was for naught–a large shipment of goods was being sent to Venice and those returning with the profits were expected back at that time. They should be passing through the gate around the same time a throng of rowdy football fans would be pouring into the streets in that part of town, an obstacle better than a fallen log.

Her father had taken her to see the sport played once, but he had not cared for it. While originating in Florence and being widely popular there, Milan had adapted their own version which had soon attracted a wide following. Florentina found Calcio rather barbaric, but she could understand its appeal to the masses. Two teams of musclebound athletes, competing without shirts–a more modest version of the ancient Olympic Games while still allowing athletes to show off their physiques–each tried to get a ball to the other end of the field. They could throw, kick, or run with the ball, but those were basically the only rules. Fighting was not only allowed, but expected; therefore it was quite a blood sport, enjoyed by men for that reason, and by women who gushed over the physical attributes of the players.

Milan boasted four official teams, one from each quadrant of the city. While many youths threw together unofficial bouts in any large empty space they might find, the recognized teams could only draw their competitors from the ranks of the upper class and nobility. As Florentina recalled, Giovanni Sacchi's son Pietro was a star player on the Minotaurs, the team representing the southern district. Anyway, the sport was of no import to her plan, but the huge event was crucial; everyone was talking about it and the streets would be jammed with people.

The Night Flyer, in full gear, crouched above the eastern gate watching and waiting. The city walls were made of thick stones and spread twenty feet wide with an avenue atop it. The walkway was only accessible to soldiers and city guards and sported four and five foot high battlements along its length. But the war Spain and France fought over the Duchy was being played out far away posing no military threat to Milan, thus all the soldiers had been sent to the front. The guards were gathered over a hundred yards away observing the sporting event from their free perch.

But Florentina's focus was set outside the metropolis where lay fields of grain, pastures of grazing livestock, and the highway from Venice. The time spent waiting was used to review the order and elements of her plan as well as to contrive contingencies for every eventuality. The other Night Flyer attacks, besides at the warehouse, had been away from town; therefore, Florentina suspected that once the city was in view, the caravan would relax assuming the danger was passed. After all, who would attempt to carry out so daring a robbery with thousands of people to witness it and with constables near at hand? Yes, they would let their guard down, feel safe, and then she would strike.

She double checked her equipment; everything was where it should be, including a new addition. Because her backpack was occupied by her flying device, she had purchased and modified a black leather bag to wear strapped across her chest into which to deposit the coin bags she would collect. She also considered they may change how they transport the money after the coach robbery, but she speculated that Stefano would be closest to the cache.

The Night Flyer heard the roar of the crowd from the stadium nearby as the sun sank low in the sky. *The game must be almost over by now,* she thought as her eyes studied the road. There had been little traffic through the gate, but at last she spied some riders approaching. She heightened her senses and held a spyglass to her right eye, turning the adjuster to gain the correct focus. There were no wagons or carriages, but ten men on horseback riding in twos. *That is definitely a purposeful formation,* she considered. *I don't see a banner but they are wearing Viscardi colors. Ah ha! Stefano!* Her heartbeat accelerated and she sensed energy shoot through her body.

"Hey, what are you doing here?" The sound of the deep booming voice had her momentarily stunned. She swallowed hard forcing her brain to remember what to do if discovered.

Don't panic. You planned for this possibility.

Leonardo had devoted much of his time and genius to the field of anatomy and medicine. That is how she had learned about the ingredients to mix in her gas cloud potion. Additionally, he had kept many books copied from ancient writers lying about and her knowledge of Latin made it easy for her to soak up as much information as possible. Two of the medical books she had read were by the Roman scholar Aulus Cornelius Celsus and the Greek surgeon Galen. They had written about a technique to administer ointments and liquids in a manner similar to how a snake injected its venom, by filling a tiny glass vial with the appropriate substance and pushing it into the body of the patient through a needle at one end. Modern physicians did not employ the technique because they didn't know enough about it and had sworn by the words of Hippocrates to first do no harm.

Florentina didn't want to kill people if avoidable; after all, this watchman hadn't murdered her father. But she did need to employ techniques that required minimal physical strength and would create a result as quickly as possible. Therefore, she had fashioned a few of these needle vials and filled them with opium, an Oriental drug made from the poppy plant. Leonardo said that opium was once used to induce sleep for surgeries, but that its use was discontinued because patients kept wanting more of the opiate long after their ailments were healed. Florentina was not worried about the guard developing an addiction as he would have no idea what drug was used on him.

She took a deep breath and carefully removed the wrapped vial from a pouch on her belt. "Just wanted to watch the game," she said knowing that she was on the wrong part of the wall for that. It was a ploy to buy time.

In an instant she swung her arm and torso around, stabbed the needle into the man's leg, and pushed the plunger.

"Hey!" he cried and stepped back before she could withdraw it. He reached down and swatted at the vial protruding from his calf breaking the needle off in his muscle.

"You shouldn't have done that," the Night Flyer said as she remained in her crouch. "It's going to put you to sleep. Don't you feel sleepy?"

A strange smile crossed his face as his eyes became unfocused. "I feel, I feel good," he mused and slid down the battlement to sit on the stone walkway a few feet from her, his legs splayed out in front of him. "I feel... wow," he added dreamily. Knowing that the drug was doing its work, the Night Flyer returned to the mission. Viscardi's men were beginning to pass through the gate. It was time.

Stefano rode in the middle of the line beside some brutish looking bearded man who was heavily armed. Both riders had bulging brown leather saddle bags hanging across their mounts' hind quarters. How would she collect all the coins?

Florentina's mind raced as she secured her grappling hook around one of the stone battlements a few yards to the left of the open gateway arch. She had drawn and measured the arc she would need to create on paper back in her room while designing the plan. If she could maintain her speed she should be able to complete the arc twice, thus allowing her to collect both saddlebags. If it didn't work, she could always run like hell! One more glance down to estimate the distance: the wall was twenty feet high, add five feet for the battlement, subtract five feet for the height of the horse's back, and she stepped off eighteen feet of rope, wrapped it around her wrist gripping tightly with her gloved hand, and looked down again. Stefano and his companion had just cleared the gate; she jumped.

Phase one was to catch one foot in the cord so that her head and outstretched arm were facing downward. She had practiced this move with her rope tied to a tree branch, so it went rather smoothly. Part two, grab Stefano's saddle bag without interrupting the flow of her arc. *Yes!* It was heavy, but that only added to her momentum as her swing brought her up toward the top of the wall on the other side of the gate. As she saw herself almost level with the top, she threw the bags with the thrust of her swing and they landed on the rampart.

Having reached the peak of the sweep, the Night Flyer started to descend, her motion carrying her back along the same path she had just taken, much like the pendulum on a clock. With her right hand secured in the cord, she reached with her left to snatch the other saddle bag but was met by the edge of Zuane's blade. It scraped across her arm but because of the speed of her motion did not cut too deeply to prevent her from grasping her prize. Up, up, the rise of her arc took her, and she tossed the sack over onto the top of the wall.

The next step was to launch herself onto the wall, which was the more difficult part. Having made two sweeps already, her momentum was waning, so to add more thrust she unwound her foot from the cord, slipped right side upwards, and kicked off the stone fortification. This threw her arc outward over the crowd and away from Viscardi's men. Now clinging to the rope by both hands, she readied her feet to strike the side as she sped toward it. *Success! Now just run up the stones a few steps and there!* She tumbled over the wall in a heap.

There was not a moment to waste. The entire heist took less than one minute but it had attracted a great deal of attention. The Night Flyer scrambled to her feet, scooped up the first saddle bag and ran away from the group of guards toward her grappling hook and the other bag. Pausing to untie the hook and cord from the battlement, she glanced back at the pursuing watchmen. There was about a dozen of them, most with swords or pikes and a few attempting to arm their arabesques. She wasn't worried about those. Leonardo had drawn plans for improvements, but the novel firearms were notoriously off target. The lead balls they shot were not made to precise sizes and often rattled around in the barrels exiting with a bizarre spin. Additionally, the barrels themselves if not cleaned regularly would contain particles that threw off the shot. Add to this the fact that the shooters were moving as they fired and she was not concerned about those weapons. But it was essential that she be off the wall before the armed men reached her position.

She stuffed the grappling hook into her belt and then raced to the other saddlebags. Kneeling down, and keeping one eye on the advancing guards, she transferred sack after sack of coins into the bag she had strapped to her chest. It was soon apparent they would not all fit, so she made an instantaneous decision.

The streets below were jam-packed with the crowd leaving the ball field and she could hear Stefano shouting obscenities at her. But Viscardi's men on horseback were surrounded by a sea of Calcio fans and may as well have been stuck in a tar pit. However, a few of them did have crossbows which would be a problem once she stood up. So before doing so, she lifted out four coin pouches that she had no room for and began heaving them over the wall as far into the crowd as her feminine muscles could manage.

Immediately, young, old, poor, rich, middle-class, male, female, and even clergymen descended upon the spilt bags of coins like ants onto a drop of honey. She grinned from an opening between the battlements, then saw the troop closing in on her. It was awkward running with the heavy pack bouncing against her core. *I wonder if this is what it feels like to be with child?* her mind conjured. As she neared a bend in the wall, she pulled the handle that deployed her gliding wings just as the sound of an arabesque rang out. She leaped off the side and began soaring over the city.

Excited voices sounded from below and people started pointing at her. She couldn't hear any individual, only a wild cacophony. Once she steered herself over one of the busy streets, she released the left handle and began pulling out coin pouches and dropping them amongst the excitement below. The crowd, with all eyes toward the sky, parted as each bag fell, then pounced like ravenous vultures as it burst onto the cobblestones. She needed to do this as quickly as possible as the excess weight caused her to descend faster than usual.

She maneuvered over the shopping district and managed to land safely on a rooftop in an area where the buildings were all crammed close together. Then she pulled in her wings and bounded across terra-cotta tiles, tossing out all but one of the coin bags. *Now, time to disappear.*

She followed the roof tops, sometimes having to scramble to a higher plane and others needing to hop down to a lower one, until she neared the slum district. A few die-hards were still running behind on the lane below, but since the Night Flyer was no longer showering them with money, most had given up. She leapt a few narrow alleys, landing hard on the rooftops, but managing to keep her balance. With the adrenaline rush waning, she noticed the cut on her arm. It was still bleeding. *How will I explain that to Maddie?* was her biggest concern. She had a small bottle of carbolic acid along with other potions in a drawer to her trunk back home with which to cleanse the wound as the Greeks Galen and Hippocrates had advocated, and a honey based ointment to coat it with. She didn't have bandages, but who would notice if a few cloth napkins went missing from the linens?

By the time she got to Slues Street, no one was following anymore. The sky was almost completely dark with a cloud covering the moon. She slowed her pace watching her steps closely in the dim light. Then she noted the glow of a fire ahead and followed it. Below in the alley was a small gathering of unfortunates near a blaze contained in a large, low-sided clay pot that was normally used for planting a decorative shrub.

Florentina wondered what they were saying and if the woman with the cough had secured her medicine, or if the crippled man had received a proper set for his leg. But Madelena would have long been back from her women's meeting by now, and she needed to tend the cut on her arm. She dropped the last bag of coins into their midst and turned toward home.

CHAPTER 19

$\mathcal{M}$adelena waited in the ladies' parlor admiring the wooden puzzle box Florentina had crafted for her while Portia sat across the way showing her teenaged daughter, Pollonia, some finer points of embroidering. It was after dark and Maddie's foot tapped absently in impatience. The piece in her hands was exquisite, and she was reluctant to disassemble it lest she lose a part or be unable to fit them back correctly. She had opened and closed it many times, but she lifted the lid once more. Inside was nestled a pressed and dried red rose that would never wither nor fade. She raised the box to her nose and could catch the faintest whiff of the flower within the strong cedar aroma. It was nearly as special as the woman who carved it, except she was late, and where could she be?

All three were jolted from their evening activities when Bernardo barreled through the front door shouting, "Mama, Mama, guess what!"

Madelena carefully set down her treasure and Portia laid aside the needlework. Bernardo had to grab the doorframe to slow his momentum as he slung himself into the room out of breath but with eyes gleaming with excitement. "You'll never guess what just happened!"

"No, we won't," Portia agreed. "So please, do tell. Did your favorite team win the game?"

"No, the Alpine Bears, that's not it," he panted as he let go of the frame and tramped into their midst. "The Night Flyer!" He had to stop to catch his breath, bracing himself with his hands on his knees.

"Did he attack you?" Portia leapt to her feet and was at her baby's side in an instant.

"No, no, Mother, don't be so-" he protested as he shooed her off of him. "No hugging!"

Portia lowered her arms with a look of dejection emphasized by a pout. Bernardo was finally taller than his mother and Maddie suspected he wanted to be treated more like the man he hoped to be one day than the baby cradled in his mother's embrace.

"Tell us!" Madelena's attention was riveted to gain a first-hand account of the enigmatic vigilante's activities.

"The game had just ended, crowds everywhere in the street, and suddenly overhead, there he was–flying above the city dropping huge bags of coins! Everyone was racing and grabbing what they could, and then he disappeared over the rooftops somewhere. But I *saw* him fly, on big black wings; it was the pinnacle!" Bernardo finally had his breathing down to a fast normal, but his face positively glowed.

"See, I told you Portia," Maddie said. "He is not a notorious criminal. He only robs those who deserve it."

"I didn't see who he robbed," Bernardo added. "But the money had to have come from somewhere."

"I hope he doesn't stop by here again," Pollonia said, her brows furrowed with apprehension. "It makes me nervous."

Madelena was struck with a sudden concern. "The constables and watchmen will be out chasing him."

Bernardo laughed aloud. "No city guard can catch him–He's the *Night Flyer!*"

Just then a knock sounded at the front door which Bernardo in his excitement had left standing wide open. "Is all well with you?" called the voice of watchman Salvador Sfondrati.

"We're good," Bernardo shouted down the hall to him. "Grazie!"

"Have you heard that the Night Flyer is on the prowl?" Salvador asked taking a step inside the door. "I wanted to be sure you were all safe." By then Luca, Livia, Angela, Bianca, and the rest of the staff had gathered in the entry hall to discover what the commotion was all about.

* * *

AMID THE WHIRL OF EXCITEMENT, Florentina entered the kitchen through the roof access ladder and tiptoed to her empty room. She quickly changed her clothes and pushed her gear into the secret drawer in her trunk. She tended the cut on her arm, using a washcloth as a bandage, and pulled her sleeve down to cover it. Satisfied that she looked presentable, Florentina used the staircase farthest from the entry to descend so it would appear she was just returning home through the back.

Upon joining the gathering, who all seemed to be talking at once, she asked innocently, "Did I miss something?"

* * *

It took an hour for the household to return to normal. Even Betta and Matteo were excited hearing about the extraordinary character. With Salvador gone, the children put to bed, and the servants retired for the evening, Madelena invited Florentina to her room and locked the door.

While Maddie was loosening her hair, Fiore said in a teasing manner, "Your excitement over this masked man is starting to make me jealous again."

"Oh, and I can't be jealous of something or someone, too?" she replied in her own flirtatious tone. "You disappear for hours, sometimes all day; how do I know you aren't meeting your other lover in some clandestine locale?"

Florentina's laugh was so genuine. *Does she think no one else could ever find her attractive? Is the idea of other suitors so absurd to her?* Her response, however, was languid. "There is no chance of that."

Madelena turned, scrutinizing the tall, lanky woman who stood before her. Before she had finished formulating her words, Florentina took a step closer. "I only have eyes for you, Madelena. You are my heart, my treasure. I would never betray your trust."

Looking into those deep pools of liquid honey, Maddie saw something shimmer. "But you do have secrets."

"Doesn't everyone?" They each stepped nearer and Florentina's lips took possession of hers. Maddie felt a whirl of emotions vying for prominence—love, passion, suspicion, doubt. *What secrets are you keeping from me, Fiore?*

She noticed something wet on Florentina's sleeve and stepped back with a frown. Then she took the arm to examine it; Fiore let her. "I cut myself on a piece of equipment at the production house today. I know, I

127

was careless, silly me," she chided. "Saturday is the best time for me to see that everything is in good working order, and especially with Don Alessandro being gone, and I suppose I was in a hurry and didn't take enough care."

Maddie sighed and gave her a cross look. "We should have a physician tend it," she urged. "That is a deep cut; it will leave a scar. What if it gets red and fills with pus?"

Florentina's smile was amused but also comforting. "I trust my own treatments more than those of any physician. I promise we will not need an amputation—no ancient Roman statuary for you, my Sweet."

That drew a grin from Madelena and she retied the cloth. "I can at least find you some proper bandages."

"That would be appreciated."

"We should have an outing tomorrow," Madelena pronounced with sudden inspiration. "A picnic with the children after Mass, if it isn't raining."

She watched Florentina's eyes light up. "I would enjoy that very much." *The warmth just flows from her,* Maddie thought. *No pretentiousness, no games, no demands.* She realized that most lovers would not want the children around, would not settle for something so simple, but Fiore was immeasurably easy to please. Whatever Maddie suggested, she was over-joyed with. This had not been so in her previous relationships. The household maid hadn't lasted long as a lover; she began to feel entitled and push around the other servants. Her father had to dismiss her. With her brief courtship and subsequent marriage to Vergilio, he seldom considered her suggestions as he believed it was his place to make all the decisions. No, this relationship was different, more equitable. Fiore did not behave as her superior nor inferior, but more like a partner. They alternated taking the lead, voicing suggestions, initiating intimacy, and they made decisions together. She found the arrangement exhilarating.

"Then it is settled." Madelena brushed her lips to Florentina's and was met with a rush of pleasure as her thoughts and emotions began to merge into even more wonderful feelings of love, belonging, comfort, oneness, and passion. The kiss deepened into an urgent need, a desire to give everything she was to this woman, to possess all that she had in return. *Not yet,* she warned herself. *Don't go there too soon.* So she held to her, caressed her skin and drank from her lips, letting herself savor every step of the journey like a fine wine.

CHAPTER 20

*C*ool days with chilly nights accompanied by frequent fog and a fair amount of rain were typical weather for Milan in November, and despite the windy gray of the day outside, within the hall of the *Gilda dei Maestri Mercanti* was color and warmth as fires blazed in its two hearths. Banners and tapestries hung along the walls to the high-vaulted chamber large enough to fit the membership comfortably. The room was abuzz with conversation as Giovanni Sacchi strolled amid the assemblage. He rose the two steps onto the small platform that separated the council members' seats from the rank and file.

Giovanni had been in a particularly good mood since returning from his visit to Venice. No, he had not bought Julia a seaside villa, but she was as pleased as pudding with the new jewels he did give her. Color rose in his cheeks as he recalled how exuberantly the younger woman had thanked him. Upon reaching his seat in the middle of the dais, he lifted a hand to adjust his spectacles as he eyed the crowd. He wore his knee-length red and ebony pleated giornea with its puffy mutton sleeves open exposing a brocade buff waistcoat and black leggings and shoes. He had acquired his new clothes in Venice and wished to project the style and elegance of his position.

"Gentlemen," he announced raising a hand in gesture. "Let us take our places and commence with our meeting. We have several important issues to discuss."

With chin raised, he waited for everyone to sit before he settled into the middle Savonarola armchair. Giovanni noted the session was well attended, however one of the prime seats on the riser was empty. *Alessandro has not returned from his journey,* he noted. "I call this meeting of the Master Merchant's Guild to order."

Immediately Don Benetto stood, impatience and hostility radiating from his core. "The first and foremost issue before this assembly today is that damned Night Flyer. Something must be done about him!"

A few murmurs arose from the floor. "And what do you propose the guild should to do about a thief and vandal? Is that not the purview of the city government?" Giovanni asked.

"He is a menace, a threat to us all!" Benetto paced back and forth in front of the membership, looking out into their faces and then turning to the council members. "Next time he could strike you, or you, or you—nobody is safe, and the watchmen are afraid of him. I am the only one who even attempts to kill or capture him."

"You are the only one he seems interested in harassing." sounded an amused voice from the midst of the assembly. The comment was met with chuckles.

"This is no laughing matter!" Benetto fumed, his face a twisted mask of indignation.

I wish the Night Flyer would stop toying with Benetto and kill him already, Giovanni thought to himself, irritated that the man was co-opting his meeting. *Then I would inherit his arms clients and easily become foremost of all the Merchants of Milan. Who would miss him anyway?*

"I'm certain you have all heard of this latest theft, in broad daylight in front of hundreds of witnesses," the grievance continued. "And who will cover my losses? I need securities, insurance. I propose the guild provide assistance in these matters."

One of the younger members asked from the floor, "Are you suggesting we take up a collection for you? Are you in need of our charity?" More snickers followed and Benetto seethed.

Pointing at the young merchant he shouted, "Just wait until the bastard is breaking into your warehouses and taking away your hard-earned profits!"

"Don Benetto." Giovanni spoke patiently, trying to calm the man. "We are all very sorry for the troubles you have encountered, but I fail to see what the guild can do about them."

"Sorry?" Benetto spun toward Giovanni and pointed a finger at him in front of the assembly. "You are the one who will benefit most if my House falls. At first I suspected Alessandro but then I saw he had nothing to gain; you do!"

Unease shifted through the membership as one council member stood accusing another of multiple crimes. Giovanni lifted his palms innocently. "Surely you do not think that I am this notorious flying bandit? What a miracle that would be! Besides, I was in Venice on business during your latest robbery."

"No," Benetto sneered, "not you old man, but your son is an athlete. He could easily perform the acrobatics displayed by the Night Flyer!"

A few whispers arose as men voiced their soft-spoken opinions. Giovanni shook his head. "Do you forget? Pietro competed in the Calcio championship game in front of thousands of spectators. He was being applauded and congratulated at the same time your mystery marauder was swinging from the city walls."

At once the membership all agreed, many of them having seen the game. Giovanni sighed wearily and motioned for Benetto to take his seat. "Come now, my old friend, and be seated. It is not good for you to remain so agitated. Think of the damage to your heart. Speak with the city magistrate tomorrow; we have guild business to attend to, such as how the war is affecting our western trade routes."

Benetto grumbled, cursed under his breath, and reluctantly returned to his chair to sulk and smolder while Chairman Giovanni proceeded with the affairs of the guild. *No, I am not the fabled Night Flyer, nor is my son—though I would be quite proud if he was. I shall have to keep an eye on this masked mischief-maker,* he thought with a twinkle.

* * *

THE SECOND SATURDAY OF NOVEMBER, a week and a day after leaving for Bern, Alessandro viewed his majestic city from his seat on a gondola passing effortlessly through the still water. He had taken the craft to and from the canal's terminus at the base of the Alps and from there arranged travel through the pass. It was faster and more comfortable than making the entire journey on horseback.

Although Leonardo da Vinci had drawn up plans for a paddle-boat to use on the canals twenty years ago, no transportation line had chosen to build one. Alessandro rode on a traditional nearly flat-bottomed boat operated by a single oarsman standing at the stern. Three other passengers joined him. They had passed many barges laden with cargo headed to destinations near and far–some of them probably his own merchandise. He was pleased with how his meeting had fared and was happy to be returning home.

Hues of orange, red, and violet were painted to the west as if a huge brush dipped into a rainbow and casually swept the colors across a blue sky, while to the east the first evening star twinkled against a twilight canvas. He was thinking about seeing his lovely wife and daughter again, how they would give him grief for being a day late, and about how grown up Bernardo was becoming... and wondering how Antonio fared. *Is he still in training or have they moved to the front? Surely he would train for more than a few weeks.*

A loud boom rousted him from his musings. He and the other passengers turned, craning their necks to peer up the canal behind their gondola in the direction of the blast. The shocked and shaky oarsman grabbed his hat with one hand and clung white-knuckled to the oar with his other. "D-don't panic, e-everyone. We, we are safe!" he stuttered.

About a mile to their rear shot spectacular flares followed by countless reports and then more flames forming a dark cloud at their apex. This was quickly accompanied by another loud boom and it seemed as though the canal water burned a clear distance to their stern.

"What is that?" gasped a middle aged woman as she clutched the arm of a young man, presumably her son.

"I don't know," the youth replied in a curious tone, "but it is too far away to harm us."

The oarsman began to push the small craft with renewed energy. "We must hurry to the docks so I can report this," he huffed out.

Alessandro turned his attention back toward home. *It is fortunate we were well beyond those Viscardi barges we passed before the Night Flyer struck... then again, I suspect he waited for us to be out of harms way before blowing up the munitions. Interesting fellow; I look forward to meeting him one day.*

* * *

ALESSANDRO CREPT in through the front door to surprise his family. He discovered Maddie, Portia, and Pollonia gathered in the ladies' parlor playing a game of Frussi with a deck of patterned cards. "Ah ha!" Pollonia cheered with a wide grin. "Four threes, I win!" Her enthusiasm more than doubled when she spotted him peering through the open door. "Papa!" She tossed the cards on the end table and flew across the floor into his arms for a warm hug of welcome.

"Alessandro, you're home!" beamed Portia as she glided toward him. Halfway, she halted and gave him a disapproving stare. "You are late. I have been worried all day. I think perhaps I should be cross with you."

"It snowed one day on the return and we had to wait it out," he explained innocently. "But here I am, all in one piece, humbly asking for your forgiveness."

Madelena had already reached him for her welcome home hug. Then she turned to Portia giving her the eye, and his wife relented. "Drivel," Portia uttered bashfully. "Naturally I forgive you." The pout was replaced by a glowing smile and he enfolded her in a tight embrace before planting a kiss on her lips.

Pollonia still bounced. "I'll go get Bernardo," she bubbled. "And does he have a story to tell you!"

Alessandro laughed as she bounded off. "And where is the versatile Florentina this evening? Entertaining the children?"

"No," Maddie scowled. "She seems to believe the entire production process was her responsibility while you were away. I think she has spent more time over there refitting looms than she has conducting lessons for Betta and Matteo."

He gave her a knowing wink. "It is after dark; she'll return soon. Actually, I am quite impressed that she has been so diligent with her tinkering work. With the profits we stand to make from this deal, I may have to consider raising her wages."

"Ally," Maddie said with a change of expression, "there is something I wanted to discuss with you concerning profits."

"Are the books in order?" he asked with concern, one arm still wrapped around Portia's petite frame while she clung to him possessively.

"Yes, all is in order," she said hesitantly. "It can wait until Monday," she admitted and waved the matter aside. "Go take Portia upstairs before she bursts."

More laughter ensued, followed by Bernardo's retelling of the football game and the Night Flyer's exploits, and just before Alessandro could sweep his wife off her feet, Florentina appeared in the doorway looking positively radiant.

"It is good to have you home," she said. The smile she offered him was sincere, but when her gaze turned to Madelena, he recognized the ardent devotion her eyes conveyed.

"It is good to be home," he replied as he reveled in the love of his family.

CHAPTER 21

*D*on Benetto paced the length of the portico outside the magistrate's office for almost an hour waiting to be admitted. What was the wait for? He had made an appointment. *And after I have shown nothing but support for the French*, he thought impatiently. Even when Ludovico Sforza had briefly retaken control of the Duchy before he was finally defeated and imprisoned, when everyone else flocked to embrace him, the Viscardi family stood by King Louis XII. *So much for my loyalty being rewarded!*

"The magistrate will see you now," an aide announced at last. Benetto followed him through the arch and across a carpeted foyer to a closed door. The aide opened the door and ushered Benetto through.

Seated at a large walnut desk in front of a window looking out into a central courtyard sat a Frenchman some ten years younger than Benetto. He knew the man's name as he had done business with him. Girard Delafosse rose from his seat, set down a clutch of papers, and deliberately strode around his desk. "Ah, Don Benetto," he greeted with an outstretched hand.

Benetto shook it appreciatively. "Thank you for seeing me on this most urgent matter."

Girard Delafosse was most decidedly French, from his accent to his style. His black hair was cut short, and he sported a thin moustache and goatee. A high ruffled white collar which obscured his neck stood out in contrast to the black velvet jerkin and accented his matching white hose.

But the entire ensemble was overshadowed by his prominent codpiece–an addition which was yet to come into fashion in Milan.

"Indeed," Girard agreed. "Most unfortunate circumstances." He shook his head with a serious deportment.

"I implore you to commit more resources to dispatching with this dangerous criminal known as the Night Flyer. He is wreaking havoc on the city." Benetto had rehearsed his speech and was intent on maintaining his composure.

"Certainly, certainly," he agreed with a hand stroking his tiny beard. "He has dealt you quite a blow, has he not?"

"I have lost some merchandise and money, but nothing that cannot be replaced." Benetto did not want to appear desperate to the French representative. "My biggest concern is the damage he could cause to all the merchants, to the city itself. No doubt he is targeting the wealth of Milan as it is known around the world."

Girard half sat on the edge of his desk shaking his head, then looked to Benetto dismissively. "King Louis does not agree."

Benetto's eyes grew round and his voice rose a level. "The king has heard of this?"

Ignoring his question, the magistrate continued unemotionally. "The evidence tells a different story. This masked felon only attacks *your* shipments, only steals *your* coins, and only displays any intent of harming *you*. Therefore, it would seem he is *your* problem–not Milan's, and certainly not King Louis'. The crown wishes me to seek another provider for our army's weapons since you have become… unreliable."

"What?" Benetto fought terror and temper over the pronouncement. The French military was his biggest client. Without them, how could he maintain his prominence? His heart raced even as his previous countenance of expectation was supplanted by a contortion of desolation. "No, no, please, Your Honor, I can deliver, truly I can!" Don Benetto had never begged for anything in his life… until now. "Give me another chance, I beseech you. I will hire an army if I must and destroy the Night Flyer myself-"

But Girard only shook his head. He stepped back around his desk, placing his hand on its smooth surface. "The French government along with the administration of the city of Milan do hereby cancel any and all contracts with Viscardi Arms and Weapons. I am sorry, Don Benetto, in truth I am, but we must be practical. Wouldn't you do the same?" The Frenchman sighed and sat again on his cushioned chair.

Benetto's shoulders slumped, and he cast his gaze to the tile floor. Undeniably, he had done the same many times. He habitually ignored the pleas of others, always made decisions based upon his best interests, and if a customer couldn't pay or a supplier not deliver… they would be fortunate indeed to only have their contracts cancelled and not their lives. Resigned to his fate, he turned and walked out of Girard's office. *I'll regain my reputation and my fortune–as soon as I can kill that Night Flyer!*

* * *

"Wow, this stuff is amazing!" Matteo cooed as Florentina escorted the children around Alessandro's office. "Look at all these weapons."

"Don't touch anything," his tutor commanded. "Your Uncle Alessandro has allowed us in here today to study the globe and look at maps for your geography lesson. We want him to let us come back another time, don't we?"

"Yes, we do," asserted Betta with a nod of her precious little head.

"I didn't know he had this collection," Matteo commented as his wide eyes passed over each historic sword, ax, bow, and spear.

"They are here as a reminder," Alessandro spoke pleasantly from the doorway, "of just how terrible war is and why we should always seek to prevent it." He nodded to Florentina and then stepped away.

"Come here," she said standing beside the large sphere resting in its wooden frame. Betta and Matteo gathered around in curiosity.

"Is that the world?" Betta's big blue eyes grew one size.

"As much as we know about it so far," Florentina explained. "When I was your age, everyone thought it was flat and that if ships sailed too far from land, they would drop off the edge."

"That's silly!" Matteo exclaimed with a laugh. "If that was so, wouldn't all the water just fall over the edge too? And then there wouldn't even be an ocean."

Florentina smiled at him. *Such bright children! Just like their mother,* she thought. "Here we are," she said pointing to the northern part of the Italian peninsula just below the drawn in mountains.

"It looks so small," Betta noticed.

"Compared to the whole world, it is," Florentina explained. "This is the Mediterranean Sea," she said pointing and had them repeat its name after her. "Over here is Spain and France." They followed her finger and then placed their fingers on each country saying their names. "Because like Betta said and our land looks so small, we are going to open one of these map books."

Florentina removed a large volume from the shelves, opened it to the correct page, and laid it on a table. "This is a bigger image of just the Italian city-states," she said as they peered at the colorful map.

"I see the word Milan!" Matteo exclaimed excitedly.

"Very good! Now, what we are going to do today is, on your own paper that I will give you, draw a copy of this map as best you can and then print the names of Milan, Venice, Florence, and all the rest into their spaces. And when we are done with that, we'll take our papers back to your room and I have some watercolor paints for you to both color your maps. Won't that be fun?"

Two young faces beamed up at her. "We'll be like geography artists," Matteo said with a grin.

"Say, 'cartographers'," Florentina instructed.

"Cartographers," they parroted.

I love these children, she thought in wonder. *It is likely I will never have a baby of my own, and actually I never gave it much thought. But what I feel in my heart for Betta and Matteo—if I ever did bear a child from my own womb, I couldn't possibly love it more than I do them. If I am fortunate enough to be able to stay with Madelena, then in a way it would be like they were my children, too. She is such a good, loving mother! And I love her; God help me, but I do. I just wish... no, not wish. I pray that I can remain a part of this family, even if intimacy with Maddie must stay secret forever.* And speaking of secrets, hers was the one thing she feared may ruin everything. *If I'm not honest with her, how can I expect our relationship to grow? Then again, how can I tell her that the only reason I applied for a position with her House was to best serve my own vendetta, that I have lied to her this whole time, and that I am the Night Flyer?*

* * *

ANTONIO INTERPRETED as the older and more experienced sergeant led the artillery squads through the aiming and loading practice again. Sergeant Beaufort was a sturdy man with serious dark eyes, short sandy hair, and a beard tinged with russet highlights. He gave instructions in French, and it was part of Antonio's duties as Standard Bearer to translate for those recruits who had not been fortunate enough to have gained an education. It would also be his task to command three cannon crews in the field, police their actions when they were not at their posts, and ensure than none of them ran away in the face of stampeding Spanish cavalrymen's lances. To accomplish that, he must gain their trust and their respect, a demanding charge for a young man of eighteen years. Fortunately, Antonio had been raised to become a leader; he had been challenged, encouraged, and afforded opportunities to assert authority over members of the household staff and employed laborers at the production house. *Father has been grooming me*, he thought. *He just didn't know it was for this.*

"Not bad," Sergeant Beaufort said in faint praise, "but faster; you must move faster. Let's give it one more try. If you can beat my count, I'll stand you all to a round," he promised. Antonio repeated the instruction and the enlisted artillerymen cheered. They moved with renewed vigor and Antonio smiled. Despite the fact that he technically held a higher rank, there was much he could learn from his sergeant as well.

Beaufort completed his countdown just as the last cannonball was fired. Four squads drilled that afternoon, Antonio's and three others, for a total of twelve cannons. Of those under his charge, two hit their marks and one was off by a few feet. "Much improvement from your gunners," Beaufort said to Antonio, who could not determine if the man's lips, camouflaged by the thick whiskers, lifted into a smile or not. Then he called to the company, "Recruits to the hall for your reward; Standard Bearers to me."

Happy shouts arose as the soldiers trotted off to get their refreshment and the other three junior officers gathered with Antonio around the sergeant. "I have news for you all," he began in a sober tone. Since the other Standard Bearers were second, third, and fourth sons who would not inherit their fathers' titles or businesses, they had been privy to a similar education as Antonio and were just as fluent in the all-important language, so he no longer had to repeat words in Italian.

"We have received orders to move out tomorrow, so pack light, but be sure to bring everything of importance. The battalion is being called to Barletta, where the Ofonto River empties into the Adriatic, in the Kingdom of Napoli. We will bring our artillery and ammunition by ship to reinforce the city. Since negotiations between King Louis and Ferdinand of Spain fell apart this past summer, you know we have been at war," he explained briskly as he stood in his traditional straight postured stance with his toes pointing outward at forty-five degree angles. "We will not let Napoli fall into the hands of that double-crossing Spaniard! When your men have had their drink, tell them to pack up. We leave at first light."

"Yes, Sergeant," they all confirmed.

After exchanging the obligatory small talk with his peers, Antonio drifted away toward the dining hall to give his squad the news when he saw something that caused him to stop dead still. His mouth fell open, and he blinked his eyes. *A mirage,* he thought. *A waking dream. Surely it isn't... it couldn't be.*

* * *

AGNESE STOOD beside the back wall of the garrison dining hall at the edge of the practice field. She had been gazing longingly at her handsome soldier, memorizing every detail from his red felt cap to his knee-high mud brown leather boots. Only cavalry and infantry wore armor; ranged weapon wielders such as arabesquers, archers, crossbowmen, and cannoneers did not. Antonio's cap identified him as a junior officer but the knee-length green tunic over a black and white long-sleeved shirt and matching two-toned leggings were those common to Italians serving in the French artillery. She recognized his personal rapier in its ornate sheath hanging from the left side of his belt and a new compact firearm–a wheel lock she thought it was called–snuggly tucked into the middle of his belt. She supposed the subtle leather pouch strung to the side held the balls, gunpowder and such needed to fire the mechanism. Agnese had made discrete inquiries and learned that officers were issued close range weapons for defense in case the infantry lines failed. She prayed he would never have to use them.

Her face lit as radiantly as a harvest moon when their eyes met. It was all she could do not to dash across the field and throw herself into his arms. Instead she offered him a coy smile and a bashful wave. Unable to completely hold back a giggle at his stunned expression, she lowered her waving hand to cover her mouth. He didn't run either, but once recovered he picked up his pace and lengthened his stride.

She did take the final few steps to meet him with a vital, unbreakable embrace. His arms felt strong and comforting as he held her to his chest and laid his cheek to her hair. For a long moment neither of them said a word; they simply soaked in the feel, smell, and presence of each other. It had only been a month; how had she thought she would last the rest of her life without him?

"How did you know to come today?" he asked after a time. "I didn't expect you would be here to see me off, but I am so glad you did."

Agnese loosened her hold and stepped back, looking up into his face with unease. "See you off? Are you to leave for the war?" Her heart had begun to race, and she groped about for the strength to keep her lip from quivering.

"Tomorrow," he replied calmly. "I thought that is why you came."

"I didn't know," she answered, her voice weakening. *No, I will not fall apart. That is not what he needs. I must control my emotions.* "But this was my best opportunity to get away. Father is completely distracted by the Night Flyer and has gone to see the French magistrate."

She recognized the dreamy look in his dark eyes that threatened to break through every barricade, every sensibility she possessed and undo her. "It is fortune, then, or an answered prayer. Were you to come tomorrow I would be gone. As it is, I can sail with a joyful heart, and perhaps your favor."

Love radiated from his body like heat from a summer sun, and Agnese smiled despite her anxiety. Reaching into her pocket, she withdrew a powder blue laced handkerchief and tied it to the hilt of his sword. "There you are, my knight with no armor; you shall carry my favor with you to battle." As the weight of her words which were meant to be light landed heavily in her heart, a tear began to form.

"There now." Antonio drew her back into his arms and kissed the glistening eye, then her cheek, finally lighting his lips on hers in a sweet, tender kiss of innocence. "All will be well. We are going to Napoli, and no, I do not know when I will return, but hear me, Agnese," he instructed pinning her with intense eyes. "I will return."

"Please be sure that you do," she commanded in a rare display of authority. Then she sighed. "Why, Antonio? Why?" She gripped his upper arms tightly and steeled her jaw to hold back the flood that threatened. "Is it my fault? I never meant for you to-"

"No, no," he admonished in the sweetest, most gentle tone she had ever heard resonate from the mouth of a man. "Shh, nothing is your fault. I know that. You must never blame yourself for anything I or another person chooses to do. You did what you thought was necessary to keep us both safe; I am doing the same."

"But-" He cut off her protest with a deep and passionate kiss that aroused both longing and contentment in her soul. When Antonio slowly pulled back, he left her head swimming.

"I need to do this for me," he explained, "to become the man I must be to stand up to your father and demand he allows us to wed."

Her chin fell. "He thinks you are a foolish boy who will get himself killed."

Antonio lifted it again with an affectionate hand. "He may think me a foolish boy now, but when I have matured and gained the skills and fortitude required to do battle unto death, he will see the fearless, capable man who returns as his equal. And if he does not, I will be prepared to fight him to have you. Would you object to that?" Now his voice was as determined as stone.

She swallowed remembering all the nights spent hiding in her room, all the horrors she tried to block from her mind. "No. I would not object to that at all."

CHAPTER 22

*a*fter days of unseasonably warm conditions, Florentina suspected that the first winter storm would blow in soon. It was the beginning of December and predicting weather was a tricky proposition for the most progressive atmospheric scientists, but Florentina had taken note that strong storms often initiated or followed unseasonable temperatures. Speaking of which, the wind had started to gust outside and the evening air was cold enough to warrant the first fire in the hearth all week.

Madelena rolled her two dice. "Double fives!" she exclaimed and began moving four of her checkers over the center bar and onto her home board.

Florentina laughed and shook her head. "I may win more often at chess, but you are the queen of Backgammon," she declared as Maddie joyfully advanced her pieces.

"That's because Backgammon is just a luck game," Maddie replied.

"Not so," Portia corrected from her seat across from them as the women spent the evening in the ladies' parlor. "There is some strategy involved as well as luck."

"I suppose," Maddie shrugged.

"Luck or skill, there is no way I will ever catch up in this game," Florentina commented as her calf rubbed amorously against Madelena's.

She noticed the ghost of a smile from Maddie's delicious lips. "The night is young," Madelena noted speculatively. "You could always challenge me to a rematch."

"I thought I was going to play the winner," Pollonia spoke up.

"And you shall," Florentina confirmed. "The change in weather is making me sleepy and I think I shall have to turn in early tonight." Maddie's flirtatious smile dried up, and she tilted her head questioningly toward Fiore as she completed her double move. Florentina rolled her dice. "A one and a three," she sighed selecting two checkers to advance. "No, no chance of me catching you."

Madelena slid her leg away from Florentina's beneath their full skirts. "The weather has made you sleepy you say? Drivel! You are simply embarrassed to lose twice in a row." She shot Florentina a hopeful glance.

Not tonight, my love, Florentina thought to herself. *The time has come for the Night Flyer's final act.* Alessandro had mentioned at dinner that Viscardi's warehouses were filled to bursting with weapons of every variety as the French army had cancelled all their orders and he was frantically seeking out new buyers. "He was so angry he even considered selling to the Spanish," Alessandro had laughed. They all knew Antonio had been sent to Napoli, to the war, but no one dared speak of it around Portia.

Florentina glanced at the petite blonde who feverishly pulled a needle and colored thread through fabric in an attempt to busy herself before turning her eyes back to Maddie. "It is a scientific fact: weather can and does affect people's mood. It could also be because I haven't had enough sleep recently," she added with a subtle wink.

Madelena rolled her dice, biting back a giggle. She flashed those dazzling verdant green eyes of hers at Fiore before returning them to the game. "Six and four," she declared and moved her final two pieces onto her home board. "But you still have a chance to catch me," she teased as she rubbed her leg against Florentina's again and smiled invitingly.

Florentina met her gaze and every emotion of joy, pleasure, and exhilaration they had been sharing in private moments flooded over her like a tidal wave. She had never known she could feel so happy, so alive, or so terrified. *Once I finish with Viscardi, I can put this whole vendetta and the persona of the Night Flyer behind me. Then I will no longer be keeping secrets from you, no longer forced to explain myself with white lies, no longer sharing my nights with a mission rather than you. It ends tonight, and then I'm all yours.*

"I'm willing to bet a storm is on the way in just a few hours,"

Florentina predicted, "and we should all be tucked warmly in our beds before it arrives."

"A frigid wind has picked up outside," Portia noted with a backward glance toward the darkened window.

"That it has," spoke a resonate male voice from the doorway.

"Papa!" Pollonia hopped up and ran to him. "Your hair is mussed." She stretched her hand way up to smooth it for him.

"Yes, I have been outside checking on things and I must agree with Florentina. A storm is brewing for certs. May I suggest we retire for the evening?"

Portia lay her embroidery aside and flowed to him on delicate feet. "I'm ready if you are," she agreed taking his arm.

Madelena gave Florentina a disappointed look and sighed. "Pollonia, it seems we will have to have our game tomorrow night." Then she proceeded to roll double sixes and march all of her playing pieces home.

Florentina laughed and brushed Maddie's arm incidentally. "No catching you tonight," she delivered cryptically, with a barely contained smile pulling at the corners of her mouth and a sensual gleam in her eyes. "Perhaps another time I'll come out on top."

"You come out on top often enough," Maddie replied flirtatiously. Then she stood with a sigh. "But Alessandro is correct; we must all be off to sleep. Good night Ally, Portia," she called after them as they left the parlor with their daughter. "And good night to you, too, I suppose," she said quietly to Fiore.

Florentina stood, and they walked out together close enough for their shoulders to brush and for her to detect the electric rush she always felt at Madelena's touch. "Sleep well, Maddie. I'll see you in the morning." Maddie reached to give her fingers a little squeeze before they turned toward their own portions of the residence.

It was exceedingly difficult to walk away. Such a night was perfect for snuggling in bed with the fabulous woman she loved. And if the wind howled and rain beat upon the window panes, it might indeed provide the impetus for them to take the plunge. *I wonder what it will be like?* Florentina thought as she climbed the servants' stairs. *The pleasure, the wonderfulness that I feel just kissing her, touching her, holding her in my arms is beyond description... what will it be like to experience ultimate ecstasy? I don't see how I could contain even more sensations. Will I dissolve into a puddle or explode into a million pieces? I don't know if I can stand it.* Then she smiled to herself. *Oh, but do I want to find out!*

* * *

THE NIGHT FLYER stood in an alley two streets over from Viscardi's block, obscured in the dark of a moonless, starless night. It was well after midnight and between the wind and first drops of freezing precipitation, the streets were deserted. She moved into the middle of the lane, held out her arms, and closed her eyes letting a gust blow over her. The weather could help or it could hurt her plan. A strong gale could catch neighboring buildings ablaze, but rain could reduce the chances of that happening. *Wind is coming from the north,* she reasoned. *The only thing south of Viscardi's warehouses is his mansion. That has to be destroyed as well, but his wife and daughter and any servants must be evacuated. I have only one target and don't want innocent bystanders harmed.*

She had all of her regular gear along with a few new additions. The black bag that had once held sacks of coins was now filled with sealed clay jars containing crude oil, an inky thick liquid from Constantinople. The Italians called it naphtha, and her father had kept a small quantity for experiments. Together with the pouches of sulfur, saltpeter, charcoal powder, and quicklime, Florentina brought with her the ingredients for Greek Fire. *They can throw as much water on it as they like,* she thought, *but that will only make it spread. Tonight House Viscardi burns.*

Leonardo da Vinci had never written down the formula, but he could not resist the challenge of discovering it for himself. Fortunately for Florentina, the master's focus was so singular when he worked that he was often oblivious to the world around him, and the people in it. Add that to his penchant for talking to himself as he worked, and she had learned more from the master than he ever imagined. When he did notice her in his workshop as the euphoria of success lit his eyes, he swore her to secrecy. "It was one thing for the Byzantines to use this as a defensive weapon against enemy ships encroaching upon their shores," he warned her gravely, "but can you imagine the potential for civilian casualties if our modern warlord kings were to unleash it on a city?" She shuddered just remembering his tone. Leonardo may have made the majority of his income from weapons contracts, but he would never allow this secret to fall into the hands of politicians or generals.

She hoped the freezing rain would prevent the fire's spread, but at least other buildings, were they to catch, could be put out with water; only the warehouses and mansion where she would plant the unstoppable inferno would burn into ashes.

Florentina stood for another moment, arms outstretched feeling the ice droplets pelt her body and took in a deep breath of cold air then slowly let it out. She repeated this several times to calm and steady herself for what lay ahead. She had a plan, but would most certainly be called upon to improvise. *It is time.*

The night was perfect. Total darkness, save for a few street lamps, hid her approach, and the noise from the storm drowned out all other sounds. First she rounded the farthest structure, scouting out the placement of guards huddled into doorways. Each entry to the three warehouses sported two guards, but she was not certain how many waited inside. *Noticeable surge in security there, Benetto; are you afraid of someone?* she thought in proud amusement.

The Night Flyer circled back to the alley side of the farthest warehouse which had only one door. She crept closer and felt a chill as cold moisture penetrated her clothing, but the blood pumping through her veins was red hot. She crouched against the wall only a few feet from where two hired men who had no stake in Viscardi's fortunes hunched with woolen cloaks wrapped around them trying to avoid the numbing, wind-driven sleet. They both had swords hanging from their belts and a spear was propped against the building as they rubbed their hands together to keep warm. She waited.

Presently one said, "I have to step inside for just a moment, get something hot to drink. Do you want I should bring you a cup?"

"Si, si," the other eagerly agreed. And then there was one.

Florentina withdrew a dark brown bottle from one of the pouches on her belt and damped a cloth with the ether. In a swift, sudden move, she lunged from her crouch, grabbed the guard from behind, and pressed the wet rag to his face. He tensed and tried to struggle for an instant. He was not a big man, actually shorter than she was, though a bit thicker. In just a few breaths he fell limp in her arms, and she dragged him away from the doorway and laid him out on the sidewalk. Then she moved to the side of the doorway, plastered herself with her back to the wall, re-dosed the cloth, and waited.

"Here you go, Teodor," a voice sang out. "Nice and hot. Teodor? Where are you?" The figure stepped through the lintel searching for his counter-part. She pounced, and two cups of steaming liquid clattered to the paving stones. His limp, unconscious body soon joined them.

Cautiously, the Night Flyer eased inside. The vast, high roofed structure was dark, save for a small sliver of light passing through the windows on the opposite side facing the main thoroughfare. Outside a lone oil street lamp's flame flickered safe from wind and wet inside its glass dome. The warehouses were constructed with many windows to allow maximum natural light, as it would be infeasible to light the huge expanse with candles and oil lamps. Since almost all work was done during the daytime, it was the sensible architectural devise to employ.

Her eyes were already adjusted to the dim illumination, so she used them to scan the chamber while listening intently for any sounds. The indomitable rat was the only creature her keen senses detected, so she slowly made her way toward the center. *Full to the brim,* she noted as there were crates, boxes, barrels, and bags stacked from wall to wall about waist high leaving walking trails between them. Once she judged herself to be about in the middle, she stopped and used a hook on her grappling device to pry open a crate. This one held wooden handled lances with steel points. *Perfect,* she thought considering the flammable product.

Florentina removed two clay jars of naphtha and set one inside the crate. She opened the other one and proceeded to pour a small trickle forming a line about ten paces to the north, then returning to ground zero, she did the same in every direction, some paths crossing crates and others along the floor, until the jar was empty and she had created a design akin to spokes radiating from the hub of a wheel. Next, she opened the second jar and measured out a prescribed portion of the power ingredients and stirred them in with a wooden spoon she brought from their kitchen for this purpose.

It was all prepared, everything laid out correctly. In moments the entire building would be engulfed in an inexorable conflagration. She had left herself a path of retreat, of course, back to the door from which she entered, and had been extra careful not to spill a drop on herself. She had no intentions of bonding with St. Joan in that way! Florentina drew out the small tin containing her sulfur matches. While the original Greek Fire had been spewed from a distance as a burning liquid, she planned to simply ignite it in place.

The Night Flyer broke the jar of prepared oleaginous fluid over the lances in their crate, but before she could strike the match, she heard the scuffle of feet.

"Stop, you!" shouted a deep voice. She turned and saw four guards spread out blocking her escape route. Still holding the match and box at the ready, she took a deep breath. *Time to improvise.*

CHAPTER 23

 wo guards drew swords while the other pair fumbled to load and ready crossbows. The Night Flyer struck the match and let it fall. She dropped to the floor and rolled away as a booming sound accompanied the flaming cloud that surged toward the high ceiling. Springing to her feet, she watched rows of fire burst forth from the hub, streaking out along the oil lines filling the chamber with light, smoke, and a starburst of flame. The guards stepped back, instinctively raising a free arm to cover their faces. One, however, had been standing on a line of naphtha that caught his boots afire straightaway. She heard his scream and saw him leap into a terrified dance as his sword clattered to the floor.

"Kick off your boots, you oaf!" Florentina shouted in a low-pitched voice. "And stop hopping about unless you want to burn to death." She rapidly weaved through crates, some of which were beginning to blaze, toward a row of windows. "If there is gunpowder in here, I suggest you run!"

Two crossbow bolts whizzed past her, one lodging in a crate and another into the wall. Smoke obscured the air between her and the guards giving their shots slim chances of striking their mark.

"Help me!" The frantic man plopped to the floor amid rivers of fire and burned his hands tugging off his fiery boots. One of his cohorts rushed over, caught him under his arms, and began to drag him away toward the door. The other two dashed out ahead of them sounding the alarm.

Florentina tore off the lid of a wooden box and slammed it through the windows across the large room from where the guards made their escape, sending shards of glass shooting out into the frigid night, followed by a figure in black. Bells began to ring and shouts went up as smoke billowed forth and flames shimmered in a macabre dance. *One down,* she thought, and vanished into the darkness.

* * *

Benetto was awakened by the uproar and had just thrown on his clothing when Stefano burst through his bedroom door. "One of the warehouses is on fire!" he hollered breathlessly after running up the stairs.

"I gathered as much," Benetto spat out in bitter reply. "You stay in the house," he commanded his wife. "I'll deal with this."

"It's the farthest one," Stefano continued the report as his older brother followed him out. Benetto's man at arms, Zuane, had rushed in and met them at the bottom of the staircase.

Benetto barked orders to him. "I want half of our men putting out that fire. Then divide the rest between guarding the other two warehouses and chasing down that damnable Night Flyer. No excuses this time!" he bellowed. "Burn down my warehouse, will you," he muttered to himself as the three men marched toward the front door of Casa de Viscardi. "I'll kill you myself," he hissed between clenched teeth.

Zuane rushed off to distribute the hired men to their tasks and Stefano grabbed the butler who had ventured into the entry hall. "You go find a city watchman and call for a fire brigade," he instructed. The startled butler nodded then scrambled away, dashing down the street.

"He picked the worst night of the year," Benetto complained as he stepped out into the frosty air and icy precipitation. "But the freezing rain will help extinguish the flames."

"I guess he wasn't so smart this time," Stefano commented. "We'll get him for sure."

Benetto said nothing, only crossed his arms over his chest and scowled as he looked toward the burning warehouse. He wasn't certain. That tricky bastard was up to something; he didn't make simple mistakes. A strange and disconcerting feeling began to boil in Benetto's gut, twisting his insides painfully even as his hatred rose. What if this was it?

What if Don Benetto Viscardi was beaten at last, and by whom? Some masked highwayman? No. He must have been sent by *them*... a nameless, faceless marauder sent by a nameless, faceless secret society that for whatever reason wished to destroy him. How could he fight such a foe? But he would, by God; he would fight!

* * *

THE BURNING WAREHOUSE lit up the night and men were dashing toward it, some with buckets of water and others with weapons. "Spread out!" shouted Zuane. "Get water in there and put that fire out. And you, hunt down the Night Flyer."

Florentina wasted no time. As soon as the last of the brigade rushed past her position crouched in the shadows of an alley across the lane from the second warehouse, she sprang and raced toward the deserted building. She could still hear Zuane barking orders when she pulled a small bomb from her pouch. She zipped around the corner and squatted on the cobblestones with her back against the wall to warehouse number two. "Search every backstreet, every rooftop, behind every feckin' bush!" the security chief bellowed. She lit the fuse.

The Night Flyer trotted back around the corner to the windowed wall of the second warehouse with a lit explosive sphere in her right hand. She had just about reached the middle of the block-sized structure when a voice rang out, "There he is!" She reared her arm back and launched the lead ball through a glass pane, immediately streaking away from her pursuers and toward the third warehouse.

The initial boom was followed by a tremendous explosion that blew the roof from the building and sent glass particles cutting through the wintry mix like tiny razors. Clay tile shingles rained from the sky and the guards who had not been flattened by the power of the blast were forced to take cover. *Well, we know where the powder was kept,* Florentina surmised as she hastened to the unattended side doorway of the last warehouse.

It was locked, and there wasn't time for subtlety. The Night Flyer lifted her grappling hook from her belt, held a length of rope in both hands, and swung the hook end through a window. With the cacophony of shattering glass and gunpowder kegs blaring through the night, who would notice anyway? She leapt through the hole and crouched inside beneath the row of windows while she rewound the rope.

They will come here next, she concluded. *While some are spreading the first fire in an attempt to put it out, others will be chasing me and they saw the direction I took. I don't have time to neatly lay out the oil like before, so...* There was enough light now to see the interior of the extensive structure. The south end was divided into three floors where the offices and other rooms were situated closest to Casa de Viscardi. She had been up there before. The big room she currently occupied was more crowded with merchandise than the first had been. Here scaffolding had been erected to store boxes and crates high off the floor which was filled with large items such as cast bronze barreled cannons with wide spoked wheels, smaller mortars, and heavy artillery carts designed to transport the cannonballs and powder kegs to the field. She instantly thought of Antonio; he could be using weapons like these purchased from Viscardi before the French cancelled his contracts. Then she recalled Alessandro's comment, "He was so angry he even considered selling to the Spanish." Her blood boiled at the notion that Benetto may have plans to sell these weapons to an army that would use them against Madelena's nephew. *Alessandro, this is for you.*

There was no time for careful mixing of the formula nor artful arrangement of naphtha. She opened one of the jars and dribbled it behind as she jogged through the warehouse aiming for the opposite doorway. Before the jar was empty, Viscardi's men were pouring through the front door. "There!" one shouted and pointed.

She ducked behind a munitions wagon, hurled the jar toward them, and pulled up her revolving crossbow. The Night Flyer stood and fired off several bolts in the guards' direction forcing them to take cover, then she stooped back down to light a sulfur match. When she perceived the stomp of boots, she stood, dropped the match onto the end of the oil stream, and pushed her way through the stockpile of artillery pieces toward the nearest exit, which in this case was the back door leading in the direction of the engulfed second warehouse.

"I've got him!" sounded a man's excited shout just as the whoosh sounded and flames started to race down the black line of oil. She heard the report of his arabesque and the alarmed voices of others as they made exclamations about the fire.

Once she reached the door, Florentina bent down and turned toward them, a lead ball in her hand. "I'm going to give you fellows a fighting chance," she called out. "This bomb has a ten second fuse. If you run, you'll make it out."

She counted maybe six of them, and every one stopped and stared as she lit the cord and tossed the bomb into middle of the building. It hit the floor and started to roll, a hissing fuse burning its way toward the powder inside. The Night Flyer pushed open the door, and the men dashed away, racing each other back to the entrance whence they came.

Florentina's boots ran over pieces of burning wood, broken glass, and shattered roof tiles. She dodged a flaming beam and stumbled around piles of bricks in the narrow alley between the destroyed warehouse and the one about to blow, just barely clearing the requisite distance before hearing the loud report. With the explosion of the third warehouse drawing attention, she sprinted across the street and down a neighboring backstreet, then two blocks south to skitter up a drainpipe onto the roof of some anonymous person's dwelling to survey the situation.

Three warehouses burned, one totally destroyed by a gunpowder explosion, and two more that would be impossible to extinguish. Pausing to catch her breath, she noted that the wind was dying down but the wintry mix of ice, sleet, and snow persisted. The fires had been contained and no other structures were in peril. That triggered a sigh of relief. Now to implement the final strike–Casa de Viscardi and Don Benetto himself.

* * *

BENETTO COVERED his face with his forearm and turned away when the bomb blew inside the warehouse across the street from his front door. He watched as six of his guards streaked out the door dispersing into the thoroughfare. "Where is Zuane?" he called.

One of the men paused long enough to answer. "He was back by the first one hit a minute ago."

"Go get him and bring him here," Benetto commanded. The hired man nodded and trotted away. Then he turned to his brother, "I want you to stay here and protect the mansion. I must survey the damage myself."

"Don't worry, Benetto," Stefano assured him. "No one is getting in the house."

Benetto strode away leaving his stalwart brother blocking the doorway with his broad-shoulders, arms crossed over his chest. He shook his head as he raked his stinging eyes over flames and destruction. The fire brigade had finally arrived, but it seemed the more water they threw on the blaze, the more it spread.

The errand guard met him with Zuane in tow. "We can't seem to get the fires out," Zuane reported in dismay. "Some of the men claim they gave chase to the Night Flyer, but each time something blew up and they were forced to retreat. I've got a dozen more spread out over several blocks searching for him."

Benetto stared dry eyed as he watched his dream literally turn to ashes. He had no words, no sure course of action. For the first time he could remember, he was truly afraid, convinced some shadowy, underworld order had marked him a dead man. He simply felt numb.

CHAPTER 24

With her dagger drawn, Florentina crept on velvet feet, as silently as a cat on the prowl, through the servant's entrance at the back of Casa de Viscardi. Candles and lamps had been lit and a sense of tenuous fear permeated the mansion. She paused to listen and ducked into a closet upon hearing tiny, rapid footsteps approach. Peering through the cracked door, Florentina spied a middle-aged woman in a maid's attire scurrying past.

The Night Flyer darted out behind her and clamped her left hand over the woman's mouth while brandishing the knife where it could be seen. "Don't make a sound if you wish to live," she whispered in a gravelly voice.

The terrified servant squeaked and quivered, but did not faint. "Nod your head if you understand me. Do not make a sound. I am not here to harm you, but to save you." Slowly the woman nodded her head.

Florentina turned the woman toward her and leveled a grave gaze into her ashen face. "How many servants are in residence?"

The maid's eyes flew wide, and she covered her own mouth in an effort to obey the order to remain silent. A small gasp escaped her lips, nonetheless. She took a steadying breath and held up eight fingers.

"And your mistress and her daughter?"

The maid nodded, but her breathing began to steady and her shaking eased. "You're a-" she sounded in a whisper.

"Never mind that," Florentina demanded, holding the servant with intense brown eyes. "I am the Night Flyer, and in five minutes this mansion will be in flames. Do you understand?"

She nodded, a look of curiosity now replacing the previous panic. No one had ever seen the Night Flyer up close; therefore, everyone had assumed the prowler to be a man. Florentina supposed that with scarcely twelve inches between them her gender was more easily detected, but there was no time to speculate about that.

"Go up and collect your mistress and her daughter along with the staff and bring them out through this back door, and this door only. Do you understand? Not the front or a side exit, but this one. It will be the only safe path of retreat. Then head for the nearest chapel."

The maid nodded her head. "Gather everyone and bring them out here," she repeated in a discreet echo.

"I will see you and I will count. Do not alarm Don Benetto nor any enforcers," she warned. "If you do, then none will leave this house alive. Is that clear?" Florentina had no intention of harming anyone save her father's murderer, but she hoped the warning would convince the maid to comply. Once she saw the nod of agreement, she announced, "Four minutes now. Make haste."

The woman's eyes widened once more, and she turned to dash up the servant's stairway. The Night Flyer shrank into the obscure closet to wait once more.

She had almost counted four minutes in her head when she heard footsteps and whispers on the narrow stairs. Through the cracked door she observed those exiting the abode. A nervous plump woman with blond hair donning an expensive silk-lined wool cloak over her nightgown clutching a carved box, presumably filled with jewelry, skittered out first, followed by a youthful girl just old enough to be considered a woman wearing similar attire carrying a small painting, a pillow in an embroidered satin slip, and a book. *There's the mistress and her daughter. Is that one of Antonio's paintings?* she wondered, straining for a better view, but for naught. Next came a parade of two men and five women in various stages of undress and bringing up the rear was the maid with whom Florentina had spoken.

The Night Flyer materialized into the room, gave a nod of approval to the startled maid, and closed and locked the door behind them. She took a deep breath and proceeded to work her way into the main part of the structure. The layout was similar but not exactly like Casa de Torelli.

Still, it was not difficult to locate key rooms. She needed to set her Greek Fire in a central location filled with combustibles to fuel her inferno. *The dining room would be fitting,* she mused, *since that is where he poisoned Papa.*

Soundlessly she placed soft-soled boots one in front of the other as she explored the first floor of the now empty house. *Perhaps through this sitting area,* she thought, *those double doors.*

Florentina slid aside one of the heavy doors that glided eloquently into its wall pocket. She smiled as she surveyed the rich furnishings of the dining room, then hastened to the heavy walnut table. She withdrew the last of the clay jars of crude and began mixing in the sulfur, saltpeter, charcoal powder, and quicklime in the prescribed amounts. Next she dribbled out a circle of the tincture on the table top followed by another around it crossing each chair. With the jar tilted enough to pour a thin line, she retraced her steps through the sitting room and hallway. She continued the trail down an exquisite Persian carpet into the entry hall and to the base of the grand staircase.

The Night Flyer spun about abruptly when behind her the front door flung open and the brawny Stefano strode through it. "What's that smell?" he said wrinkling his nose.

"I don't care about smells," the man-at-arms dismissed in a gruff tone. "Don Benetto wants his coat and sent me to bring it—hey!" Wide-eyed and slack-jawed he pointed at the masked intruder.

Florentina had back-stepped halfway up the stairs before she was spotted. Her rotating crossbow was in her hands and it still held two bolts. Why hadn't she thought to reload it? How stupid! Stefano was standing directly below a large silver candelabra that must have weighed at least twenty pounds. She made a split second decision and fired the two shots at the canopy where the chain holding it was connected to the ceiling. It crashed down on the unsuspecting man and he fell unconscious beneath it.

But the larger, younger Zuane was already surging toward her. Florentina turned and ran. She must reason her next move, but he was gaining on her. She reached for a door handle only to find it locked. That's when she felt the blow. It rendered her head spinning and her ears ringing. The floor was rushing up toward her; then it smacked her in the face. She tried to crawl but a boot under her stomach sent her airborne and careening into a wall. Now she had no breath in her and couldn't focus her vision for all the scattering of tiny white lights in her eyes. This was not good.

"I've got you now, you little bastard," he spat out in a kind of hateful glee. "Don Benetto wants to kill you with his own hands, but I can have a bit of fun first."

While she was still trying to pull her senses together a huge rough hand picked her up by her throat. She reacted the only way she knew how in that situation, with a quick, hard kick to his groin. When the hand released her, and she heard his agonizing moan, she offered a prayer of thanks for having hit her mark.

Florentina sat sprawled on the floor trying to catch her breath knowing her reprieve would be short-lived. *He is so strong. I can't fight him, and I can't run away.* There was only one alternative, one she had hoped to avoid.

"Now you've done it, you miserable scrap of shit." The words spewed from his lips as he braced himself against the wall only a few feet across from her.

Her heart pounded in her chest, her head was spinning, and her gut throbbed with pain, but she managed to suck in a bit of air and focus her eyes on his hulking form. Florentina heard more than saw him pull a sword from its sheath. She bent over so he wouldn't see her draw her own weapon. Catching the movement in her peripheral vision as he made the preparatory move before the strike, she rolled.

The Night Flyer sprung up on Zuane's left side, and with both hands clamped on the hilt, plunged a double-edged carbon steel dagger into the big man-at-arms' chest. His eyes widened as he gasped to breathe and turned his dying face toward hers. Their eyes met as his sword clamored to the floor. He clutched at his wound but his hands ended up tightening around hers as she still gripped her weapon. Then he fell limp and his body dropped away from the knife with a disturbing sucking sound.

Blood covered Florentina's hands along with her blade. She stood there staring at his body for a moment. *I didn't have a choice. He was going to kill me. This was self-defense.* Snapping back to the reality of the moment, she reached down and wiped off her dagger and her hands on the edge of Zuane's coat. Florentina set her jaw and pushed herself to an upright position. She tried twisting her torso and decided that nothing was broken. Then she purposefully stepped over the lifeless frame at her feet and marched downstairs.

Stefano was unconscious, lying directly inside the front door. That would not do; this is where Benetto will enter and his brother can't be here. So Florentina grabbed him by his feet and started to drag him toward the back door. He was heavy, and she was hurting, but she managed to get him all the way to the closet near the back door. Looking down at him she noticed the black smudges on his coat. Sure, he was the murderer's brother and had most likely carried out murders on Benetto's bequest, but in the end it was Benetto himself who was responsible. *I've already killed his man-at-arms; I don't intend to kill his brother, too.*

It was an awkward struggle, but she managed to pull Stefano's oil smeared coat off of him. Satisfied that the rest of his clothing had no flammable liquid soaked into it, she tossed the garment into another room. *He won't be out for long. If I have to, I'll come back for him,* she reasoned.

Resolutely, Florentina strode to the front door, closed it, and flattened herself against the wall just inside the doorframe with a large knife clasped in her right hand. She forced every thought save completing her vendetta and avenging her father's death from her mind, and like a lioness on the Serengeti, she awaited the arrival of her prey.

CHAPTER 25

"What is taking Zuane so long," Benetto muttered while sleet bounced at his feet and fat, sloppy snowflakes melted into his tunic. He shivered, then turned away from the gloomy scene of destruction, holding his arms around himself. Men battled to put out the fires to no avail, and no one had brought him news of the Night Flyer's capture. Benetto was totally despondent, but he did not care to freeze to death. *I'll rebuild,* he said to himself as he trudged back toward his home. *I did it once; I can do it again.* But he didn't actually believe it. He understood that he had inherited the bulk of the business and clients from his father, not to mention the mansion and vineyard. But he had been a shrewd businessman in his own right. He had increased the fortune, not squandered it as so many did.

I'll put a bounty on the Night Flyer's head, he considered. *Hire assassins and spies to hunt him down. Mayhap I'll sell the vineyard and use the proceeds to rebuild the warehouses.* But he knew no one would buy the property now that it could not produce usable grapes. *I'll take out a loan. I could use Casa de Viscardi as collateral. The bank would not deny me.* That idea made him feel a little better.

But when Benetto reached the front door of his mansion, Stefano was nowhere to be seen. *Zuane didn't need him to go find a coat; my brother should be at his post doing his job.* He scowled at the unguarded entry to his personal castle before being struck by a wary suspicion which hurriedly regressed into panic. *Why isn't Stefano standing watch?*

The seasoned master merchant clamped down on his emotions, willing himself to steadiness, but his heart still raced and his palms began to sweat. *Why isn't Stefano at the door? It could be nothing... it's probably nothing. He just went in to show Zuane where to find my coat. Or he got hungry; you know Stefano–always thinking of his stomach.*

Nevertheless, every one of Benetto's senses shot onto high alert as he placed a tentative hand on the door handle and pushed it. Cautiously, he nudged open the solid oak door, its copper hinges whining an indignant creak. The entry hall was bathed in pale light from a distant lamp. "Stefano?" he called out in a question, but it was the odor that struck terror through his heart. While he couldn't name the ingredients in the pungent combination, he recognized it from one of his burning warehouses. At once his muscles tensed and he shoved hard at the door, whipping an alarmed gaze from side to side. All he caught was a black streak before a solid object hit him in the head. The sharp pain was accompanied by stars before his eyes.

Instinctively, Benetto reached out his hands with the intent of grabbing something to steady himself, but a foot blocked his right leg from stretching forward. His advancing momentum ensured that he hit the floor with a solid thud sending a stunning shock through his aging body. Still trying to clear his vision, he placed his palms to the wooden planks attempting to push himself up, but his arms were shaky and he feared the worst fate for his missing brother. Then the door slam behind his splayed feet.

"Who-" Benetto sputtered. A hand gripped his shoulder and rolled him onto his back. He sensed pressure on his chest which he at first took to be the onset of a heart attack, until he discerned the cold, flat steel of a knife blade against his neck. He blinked his eyes several times and was finally able to see the masked face hovering above his.

"Night Flyer," he uttered and fell limp. He was still conscious but recognized nothing was to be gained by a vain attempt at struggle. "My brother?"

"He's alive," the tenor voice clipped. "Can't say the same for your other man."

He bested Zuane? A new wave of panic flowed through him as his enemy came into focus. The lean figure all in black had a knee crushed against his chest pinning him to the floor and his right hand pressed a dagger to his throat. He recognized the glare of loathing in the hard brown eyes that stared through him, and he realized he had lost.

"My wife and daughter?" he choked out.

"They are safe... for now. But that could change. They say confession is good for the soul, and seeing how near your soul is to being cleaved from your body, you are going to speak the names of all the men you have killed or had killed."

"What makes you think I've killed anyone?" he asked as he stalled and tried to assess the identity of this assassin.

His eyes widened at the sharp prick of the honed blade and felt a little trickle of blood warm against his chilled skin. "I am not here to play games, Viscardi. Say their names," the Night Flyer demanded.

Benetto took a breath and swallowed carefully. "I am an important man, a respected man, powerful in this city. If you kill me the government and every watchman and constable will hunt you down."

This drew an unexpected response as the assailant in black actually laughed. "No one respects you," he declared incredulously. "And you will not be missed for a moment. Do you honestly think the leaders of Milan will call out the guard to avenge you?"

"But," he protested, more horrified by the Night Flyer's words than his steel. "I am respected. People-"

"People fear you," he interrupted. "Even your own wife and daughter are terrified of you, but fear is not respect. People will feel something at the news of your death–relief. They may even throw a party to celebrate."

"You impudent thug!" In the midst of the whirlwind of emotions anger managed to surface, most of all because Benetto supposed his words may actually be true. "Why should I do as you say? You will kill me anyway."

The Night Flyer titled his head to one side as if in contemplation. "There are many ways to die. A knife to the throat is quick with little pain. Burning, however, is neither quick nor painless." A shiver ran down Benetto's spine at the thought of the agony of such a death. "And there is the matter of your family members, or do you not care of their outcome?"

He sighed, tortured misery lining his face and dully lighting his gray eyes. Then he began a list of names and an explanation of why each was deserving of his fate, ending with the careless spy, Iseppo.

"Are you forgetting someone?" The Night Flyer's voice took on a sharper tone. Benetto looked up through clueless eyes but said nothing. "What of Luigi de Bossi, the inventor?"

"Oh, yes," he recalled. He had forgotten about him. "He betrayed me, kept stringing me along taking my money but always had an excuse why the exploding cannon shells I was paying him to develop were not ready. It was obvious that he was secretly working for one of my competitors, pretending it was taking so long all the while never intending to deliver."

"And you had proof of this?"

"Well, no." Benetto drew his brows together. "Not exactly, but-"

"You couldn't have merely dismissed him?" the outlaw taunted angrily.

Benetto drew in a breath and set his jaw, his eyes lighting with renewed fire. "No one makes a fool of Don Benetto Viscardi!"

The Night Flyer sighed and shook his head, but the knife remained pressed to Benetto's jugular and he was reminded that he was about to die. Did he deserve this? Had he been too quick to assume the role of judge and executioner over others? His heart sunk further into melancholy as he had harbored doubts, especially regarding de Bossi's guilt or innocence. *No one makes a fool of me,* he pondered sullenly, *except for me.*

"And what of Vergilio Carcano?"

Benetto's mouth slacked and confusion draped his expression. "Who?"

The Night Flyer appeared aggravated and raised his voice. "The merchant Vergilio Carcano, Don Alessandro's brother-in-law."

Now Benetto was genuinely confused. "I didn't kill him," he stated plainly. "I heard he fell from his horse."

"Come now, Viscardi," the Night Flyer pressed. "Just one more confession."

"But, why would I kill him? He wasn't important enough to kill. Honestly, I never gave him a thought."

Benetto read the mistrust in the masked man's face. Was it a man's face? A youth, perhaps. "He was very vocal with his political views," his captor explained, "which were in opposition to yours. He strongly supported the Sforza family, and you ran to the French, eager to sell them arms."

"Well, yes," Benetto replied innocently. "But I don't care about politics; I saw a good business opportunity. I stood to make higher profits from the French. I've confessed to all the others; why not one more? Because I didn't kill the man. But you have no room to judge me," he spat changing timbre. "I know you are merely a hired killer sent by *them.* But I don't understand why? Why not recruit me for your order? I could have been such an asset to your lords. Instead they want to be rid of me. I just don't understand why?"

* * *

FLORENTINA LOOKED DOWN into pleading eyes and was thoroughly thrown aback at his words. After hearing all the other confessions, she believed him when he said he didn't kill Madelena's husband. But if he didn't, who did, and why? How much did she not know?

"Who?" she pressed as she twisted her knee over his ribs, discerning his discomfort and observing the distress in his eyes. "Who do you think sent me?"

"*Them*," he answered in a whisper, shuddering as he did. "The secret underground society, the sign of the horse. I know they are men of power and means. I don't know what I did to draw their wrath."

This was definitely new information, and she needed to learn as much as she could. If he hadn't killed Vergilio, perhaps this secret order had. She turned up the corners of her mouth and declared, "Perchance you murdered someone they cared about." But she required more information.

"How did you attain knowledge about this group and their activities if they are so secret? Speak man; your life depends on your answer."

"I acquired the diary of... a madman, I think. It belonged to Galeazzo Monetario, a younger son of some lesser noble who indulged in too much wine, and God knows what else. It could be nothing more than the ravings of a lunatic. When his body was pulled from the canal last year, no one suspected foul play, but I came into possession of his writings. They mostly make no sense, but... if true there is a much more dangerous force than I working in Milan."

Florentina drew her brows together with concern and spoke briskly. "Give it to me."

She watched Benetto slide his eyes to the left and look back at her innocuously. "I don't have it with me, but upstairs-"

"No," she snapped. "It is important and you are afraid of them. Slowly withdraw the volume from your pocket Don Benetto, and hand it to me now." Her voice was low and commanding and he did as she required. Florentina slipped a small leather-bound book into a pouch on her belt, then returned her attention to the object of her vendetta, the man who not only had murdered her father but had deemed his death forgettable.

Benetto sunk into the floor in defeat and Florentina took a minute to truly see him. He looked old; he looked weak. Was he a murderer? Yes. Was he the monster she thought him to be? Maybe not. But there he was, lying helpless beneath her blade, the moment she had waited over six months for. Removing him from the earth was justice; it was what he deserved. But after all of her planning, practicing, and preparation, after meticulously devising and carrying out her vendetta, after hearing the names of almost a dozen men he had sent to the grave over the years, Florentina's heart spoke to her, and it said, *it is enough.*

She gripped the dagger tighter and gritted her teeth, bitter eyes stabbing through his, but it wasn't right. It wasn't who she was. When the final moment had come, Florentina discovered that she couldn't carry out her judgment; she couldn't execute a man sprawled helplessly beneath her, no matter what he had done.

"You are finished, Don Benetto. Your wealth is gone, your position forfeited, your crimes laid bare." She raised her blade and saw him flinch, the shadow of fear race over his face. "And it is enough." He didn't move. She felt the uncertainty, detected the disbelief in him, and she continued. "You have twenty-four hours to leave Milan, which won't be an imposition since I am about to burn your mansion to the ground. You may retreat to your vineyard and live out your days."

Then she drew the knife in a quick slice across his chin. "That is to remind you. Every time you look in the mirror and see that scar, remember that you were given a second chance."

She heard a noise from the back of the house and concluded that Stefano was conscious again. "Your brother is coming and you can find the rest of your family at the nearby church. Do not think you will get another pass from me, Viscardi. If you are not out of the city by tomorrow night, I will finish what I began."

Benetto reached a hand to wipe the blood from his chin and nodded. The Night Flyer straightened up, took two strides from him, and withdrew her matchbox. "Zuane?" a groggy Stefano called.

"In the front hall!" shouted Benetto. "Hurry!" Florentina struck the match and dropped it into a pool of Greek Fire, then stepped back as a plume of flame flashed toward the high ceiling. She was exiting the front door as Stefano reached his brother. They would both have time to get out.

While a part of her felt as if she had failed her father and failed in her mission, her heart knew she had done the right thing. He may not be dead, but perhaps losing all of his wealth and power was a fate worse than death, and maybe–just maybe–he would consider this close encounter with eternity and change his ways.

Outside in the cold, wet, fiery night, men worked feverishly to extinguish flames, guards looked everywhere except the master's house for the culprit, and the Night Flyer slipped silently into the shadows.

CHAPTER 26

*M*adelena rolled over in bed, readjusting her covers. The fire in the hearth was nothing more than a smoldering log that had broken in the middle leaving two charred ends framing a pile of ashes. The coals in her brass bed-warmer emitted just enough heat to register its existence. She missed the warmth of another human being lying beside her. Even if Vergilio had not often been emotionally intimate, his physical nearness had been a comfort. *How I would love to have Fiore in my bed every night,* she mused. That set her brain to work trying to figure a way to achieve that goal without creating a scandal. Slowly sleep eased away, though she realized she should let the thoughts go and drift back into dreams. She rolled again, this time toward the windowed balcony doors. An eyelid lifted. Instead of the stark darkness she expected, there was a reddish-orange glow in the sky outside.

It can't be dawn already, Madelena grumbled with a sullen frown. *I haven't had a proper rest yet.* But as the veil of sleep fell farther from her rousing consciousness, she realized the light did not hail from the east, but illuminated the western sky.

Sudden alarm jolted her in to full alert, and Maddie threw her legs over the side of the bed, slid her feet into padded, satin slippers, and reached for her warm, lamb's wool winter robe. She rushed toward her balcony doors while tying the sash around her wrap.

A rush of frigid air sought to dissuade her from venturing out, but adrenaline surged through Madelena's veins and anxious speculation filled her mind. She stepped through the door and her foot began to slide on the slick wood. The black iron railing was adorned with a trickle of icing along its top and tiny frozen stalactites hanging down from its underside; she grabbed it with bare hands.

She could smell the smoke and at first panic seized her emotions. Every city dweller knew of the great fires of London in 1135 and 1212. Thousands had died in massive infernos that had consumed half of the great city. Not only London, but in Lübeck, Germany and Amsterdam as well as other historic devastations. The major Italian cities of modern times were less vulnerable to wide spreading fires because they did not use straw thatch and few structures were built entirely of wood. Their brick and stucco edifices with their clay tile roofs were much safer; still, the idea of a sweeping conflagration was enough to strike terror into any urban resident.

Madelena stared at the smoke and flame judging its distance away, the part of town it was in, and something clicked in her brain. *That is Don Benetto's district.* She watched for some time noting that the blaze was getting smaller, not larger, and a wry smile crossed her lips. *It seems the Night Flyer is busy this evening, and if so, he will not allow such a fire to get out of control.*

She pulled her robe tighter and hugged herself against the wet chill as a gust lifted her long, loose, red locks and billowed them like an unfurled sail. The earlier gale had died down and as the temperature dropped rain had turned to sleet, then ice, and finally snow. Now the sky was filled with powdery crystalline flakes tossed about like goose down from a torn pillow.

Convinced that her home was safe, Madelena decided to return to the relative warmth of her empty bed when something caught her eye. A dark shadow was descending toward her rooftop across the courtyard, back-lit by the hellish glow and partly obscured in front by a swirl of white. Fixing her eyes on the opaque object, she watched it come closer until she recognized the outstretched wings of an obsidian kite and saw the Night Flyer's feet touch the terracotta tiles. Without missing a stride, he ran along the apex of the roof and pulled in the wings until they seemed to disappear, then slowed his pace to a trot.

Excitement rose into her throat and beamed on her ivory face, cheeks now rosy from the frost. She didn't understand why he evoked such strong emotion in her, nor why she could scarcely catch her breath the few times she had seen him. Was it the mystery of his identity, the skill and prowess he displayed, or the raw courage of his actions? She didn't know and at this moment didn't care. The enigmatic vigilante was striding toward her with haste. She was not afraid; he would not hurt her. But why did he come to see her? Did he share a similar fascination with her?

"Viscardi's warehouses?" she called out as the figure in black slowed and stopped on the roof above her.

"And his mansion," returned a steady reply.

"Did you kill him?"

"No. He lives, but he is destroyed. He will have left Milan by tomorrow night."

Maddie nodded. "That will do."

The Night Flyer squatted down, regarding her with serious eyes. "I came to tell you he did not murder your husband."

That was a surprise! Madelena's eyes widened and her mouth fell open. "Are you certain? How do you know?"

In an unemotional tone, he explained. "I forced him to confess his crimes, and he named plenty of men he had killed, but Vergilio was not among them. When I pressed him about it, he was honestly bewildered, replying that he was not important enough to kill. I believe him."

"I see," she answered with deep, troubling concern.

"However, I am pursuing a lead. Viscardi told me of an underground order of powerful men, dangerous men. Perhaps they are connected to his death. I can't tell you more at this time, but you should inform your brother, and get out of this freezing cold before you catch your death."

Maddie smiled at the concern in his voice. It did seem somewhat familiar, but she had no acquaintances from Venice. She nodded. "Shall I see you again?" she asked, trying not to sound too hopeful.

"Time will tell." He rose, bowed his head to her, then shifted and scampered across the roof and out of sight.

Madelena eye's trailed after him until he was gone. She sighed wistfully and turned back into her bed chamber closing the doors behind her. *Florentina will be jealous again,* she thought, shaking her head. It was silly to imagine she may have a future with this prowler of the night.

She was on her way down the hall toward Alessandro's room when she heard his voice coming from downstairs. *I should have known he would be awake, too.* She turned down the main staircase, pausing to watch him bid farewell to Salvador Sfondrati, the city watchman who had been indebted to their father. He pulled a red felt beret over his thin, short, graying hair and stepped back out into the wintry night. Madelena considered that their long-time friend looked old and tired, the lines in his square face so deep and pronounced and a stiffness to his gait.

"What did Salvador have to say?" she inquired as she took up her position beside her brother, who even in his slippers and robe towered over her. He turned toward her, leaned against the closed solid oak door, and ran a hand through his tousled brown tresses.

"You were awakened by the fire as well?" he asked the obvious, and shook his head. "It would appear that the Night Flyer has finally finished off our rival."

"No," she corrected. "He isn't dead, if that's what you mean."

His umber eyes widened, and he replied in surprise. "But Salvador reported that not only the warehouses, but Casa de Viscardi burned as well." Then he narrowed those compelling eyes at her. "What do you know and from whom?"

"The Night Flyer saw me on my balcony and stopped for a moment. He didn't kill Benetto, just ruined him." She stepped into Ally's personal space, looking up at him with eyes like a tempest sea, and reached to take hold of his thick upper arm. "He said Benetto did not murder Vergilio." She watched her brother's surprise darken into concern. "He said he forced Benetto to confess his crimes, and he did, but swore he had nothing to do with Vergilio's death and the Night Flyer believed him."

Alessandro brought a hand to her shoulder and rubbed it gently while a far-away look captured his face. "There's more," she continued. "Benetto told him about a secret society of rich and powerful men who are very dangerous and the Night Flyer is going to try to find out who they are and if they killed my husband."

As if coming back from a dream, Ally's eyes lit and he flashed a bemused smile. "Secret societies? Really? Surely you don't accept such a thing as true."

"Well," she offered defensibly. "The Freemasons are very secretive, and I've heard rumors of a group called the Rosicrucians–supposedly they dabble in the occult. And we all know about the Knights Templar, except we all know practically nothing about the Knights Templar, so it isn't unheard of. Besides, how could an order actually be secret, if everyone knows about them?"

"Sweet Maddie," he chided and placed a kiss to her forehead. "I suppose it is possible that Benetto imagines there is some deep, dark, unground cult in Milan; after all, he can be quite paranoid. But isn't it equally possible that Vergilio simply fell from his horse?"

She sighed and slumped her shoulders, a wave of defeat washing over her. Then strengthened in the knowledge that the Night Flyer was seeking them out, she straightened and raised her chin. "I will not stop searching until I have found the truth, and if it turns out to be that it was an accident, then fine. But if there is a clandestine order, the Night Flyer will find them."

Alessandro gave her shoulder a little squeeze. "I suspect there is very little that this Night Flyer cannot do. But come, now," he said taking her arm. "We should be getting back to bed."

"Yes, you are right," she concurred.

As they strolled toward the grand staircase Alessandro asked, "Wasn't there something you wished to speak with me about the finances? Is anything amiss?"

"Oh, yes!" Madelena brightened. "Nothing is wrong." She paused to consider how to word her request and assumed a more businesslike tone. "I wish to purchase a building that is for sale in the Vittore district. It was once a shop with apartments on the upper floors."

Alessandro stopped at the foot of the stairs, a puzzled look on his face. "That is a poor, run down area of town. What would you do with a building there?"

"I want it as an investment," she explained. "Not for monetary profit, rather to invest in the lives of people. We have been so blessed," she expounded passionately, "and I have come to discover that there are many in our rich city who have no home, no food, and no medical assistance."

"But don't the charity houses take care of them?"

"Some, yes, but not all. When I went over to Slues Street-"

"You did what?" he proclaimed in a louder astonished tone.

She waved her hand at him dismissively. "Florentina was with me, and she can be quite intimidating when she wishes. There is no need to bother now. I was perfectly safe with her. Florentina knows how to handle herself."

A wry smile tugged at the corner of his mouth and he quipped, "I'm sure she does."

"Oh, Ally!" Maddie swatted him on the shoulder, color rising in her cheeks. "You're incorrigible!" Then she added in a whisper, "You know that's not what I meant."

He laughed like a school boy and she brimmed with embarrassment. "Anyway, there are men and women, young and old, who have been left out of Milan's bounty and not all because they are drunks or sloths. Many are the victims of unfortunate circumstances and need a helping hand. I want to convert the building into a house of hope, a place they can have a roof over their heads, a warm bed, and a hot meal. We could provide training in marketable skills and assist them in finding jobs. Once they get a few months' pay in their purses, they can move into their own accommodations and make room for new residents. I am aware we give to the church and patron the arts, but with our wealth it seems we could do more. Oh, Ally, you should have seen their sallow faces, the sores on their lips and hands. No one cares if they live or die and that simply shouldn't be," she pleaded.

Alessandro had stopped laughing and looked at her earnestly. "You are wrong," he stated and her countenance fell. He paused, but she found she had nothing else to say. Then his elegant voice proceeded to add, "Someone does care if they live or die; you." Instantly her heart soared, and the sparkle returned to her eyes. "You will have to be in charge of this project, hire builders to remodel, secure a steward to oversee the property and residents, devise a system to determine how many and who you can take in and who will have to wait. You must acquire craftsmen to teach them skills, physicians to tend to their illnesses, and no doubt a priest to bring them prayers and sacraments. It shall be a huge undertaking and I expect you to keep up your part in our primary business affairs."

She beamed the whole time he lectured then pushed to her tiptoes to give him a gigantic hug around the neck and kiss his cheek. "I know I don't say it often enough, but I love you. I have been so blessed to have you both as a big brother and the head of my House. You are truly a treasure."

"Remember those gushing words of praise the next time I say no to one of your schemes," he pronounced humorously. For a moment he reverted to that earlier distant look as though he was deep in serious thought that transported him to another place and time.

With concern she drew back to put a foot of space between them. "What is wrong?"

He shook his head, the spell broken, and the smiling brother returned.

"Nothing. But I would ask you to name the place Margarita's Hope House after our dear mother."

Madelena took a deep breath and pressed her head into his shoulder. "I can think of nothing more perfect."

"What a night," he observed aloud. "The mighty has fallen and the humble will rise. Come, now; 'tis only a few hours until breakfast. And in case I don't tell you often enough, I love you, too."

CHAPTER 27

The Torelli household was all abuzz the next morning when Florentina entered the dining room for breakfast. Bernardo could scarcely sit still in his chair as Angela set out bowls of porridge and Madelena's eyes held a sleepy, dreamy quality. Alessandro was as unflappable as ever as he buttered his bread. "It would seem that Milan is saying goodbye and good-riddance to one unscrupulous merchant today."

"Which leaves my upstanding and well-deserving husband at the pinnacle!" Portia beamed at him.

But Alessandro held up a hand and bowed his head. "Now my Dearest, we don't want our rise to be because of a competitor's misfortune. However, in this case..." His voice trailed off, and he gave her a knowing look. "Anyway, it is likely House Torelli will not be the wealthiest for long. Don Giovanni is the one who stands to profit most as he will likely take on most of Viscardi's arms contracts. Besides, we are comfortable and have enough to sustain several generations of our progeny."

The storm had passed and the morning sun shone brilliantly through the windows lining the exterior wall of the dining room, the light outside dancing and glistening merrily across the melting icicles. "I can't believe Florentina slept through it all!" Bernardo declared and proceeded to spoon steamy breakfast cereal into his mouth.

"It's alright," Betta offered in a comforting tone. "I didn't wake up either."

Florentina smiled at the child and gave her a wink. Then Matteo joined in. "I would have gotten up to see the fire, but no one bothered to come and tell me about it."

Maddie tousled his hair and grinned at him. "You two were supposed to be in bed getting your sleep. Besides, you couldn't see anything from here but a big cloud of smoke, so it wasn't that exciting."

"I think it would be appropriate to amend today's lessons to include how to start a fire, how to put out a fire, and proper fire safety," Florentina said.

"I approve," Alessandro confirmed and winked at her. Florentina was certain that color rose in her cheeks and she wondered what that sly look of his was about. He was aware of her relationship with Maddie, but was that all he had discovered about her? She looked back to her food.

"Hurray!" Matteo cheered pumping a fist in the air and grinning through his too large front teeth. "This will be a fun day."

"Every day that we learn something new is a fun day," Florentina declared. "Fire safety is serious business. Way back in the time of cave men when humans first learned how to harness that peculiar element, they discovered–sometimes the hard way–that fire could create but also destroy; it could protect them from predators or become its own predator. It is a valuable tool and a treacherous weapon. Just like learning to swim, mastering fire is a skill every person should acquire for their own benefit."

"I don't know how to swim," Betta admitted with an anxious, scrunched-up face.

Madelena smiled at her daughter and said, "Next summer when the weather is warm, Florentina will teach you. You'll be able to swim like a fish!"

At that assurance, Betta beamed up proudly at her mother. Florentina's heart was warmed through and through. She loved her new family so much. She had truly hoped that the Night Flyer had completed her final flight, freeing her to put the deception away and focus all of her time and energy on Maddie and the children, but… should she pursue the notion of an underground order, a covert, possibly criminal organization, or let it go? At last, she had found the life she had always dreamed of; wasn't that enough? Must she solve every puzzle?

Florentina looked around the table and listened to the excited chatter. She noted the fond expressions pass between Portia and Alessandro and thrilled at the smile and batted eyelashes Madelena sent her way. She was a teacher, whose sole job was to obtain knowledge and pass it on to others—what calling presumed to be higher than that? Dare she risk everything to continue putting on her disguise and scampering across rooftops simply to chase after Benetto's mystery? No. Tonight would be the Night Flyer's last flight. Besides, even if she tried to find this obscure covey, it was just as likely they had not killed Vergilio and that he actually did meet with an unfortunate accident. She would be certain Viscardi vacated Milan, and that would be the end of it. She sighed and smiled to herself at a decision well made.

* * *

FLORENTINA'S SPIRITS rose with the outstretched wings of her miniature flying device. A plethora of stars shone above, and the cool, crisp air streaming across her face as she glided over the city made her feel alive. Here in the sky, she was invincible! An updraft caught the silk and lifted her higher and the thrill sent tingles throughout her body. Angling her wings, she soared over the burnt out remains of Viscardi's property. It still smoldered, and would for days.

Pulling on the handles, she brought herself down to a nearby rooftop and folded in the wings, careful to tuck them into her pack. Then in stealth black she shimmied down a corner of the building and crept about through the deserted neighborhood. A few youths stood around the heap of rubble and smoking coals that was once the great Casa de Viscardi.

"Come on," one prodded to his companion. "I dare you."

"I'm not poking around in there," he answered indignantly. "There's hot coals and burning tar. You go look for treasure if you want."

"I'm not stepping toe in that pitch," he echoed with a laugh. "What about you, Francesco?" he said turning to a third boy.

"What if Don Benetto returns and finds us trying to steal his stuff?" he asked nervously, shifting his slight weight from one foot to the other.

"He won't," declared the first young man. "I saw them all ride out of town in carriages this afternoon. He's gone, and he's not coming back."

"Still," Francesco hesitated. "I don't think there's anything left that hasn't burned or melted. It's just davvero forte to stand here and see it."

"Here's something!" a female voice called out. She stepped over broken bricks and roof tiles to join the group of boys carrying an object in her hands.

177

"What is it?" one of them asked in anticipation.

"I think it used to be a brass clock," she said holding it out for inspection. With light from the coals, moon, stars, and street lights it wasn't hard for them to see. Florentina even caught a glimpse of it from her hiding place across the lane.

"It's a little melted and scorched but it looks like a clock. You are probably right," the first young man concluded.

Florentina felt a prick to her heartstrings and tears began to roll down her face uncontrollably. She was able to stay quiet and refrain from sobbing, but she recognized what they had found in the burned out mansion—a clock her father had made for Don Benetto. It was not as artistically crafted as the one that showcased Alessandro's main hall, but it had been a precise timepiece with the same new spring action design.

It was silly to stand here crying. She knew it. It was only a clock. But... Florentina had been so busy planning her revenge that she hadn't taken the time to grieve the loss of her beloved father, and now all that emotion came rushing in and crashing against her senses like sea billows against a rocky shore driven by a mighty storm. She trotted further down the alley, then sat on an old, empty crate and buried her face in her hands.

She wasn't sure how long she remained in that state, allowing wave after wave of sorrow and loss to flow through her, but after a while the flood began to subside. Florentina loved her father, and he had loved her, but he was gone now. Luigi had lived a good life—a life of knowledge and creativity, science and art. He had been a kind, good humored man. He had not been truly old, but neither had he died young like Maddie's Vergilio. His had been a full, abundant life, not without its tragedies, but considering all, a satisfying one. It was time to let him go. Her father would always be with her, she believed, but that night in that alley near the scorched ruins of his killer's domain, she finally said her goodbyes.

* * *

FLORENTINA TREASURED the final flight of her alter-ego. Despite the serious nature of her mission, it had been exhilarating! And she had done some good for the poor of the city, prevented a few crimes, and become a living legend. She would miss the thrill of lifting off into the wind, soaring over treetops and edifices, and experiencing the ultimate freedom that it produced. Steering to her right, she glanced down at the streets below, empty in the dead of night.

Raising her head she then looked skyward at the multitude of stars lighting the sky. She was familiar with Ptolemy and Aristotle's writings on heavenly bodies and had once attended a lecture by the famous Italian astronomer Domenico Maria Novara da Ferrara, professor at the University of Bologna. Many a night as a child, Florentina lay on her rooftop gazing up at the stars wondering about them. She was able to calculate the phases of the moon and follow the major constellations through their courses, but there was so much about the shining lights in the sky that were yet to be discovered.

The wind was waning now and Florentina had to be careful that she not drift into a tree or building on her descent, so she returned her attention to directing her flight toward Casa de Torelli. She sighed blissfully as she lighted atop the Torelli production house, her final voyage at an end. She had experienced a rare thing indeed, one that to her knowledge no other human actually had–the wonder of flight!

Folding in her wings was a bittersweet moment, and she wondered what she would do with her singular device. It was too risky to keep hiding it in her trunk, but she couldn't bear to destroy it. She would think of something. The black costume was of no great consequence, however, and she might discard it after a few days. No one would ever discover the identity of the Night Flyer, nor why he suddenly appeared and just as suddenly vanished from the skies over Milan.

Florentina sprinted across the street, keeping out of direct lamp light, and down the alley leading toward the back of the mansion. She took hold of the drain pipe stretching from a few feet off the ground up three stories to the eave of the roof and gave it a slight tug. She had climbed down it before, but not often up the metal tubing. It was not a strenuous task for one with her body build and youth, but she worried about it clanging against the wall if any fasteners were loose. Within little more than a minute her palms were pressed to the edge of the roof; she pushed, lifted one leg tucking her knee under her torso and then bringing the other foot up, she was on top.

Now the key was to walk quietly around to the narrow stairway that led to the kitchen. She didn't want to run into Madelena again, nor wake any of the staff. She had done this numerous times before. But as she crept along the terracotta tiles, something caught Florentina's eye–a dark figure on Maddie's balcony, and it was definitely not the woman she loved.

Instantly the Night Flyer snapped to full alert. Her delicate steps gave way to a desperate dash as she took off running as fast as possible without slipping and falling to her death in the courtyard below.

Oh no you don't, she swore to herself frantically as she pushed to run even faster. *Not my Maddie!* She could now see it was a man of average size wearing a dark colored waist cape and cap. He had jimmied open her balcony door and was fitting a bolt into a crossbow.

Florentina's protective instinct outmaneuvered panic and dread as her brain kicked into strategy mode. There were still several yards between them and she would have to jump down to a second floor landing; there wasn't time for all that. She drew up her repeating crossbow, slid to a halt, aimed, and fired two hasty shots. Because of that, the first one missed, but the other struck the intruder's weapon, knocking it to the balcony's base. He whirled to spot her running toward him along the roof and she saw him draw a dagger. She fired two more bolts in his direction, one of which grazed his leg and the other lodged into a floor plank, then she tossed the firearm aside.

At the moment he looked away to check the slight injury to his leg, Florentina launched herself at him from ten feet away and twenty feet above. She was confident at her speed she would make the landing; she just hoped she took him down when she did.

As gravity aided her rapid descent, the would-be assassin glanced up just in time to discern the dreaded Night Flyer closing on him. He stepped away from the railing toward Madelena's open door and Florentina thrust out her left arm in a speed-induced sweep. They both tumbled to the balcony floor. She landed like a stone and felt a vague, far away pain in her right knee, plus she was still bruised from battling Zuane the night before, but the adrenaline was pumping too hard for her to pay it any attention. Why was this man trying to kill Maddie? That didn't matter now; she had to stop him.

Florentina drew her knife as she rolled, coming up in a crouch. Her opponent poised on hands and knees in front of her and lunged. She dodged with a quick feint toward the railing and jabbed her blade in the path of his advance, but he swatted it away with a rapid motion of his powerful forearm which connected with hers. She scuttled around him crab-like, still staying low to the floor so he couldn't bat her off their precarious perch like an annoying fly.

The assassin straightened up as he pivoted in her direction and she saw him clearly. His dark complexion was accented by short black hair that stuck out from his uncovered head as his cap had vanished in the struggle. He was neither old nor young and his face was the rugged mask of a trained warrior. However his build was slighter than a traditional fighter's and he could probably match her speed and dexterity. He pulled a second dagger as he also scrutinized her with wary eyes. He was definitely a professional assassin, but it was clear that he respected the Night Flyer's reputation. However Florentina had one huge factor in her favor–this was no job for her; she was in love with the woman he had come to kill and would protect her at all costs.

CHAPTER 28

*M*adelena was in the middle of a sound sleep, after having so little the night before, when a loud noise woke her. Before she had even opened her eyes, she felt a cold gust of wind that should not be there. Once they were open, she saw that her balcony door was pushed ajar and two figures were fighting beyond it.

Alarm jolted her into full wakefulness and she leapt out of bed, pulling on her robe as she rushed toward the commotion. She stopped abruptly inside the open doorway, her breath catching in her throat, as wide-eyed she spied the Night Flyer grappling with a strange man in a menacing looking smoky waist cloak. The interloper held a knife in each hand and she immediately feared for her mysterious guardian. She must have gasped loudly, because the Night Flyer flicked her a quick glance before springing to his feet brandishing his own dagger.

She stood frozen and breathless as they circled each other, testing with short jabs and slices. There was very little room for them to maneuver and she wondered for an instant if they would come crashing into her bedchamber. Clutching her robe closed at her neck, she took a cautious step backward.

I should run! she reasoned. *I should run screaming to Alessandro's chamber and fetch him right this minute!* But she couldn't move. Maddie's concern over the Night Flyer's fate rooted her feet to the floor. She was transfixed as she watched in shock and fright wishing there was something she could do. *I can go get Ally; that is what I should do.* Still, her feet refused to budge.

The intruder struck with both knifes, one arcing high toward the Night Flyer's face and the other jabbing low toward his abdomen. Another gasp escaped her lips, but she saw her protector slide sideways and bending back avoid both moves. Then he charged into the opening, blade first, but the other man snapped his foot in a quick kick that dislodged the Night Flyer's dagger from his hand and sent it flying over the rail. She heard herself cry out, "No!" then covered her mouth and took another step backward. This couldn't be happening. *No one* bests the Night Flyer!

Madelena wanted to close her eyes so she wouldn't see her champion die, but for some reason was unable to turn them away. She recognized her fate was intertwined with his should she remain where she stood, but she could not will her gaze nor her feet from that spot. What she witnessed next was nothing less than remarkable. The assailant with his two shining blades and dark cape flapping advanced on the Night Flyer in a low, swift, powerful charge, ready to finish him. But the inscrutable vigilante dropped in a skid toward him, lay flat on his back, and thrust both feet into the stranger's gut and pushed. He continued the motion, pressing with palms on the floor boards, arching his back, and sustained the shove until he had completed a backward somersault. It happened so quickly and was clearly so unexpected that the assassin was lifted from the ground and the forward momentum of his attack combined with the Night Flyer's forceful kick launched him headfirst over the iron railing. Maddie heard a crunch and a thud and imagined from the sound she did not want to look. She didn't know if he had cried out or not on his short trip to the courtyard paving stones; she was too immersed in her own relief that her hero was safe!

Madelena tried to steady herself, return her breath to normal, slow her racing heartbeat; that was impossible! It had all happened so fast, or did it just seem that way? She willed one foot to move, discovered that it would obey, and took the few steps required to pass through her open balcony door. The Night Flyer, breathing heavily, rose to his feet and peered over the railing.

"Are you injured?" Maddie asked, reaching a hand toward him, then drawing it back in hesitation.

The masked figure in black turned to her, concerned brown eyes his only discernable feature. "No." His chest heaved up and down and it looked like he was shaking.

"Are you sure?" She took a tentative step in his direction.

"He, he was here to kill you. Why?"

She stopped an arm's length from her shadowy guardian. "I have no idea." Madelena was caught in a whirlwind of emotions, helpless to ascertain their origins nor directions. She felt a little dizzy and must have swayed because a firm hand caught her arm and steadied her. She raised her eyes to his and there she read more than casual concern. "I only know that if you had not been here…" She swallowed before continuing the sentence. "I would be dead now. So, thank you, for saving my life."

He just stood there holding her arm, drawing in deep, labored breaths, gazing into her eyes. Did he not know what to say or do? Was he as nervous as she was? She didn't understand why she was so drawn to this, this *man*. She preferred the pleasures of another woman and was perfectly happy in her relationship with Florentina. But her heart fluttered, and she felt weak in the knees. A mere "thank you" was not enough. He risked his life to save hers and nearly lost it in the process. She took that last step, reached her arms around his neck, and kissed him.

It only took a moment, and she *knew*. Madelena jumped back in total shock, wide-eyed and slack jawed, her head spinning like a top. "It's you!"

Astonishment gave way to the painful knife-twist of betrayal. Maddie understood she should be grateful; after all, Florentina had just wrestled with a man who had tried to kill them both in order to save her life. And she should appreciate no longer having her heartstrings pulled between two love interests. But she simply felt numb.

Florentina must have read her expression because fear registered in those bright, honey eyes of hers. "I am sorry, Maddie; I never intended to deceive you, but I had to keep you safe. If I had ever been caught," Florentina hastily explained, "you could tell the authorities that you didn't know, and the truth is always more convincing than a lie."

"You were convincing." She didn't intend for the comment to sound as sharp as it did, and she pulled her robe tight again.

"Please, just let me explain," she pleaded. "But not here and now." A scream sounded below as one of the servants obviously discovered the body. "I have to go, but I'll come to your room and explain everything. Then if you want me to leave, I'll go, but…" Florentina's shoulders slumped and a pained expression that threatened a flood of tears peeked from behind the mask. "I truly love you."

Madelena wasn't sure what to think or what to believe, but Florentina was right; this wasn't the time to get into it. She considered her with a cool, flat look. "And how will you return to your room to change clothes? There are already people gathering below and the roof is too high for you to reach from here." She sighed and motioned through the doorway into her bed chamber. "May as well just wait here. I have to go tell Alessandro... something. There's a dead man on our patio." She closed the door behind them, blocking out the cold and the maid's screams. Then, brushing her hand to Florentina's added, "I'm glad it isn't you."

"Please," she asked reaching for Maddie's hand. She purposefully drew it out of reach. Florentina sighed, noticeably more distressed by Maddie's mood than the prospect of a bloody death. "Don't tell Don Alessandro about me being the Night Flyer, not until we've talked at least. I trust him; I just not certain how he'll react." Madelena said nothing, simply turned and strode out of the room, closing the door behind her.

As she ambled down the hall toward her brother's bedchamber, Madelena's stomach churned and shock warped into anger. *Why didn't she tell me? She knew I was infatuated with the Night Flyer, and still she didn't tell me. No, she made me suffer through all these conflicting feelings. And if she lied about this, what else has she lied about? Do I even know her at all? To think–I trusted her with my precious children! The nerve of that woman. Was everything a lie? Sure, she says she loves me, but how can I be certain? She is accomplished in the art of deception. I am so mad at her right now I could spit teeth!*

Fury flushed over Maddie's porcelain cheeks and her eyes flashed like jade lightning. Alessandro opened his door, alarm on his face, just as she arrived. "What's wrong?" he inquired briskly. "I heard screaming."

Madelena took a calming breath. She didn't want to start gushing about this to her brother, so she would stick to the facts. "It would seem someone wants me dead."

"What!" His eyes flew wide, and he reached a hand to push hair up his forehead. "Are you alright? What happened?"

She relayed the story to him as she had seen it, leaving out the part about Florentina being the Night Flyer, and concluding with, "So there's a dead assassin in the courtyard. Maybe you can find out who he is and why someone is trying to murder me. Perhaps there is merit in the secret society of really bad people theory after all," she quipped to him. "But I still don't understand why they would want to kill *me*."

Alessandro wrapped her in a strong, supportive embrace. "I did not mean to belittle your suspicions," he conceded. "It just sounded so farfetched. I will send for Salvador and you can be assured there will be an inquiry into this matter. No one tries to kill my sister and gets away with it!"

She sank into the hold of his arms, and for the first time since she awoke the fact that someone actually came to her room in the middle of the night with the intent to kill her in her sleep registered as real in her befuddled mind. Somebody wanted her dead and hired a professional to do the deed. That was surreal! And Florentina had raced to her rescue, with no reservations, and at prodigious peril. And Florentina was the Night Flyer. Then it dawned on her; *that's the reason I was so attracted to the Night Flyer!*

"Thank you," she uttered in gratitude.

Ally released the hug and looked into her eyes with deep emotion. "I am most thankful that the Night Flyer just happened to be here at the exact time this villain was ready to strike, or..." He had to pause to swallow a lump in his throat.

Madelena sighed and patted his cheek. "I know. Me too." She now realized why the Night Flyer was always showing up at their home–she lives here. But she didn't know why Florentina had been returning at that very moment. "God's providence."

A smile returned to light Alessandro's face. "I guess He is pleased with your plan to build Margarita's Hope House."

Seeing the misty glow in his eyes, Madelena said her good-nights and began a slow stroll back toward her room. What to do about Florentina? On the one hand she did arrive at a most fortuitous moment and risk her own life to save her from that hired killer–the truth that there even was a hired killer in the first place baffled her. That did not, however, negate the fact that her lover had systematically deceived her, living a double life right under her own roof. *Why didn't she tell me? Does she not trust me? And if she doesn't trust me, why should I trust her?* So many little things all came together... the long hours "at the production house working on equip-ment," odd "shopping trips," and the cut on her arm–that was not from any machinery; that had been the night of the big game and raining coins. *I should have figured it out*, she chided herself. *But why insert herself into our household? Was that part of her plan or did she truly need the position? Had she ever loved me or was I just part of her cover?*

Maddie stopped at her own door, hesitating with her hand on the knob. Neither her mind nor emotions were settled. Someone had just tried to kill her, her lover was a vigilante with a secret identity, and it all seemed to fantastical to be real. She felt relieved and thankful, resentful and betrayed, angry and insulted, and very thoroughly confused. *Might as well hear what she has to say.* She turned the handle, stepped inside, and closed and locked the door behind her.

Only then did Madelena turn her eyes toward Florentina. A black backpack and belt loaded with pouches, a sheath, and some kind of hook and cord attached were set off to one side, while Fiore lay disposed in a heap on the floor like a discarded rag doll. As Maddie migrated into the room, Florentina pushed to a sitting position, turning haunted damp eyes up to hers in desperate hope, and all her temper melted away.

* * *

"I was coming home from what was to be the Night Flyer's last mission, to make sure Don Benetto had left the city, when I saw…" Florentina stopped to swallow and rubbed a hand under her leaky eye. "Oh, Maddie, I was so scared! If that man had killed you…" She had to swallow another sob before she could continue. Madelena's face had softened toward her and that helped. "If he had gotten to you before I got to him… I would be shattered, lost…"

"But he didn't." Madelena's voice was filled with compassion as she moved to where Fiore sat. "You saved me."

Florentina rubbed her hands down her face before lifting it back to Maddie who stooped down to take a seat on the floor directly in front of her. "I had to; I love you more than life itself! And I've been thinking, if I had returned a few minutes sooner or a few minutes later, or if I had not gone out at all; if, if… so many ifs."

"Shh." Madelena's tone was comforting, and she took Florentina's hands in hers. "You were exactly where fate intended you be, and at precisely the right moment. You know, I was frightened for you too, out there fighting for your life."

A shimmer flashed across Florentina's eyes. "But you didn't know it was me yet."

"So, why didn't you just fly away? You had to know I would recognize your kiss."

"I have wanted to tell you for a long time," Florentina began to explain. "I came to your brother seeking a post because he was Viscardi's rival, because there were rumors Benetto had killed your husband, and I thought I might do your family a favor while dispatching my own vengeance on the murdering bastard. Your House was wealthy enough to afford me and your residence held the correct balance between distance and nearness to my target. I planned everything to the last detail," she said, then gave Maddie's hands a squeeze. "Except falling in love with you. At first I thought nothing would come of it; how could it? But then... it did."

Florentina sighed and rolled her shoulders. She was sore, but all that mattered was that Maddie was giving her a chance to explain herself. "I never really lied to you," she offered innocently. "I just failed to mention a few things."

"Um," Madelena hummed disapprovingly. "Is that what you call it?"

"Truly, my intent was to protect you and Don Alessandro from any involvement in my vendetta. It killed me to keep secrets from you," she admitted with suppliant eyes that threatened to brim with tears again. Florentina sucked them back deliberately. She had sobbed enough. "Tonight was going to be the Night Flyer's last escapade—just make sure Viscardi left town and that would be the end of it, but..." She sighed, dropped her chin and shook her head.

"But what?" Maddie asked. "Your vendetta is complete. He isn't dead, but Don Benetto now knows the pain of losing all his wealth and power, driven from Milan in shame and humiliation."

"Yes," Florentina agreed. "Only now I have a new mission, to find out who tried to kill you and stop them. In the meantime, you must be protected from any further attempts on your life, and the Night Flyer is in a better position to do that than a child's tutor or even a lover," she expounded. "I understand you were angry with me, and I swear on the Blessed Virgin that I never meant to cause you pain or distress or emotional indecision. How was I to know you would be attracted to a shadowy character that people were calling a criminal?"

A bemused smile wiggled across Madelena's full lips. "You should have known, since I was attracted to you."

Florentina blushed. Then her expression turned deadly serious. "My

Sweet, I'll understand if you don't want to be with me anymore. I realize I wasn't honest with you and it has been difficult enough to pursue this relationship without that added offense. But you cannot and will not stop me from protecting you or pursuing this investigation. You can banish me from this House if you like, but I will not give up the quest to keep you safe and end the person or group who wants to harm you; that I vow."

Maddie raised a hand and stroked her cheek, a hint of sorrow clouding her verdant eyes. "Fiore, don't you know?" She leaned forward and brushed her lips to Florentina's. "Sometimes I have trouble making decisions, and when I do make them I tend to second guess myself. My moods can run hot and cold, and yes I was hurt that you didn't confide in me about this. Now I also understand why. But the truth is that if you had been killed tonight instead of that man, I would be the one shattered. You have brought joy and passion and adventure to my life, and I have treasured every minute spent with you. I may get angry or flustered at times, but please, never doubt how much I love you."

Florentina was swallowed in a wave of relief and elation. She leaned in, returning the kiss, completely absorbed by the feel of her lips, the taste of her mouth, the nearness of her breath. She boldly caressed Madelena's clever tongue and reached a hand to glide through her long locks of flame. Intoxicated by her scent, Florentina pressed nearer so that her breast closed into Maddie's. She eagerly delved deeper into the kiss, a primal urge driving her to ever increasing heights of yearning and passion. It had been an intensely emotional hour; Florentina was overcome with the need to reaffirm life. She desperately longed to hold her love so close that they melded into one. But in truth, she didn't know how.

With ragged breath, she withdrew from the kiss, her lips lingering near, and gazed into Maddie's eyes. In them she saw the same flame of desire that blazed in her own heart, and she sat on the edge, anticipation creating a tingling sensation throughout her being. Then she heard the melodious tones and magical words falling gracefully from Madelena's lips.

"Tonight, my love, I shall show you a new way to fly." And so she did.

SNEAK PEAK - BOOK TWO

I hope you have enjoyed reading Merchant's of Milan, Book One of the Night Flyer Trilogy. Here's a taste of Book Two – Secrets of Milan:

The Night Flyer had brought Florentina and Madelena together but now threatens to drive them apart. While Florentina searches for a mysterious underworld organization that has attempted to murder the woman she loves, Maddie struggles to deal with the danger Florentina is courting. Her brother, Alessandro, has become the most prominent merchant of Milan, but the Night Flyer uncovers a secret so shocking it could destroy them all.

Secrets of Milan is the second book in Edale Lane's Night Flyer Trilogy, a tale of power, passion, and payback in Renaissance Italy. If you like drama and suspense, rich historical background, three-dimensional characters, and a romance that deepens into true love, then you'll want to continue the Night Flyer saga. Look for Secrets of Milan coming soon!

To discover other books by this author, visit https://pastandprologuepress.lpages.co/

HEART OF SHERWOOD · CHAPTER 1

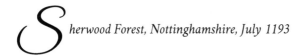 *herwood Forest, Nottinghamshire, July 1193*

BROWN LEATHER BOOTS trod softly on the dirt path beneath a canopy of oaks and birches, skirted by verdant shrubs and lush ferns that overlaid the forest floor. A covey of quail were disturbed and scurried off cooing nervously to each other.

Dusky gray woolen trousers brushed the boots of the figure draped in a dark green cloak. The hood was pulled up around the sojourner's face while a bow and full quiver hung across the back and a short sword dangled in its sheath from a leather belt fastened around a rust-brown doublet. The cream sleeves of a linen tunic were also visible, but the tall, lean traveler's face remained hidden.

Sherwood Forest itself was timeless, a mix of primeval vegetation and fresh, new growth, inhabited by a myriad of animal life. It was a place of wonder, adventure, and danger. Rumors abounded of bandits that hid out in the woods as well as mystical tales of spirits and sprites. As with all the great forests of England, Sherwood was technically owned by the crown which with King Richard away meant his younger brother, Prince John Lackland. Those caught poaching in the forest faced severe penalties at the hands of Godfrey Giffard, the current Sheriff of Nottingham who, having found favor with the Prince, had power over the shire. However, the magnificence of nature that wove the forest together, leaf and vine, hart and fowl, had no inkling that their existence was merely for royal pleasure. They continued to thrive as if kings and princes were of no more consequence than a dung beetle.

The new human interloper was no stranger to Sherwood. Each step took Robyn farther from the home of her birth and further into the unknown. Her emotions churned like the North Sea in a violent storm, flowing into anger, then ebbing into grief. Nothing was as it should be and, for the first time in her life, she felt totally powerless. She did not care for that feeling. She was so immersed in her own thoughts she did not notice the mountain of a man who stood in the middle of the narrow bridge until she was almost atop him. She halted abruptly and stared up at him with curious chestnut eyes, careful that the hood concealed her face.

"Ah, a hearty traveler," he greeted jovially in a booming baritone voice, gripping a staff the breadth of a small tree in his left hand. Standing erect, he towered over her–despite her being a tall woman–with a frowzy tree-bark beard, tousled shoulder length dusky hair, deep-set hazel eyes, shoulders as broad as a door frame, and arms as thick as Yule logs. "I must ask that you pay the toll."

Robyn narrowed her eyes, contemplating the colossal older fellow. "What toll do you mean, sir?" Her voice was naturally deep and somewhat ambiguous to gender, but she altered her accent to sound more common and less high-bred. She knew he could not make out her features beyond the lack of a beard on her jaw because of the hood she wore. That and the men's clothing she donned would give the first impression of her being a young man. "Last I heard, this was a public road."

"Ah, well, yes, you see," he began, relaxing his stance, a glint of humor in his broad face. "It seems Prince John is taxing everyone nowadays. And, while I admit the tax I charge will not be adding to His Highness's coffers, it will help me and mine to have a better meal or two. So, out with it, lad. Let me see your coin."

Under different circumstances, Robyn may have been amused or felt compelled to donate to the unfortunate bandit, but he had caught her in a foul mood and quite lacking in resources. "I am sorry to disappoint, oh mighty man of the bridge, but I have nothing to donate to your supper. So if you will kindly step aside, I have places to be."

He bellowed a roaring laugh and declared, "What an impudent little insect! I must teach you a lesson. Have you a staff?"

Robyn held out her arms, dropping a bag filled with belongings she had hurriedly packed. "You can see I do not. While I do have bow and sword, I prefer not to kill anyone today."

The bridge master, clearly feeling not the least bit threatened, replied. "I see you are a man of honor who deserves a fair fight." He stepped away to pick up a more averaged size staff from the other side of the stream. Robyn removed her bow and quiver to achieve a better range of motion, but kept her hood up. "Here you go!" He tossed the wooden rod in Robyn's direction and she caught it. "First one in the drink loses."

She let her hands become accustomed to the feel of the staff, balanced it, spun it a few times, and then settled on a grip style. She gave him a satisfied nod, putting her shoulders back confidently.

"You have grit, lad—I like that." He held his staff in a relaxed stance and motioned for the traveler to attack first. Robyn opened with a standard thrust that her father had taught her to test the giant's mettle. He moved with remarkable speed for someone his size, handily blocking the move and taking a swing of his own.

She blocked his blow, but its power sent shock waves through her hands and arms. She had spared with her brother before, but he had struck with far less force than this Herculean adversary. Robyn took a step back to re-evaluate. Why hadn't she chosen a different approach to this problem? She could have given him the money, or simply shot him with her bow. She could have lowered her hood and revealed her identity, believing he may let a lady pass. But no. She'd thought she could play his game. Now she wasn't so certain.

Robyn adjusted her stance, feet shoulder width apart with her weight on her back foot. She feigned high and struck low giving him a good rap on the shin.

"Oi!" the burly man exclaimed in surprise. "The insect can bite."

He swung out at her chest high, but she hastily ducked and sent another jab, this time to his knee. Next he swiped at her low. Being light on her feet, she jumped the rod landing nimbly. They continued to knock their staffs together until, under a powerful blow, Robyn's snapped in two.

She looked first at the severed pieces in her hands then up at her opponent. This could not be good... or could it? Two weapons, meant she could block with one while attacking with the other. She pursued this strategy, spinning and jumping to avoid any possible bone-breaking blows while bruising his shins and forearms with her lighter strikes. He was bigger than her, but she was faster. Seeing him loom to one side, she took advantage, crouching to sweep his feet out from under him with both pieces of broken staff in unison.

His weight shook the wooden bridge when he fell. Utterly dumb-founded by this scrawny lad, he toppled over the edge through three feet of air to land with a splash in two feet of clear running stream.

Robyn bent over the side, her hands on her knees breathing heavily and asked, "Are you harmed?" The summer day was warm and the water was likely refreshing, so she wasn't overly concerned.

He sat up, spitting water and wiped a broad hand down his face, then peered up at her with rounded eyes. "What the blazes! How did you... who are...?" Then, if possible, his astonishment grew as he looked at her and really seemed to see her for the first time. "I know you–you're Lady Loxley! What the devil are you doing out here in the forest alone?"

Robyn had not noticed that in the course of the fight her hood had fallen down after all. Without it, her flowing acorn brown hair and femi-nine countenance were revealed. She quickly threw the hood back over her head and began to run from him.

"Wait!" he called after her. "I know your father; I am a friend, John Naylor."

Robyn skidded to a sudden halt and hesitated.

"My friends call me Little John," he added, though he still didn't advance on her.

She knew that name from her childhood. Lord knew she could use a friend, but was it safe to expose herself when the sheriff had ordered her arrest? With some misgivings, she slowly turned to face the wet man.

John stepped out of the brook leaning on his staff with the effort. "Milady, please forgive an old fool; I didn't know 'twas you."

Her head down and covered she quietly replied, "I am no longer the Lady of Loxley. I am merely Robyn."

"Nonsense," he said and motioned to a fallen tree trunk near the road. "Come, sit. Tell Little John what the problem is; perchance I can help."

The adrenaline from the fight had evaporated, and all that flowed through Robyn's veins was cold reality. She sat beside Little John on the log and lowered her hood. After a moment of silence, she raised misty eyes to his gentle, rough-hewn face.

"I recently received word that my father and brother Thomas, were killed fighting in the Holy Land. As proof, my father's sword was returned to me." She laid a hand on the sheath at her side and glanced down at it.

"Oh no," he uttered in honest sorrow. "Dear, sweet Maid Robyn." Despite being wet, unkempt, and having just tried to knock her upside the head with a tremendous quarterstaff, Little John wrapped a compassionate arm around her shoulders. He drew her to his strong chest like she was his own long, lost child. "This is grave news indeed. Please know I admired Lord Loxley, and that I feel your loss."

Regardless of all previously shed tears, Robyn felt the lump in her throat, the knot in her stomach, and the warm, moist trickle on her cheeks. She was almost glad of his next question, and the opportunity to change the subject.

"But, why are you alone in Sherwood dressed as a boy?"

She sniffled, wiped her eyes with the back of her sleeve and raised a defiant face that smoldered with barely bridled rage, the bite of which sounded in her voice. "The Sheriff of Nottingham paid me a visit no sooner than the envoy had left the manor. He claimed he was there to pay his condolences, and to see that I was well taken care of. You may know my mother and younger siblings died eight years ago from the pox and so now I am all alone. But then the law does not allow for a daughter to inherit her father's estate. Subsequently the Sheriff offered a 'solution' to my problem: according to the law, I could still inherit the land and title if I married. But with so few young lords available, who was possibly eligible enough to wed a woman of my station?"

John shook his head with a snort. "Let me guess."

"Right. Nottingham said he would be most agreeable to marry me and take over Loxley Manor—as if I could ever abide such a thing!" Robyn reverberated with fury. "When I told him I'd rather wed a donkey, he didn't take it so well. The next thing I know he has declared me a traitor to the crown and all my title and lands forfeit." She sighed, trying to release that wave of anger. "He was determined to have Loxley with or without me; so it was without me. The problem is, I am now wanted for treason. There is no way I will be judged fairly with Prince John's friend Giffard as my accuser." She lowered her head to the big man's shoulder releasing some of her tension. "I thought I'd run away, hide my identity, and maybe somehow I'd get by with it. 'Tis only my first day away from home, but already I am found out."

"Now there, do not fret child; Little John won't tell anyone. I'll protect you; in fact…" He made a dramatic pause, his vocal inflection rising to an optimistic tone. "I have an idea."

Robyn lifted her head, her eyes gazing up at him with suddenly renewed hope.

"You see, the Sheriff declared me an outlaw, too, and put a price on my head all because I tried to make sure there was enough food to feed my family. They are still safe on the FitzWalter lands, but all because I wouldn't give him and his damnable tax collectors every penny and bag of flour–" He stopped, shook his head and gave her shoulder a pat. "Well anyway, there's a small gang of us who have taken up residence in Sherwood. You could stay with us, at least until you figure out something that would better suit you."

Excitement flashed across her fair face. But she couldn't afford to get too excited. Not yet. "You must give me your oath." She straightened up, her enigmatic eyes pinning his with demand. "I want no one else to know who I am."

He looked puzzled and absently stroked his beard. "I don't understand. These boys would show you respect. If they didn't, I'd crack their heads."

"That isn't it. I'm not afraid of being assaulted; but I fear that anyone who aids me could face a hangman's noose. It is safer for everyone if they think I am a random boy who ran away from Sir Guy of Gisborne's cruelty or was spotted stealing bread or something. Please, if you honor my father as you say you do, keep my secret."

Little John exhaled with a nod. "Aye, sweet lass, if you are sure that's what you want; I'll do it for Lord Loxley, and for you."

* * *

LITTLE JOHN HELPED PASS the time as they strolled along the dirt road by telling all about the forest and the band of men who had gathered around him.

"Deep in the heart of Sherwood," he said in his best story-telling voice, "stands the oldest tree in all of England. Huge, it is, an oak with branches reaching as far as you can see. That is where our camp is set, snug under her protection. We call her Grandma. 'Tis nothing but a tent village, but it's home - close enough to the stream for getting fresh water and far enough away to not flood when the rains come hard."

Robyn tried to listen, but stray thoughts continued to shoot into her mind like needling arrows, preoccupying her with memories and imaginings of what might have been if her father and Thomas had returned from the crusade and if the pox hadn't taken her mother and younger siblings.

"We are almost there now," she heard Little John say and giving her hood one more tug. She stood a bit straighter. "Good afternoon, fellows," he called.

Robyn smelled the smoke of the campfire and something that could have been rabbit stew coming from a large iron pot. Some of the men sat around the fire chatting and shooting dice while a few others meandered up to the group wearing curious expressions. They ranged in age from younger than herself to older than John Naylor, and they were all dirty and smelled of male sweat.

"Who's the whelp?" asked the eldest as he squinted up at them without rising.

"My friends, may I present a newcomer to our number. This is Robyn..." His face went blank as he stared out over his outlaw gang. He then glanced over at Robyn and thought quickly. "Hood. This is Robin Hood, of Nottinghamshire who, like all our present company, was unjustly outlawed by the Sheriff. Now he's a wee bit young and a little shy, so let's not all overwhelm him at once with questions, but I would like you to introduce yourselves. He's going to be staying with us a while. Alan?" He gestured toward a cheerful chap who stood about Robyn's height and held a mandolin in one hand. "Why don't you start?"

"Pleased to make your acquaintance," he chimed in a lyrical tone. "Alan A Dale at your service." He gave an elaborate bow that caused some of the others to chuckle. His sandy hair was short and choppy, and he had a wispy mustache and goatee, ruddy cheeks, and luminous forest green eyes that danced with laughter.

"Alan is a minstrel," Little John added for him. "Quite a skilled entertainer."

"Sadly, the Sheriff did not agree," Alan said. "He took a sudden and violent dislike to a song he overheard me performing." The others laughed, looking at each other as though they shared the inside story. "Would you care to hear it?"

"Another time, Alan," Little John replied waving him down. Beside the fun-loving Alan sat an even younger lad, this one in a red silk shirt with no beard at all and a sweep of black hair above intense indigo eyes like the depths of the sea in the midst of a tempest.

"I'm Will Scarlet," he offered in a friendly voice. "I promise not to pick your pocket if you'll return the favor." He crossed his heart in humorous gesture but the laughter never reached his eyes.

"Young Will here may look unassuming," Alan added with a jab to his friend's ribs, "but he is a dangerous fellow to cross."

"As skilled with a sword as he may be, that fat Friar in the back can fence circles around him," the eldest of the men added throwing a nod behind him.

"Who are you calling fat?" boomed a powerful voice. A middle aged man with his dusty brown hair ringed in a tonsure, wearing umber robes, turned with a mug of wine in one pudgy hand. His round cheeks were rosy beneath deep-set gray eyes. "Friar Tuck, lad, and I'll tell you this for free: keeping this bunch on the road to the Pearly Gates is a full time endeavor!" The clergyman was clean shaven, and did not appear to have missed many meals.

From beneath the shadow of her hood, Robyn spoke for the first time. "Why is a good friar outcast with thieves and knaves?"

"Because he is a good friar, boy," answered the same older man. He was thin as a twig with a protruding Adam's apple and scraggly gray whiskers. "I'm Gilbert Whitehand," he said with crotchety cantankerousness, "and Friar Tuck here is the finest swordsman in all of England. Why, he could beat that bloody Sheriff of Nottingham with one hand tied behind his back!"

"Oh, good sir, your words are too kind," Tuck answered with a laugh and gulped down his wine. After a proper burp, he continued. "Well, what was I to do? The soldiers accompanying Prince John's tax collectors were brutalizing my parishioners. Was I to just stand by and do nothing? I say there is a time for prayer and a time for action!" He raised his double chin and gave an approving nod.

"Unfortunately, he killed a few of those soldiers, which put him on the Sheriff's most wanted list, man of the cloth or not," Little John concluded.

"Gilbert Whitehand," Robyn mused admiringly. "I know that name. You are one of King Richard's men at arms."

"Yes, well, ancient history now," he said dismissively. "There seems to be no place for a knight loyal to Richard so long as he remains captive across the sea."

Friar Tuck took a step closer to the old man. "My friend Gilbert here came to my defense, spoke out against the Sheriff, and was rewarded for his years of service, and his valor in the Holy Land, by being thrown off his estate; his lands and title confiscated."

"Sounds familiar," Robyn muttered.

"What's that lad?" Gilbert asked. "Speak up." Then he tilted his head. "And how does a peasant boy know the members of King Richard's personal guard?"

Robyn shifted her weight thinking quickly. "I said the Sheriff is the real traitor to the crown. And you may be surprised at what a poor lad such as myself may know."

Little John looked out at them and threw a thumb at Robyn. "As much as I hate to admit this, young Robin is here because he knocked me off the bridge."

At Little John's words, the camp froze in place, not even a breath taken. All eyes turned incredulously to the beardless youth in the cloak and hood standing beside the best quarterstaff fighter in the shire.

Feeling more at ease, Robyn rattled off the names so far. "Good day to you Alan A Dale, Will Scarlet, Friar Tuck, and Gilbert Whitehand. Now for the rest of you before I lose my wits from smelling that rabbit stew!"

They all laughed, delighted, and continued the introductions. There was Much the Miller's son, who was a short man in his mid-thirties with curly honey hair and beard. David of Doncaster, the youngest, with long black hair covering the scars where the Sheriff had his ear cut off for stealing a loaf of bread, and Arthur Bland, a sturdy, ruddy fellow wanted for poaching deer in the forest. To her great relief, the rotund Tuck graciously handed her a bowl of stew and invited her to join them. Together, they were nine merry men. With Robyn, they were ten.

That night in the safety of the outlaw camp, Robyn pondered her situation. Nottingham might be sheriff of the shire, but he was not all powerful. He was under Prince John. But John was only a prince. Who really held the power?

HEART OF SHERWOOD - CHAPTER 2

*W*indsor Castle, July 1193

A FEW HOURS after sunup on the morning before St. Mary Magdalene's Feast Day, an unlikely rider on a gorgeous dapple gray palfrey returned to the stables inside King's Gate at Windsor. A scrappy stable hand jogged up to secure the horse and offered a hand to the equestrian. "Did you have a good ride, Your Highness?"

"Very refreshing!" sounded a robust, energetic female voice. The seventy-one year-old Eleanor, Duchess of Aquitaine, Countess of Poitou, Duchess of Normandy, Countess of Anjou and the Queen Mother of England was the most phenomenal woman of her time. As her riding boots touched the ground, her escort caught up.

Statuesque with a commanding air and still strikingly beautiful even in her golden years, Eleanor stood taller than the stable hand and a fair number of the nobles at court. With a gloved hand, she removed her riding bonnet to reveal shimmering silver hair with enough red left in the strands to hint at the fire they once held.

She handed the young man the reins, her intelligent dark eyes evaluating him even as she said, "I want you to rub down her legs with liniment oil; she felt a bit stiff this morning."

"Yes, Your Grace," he said with a bow and led the horse into the stables while the men at arms dismounted.

An ordinary looking, though weary, man in uniform approached the Queen Mother. "Your Highness, why is it that you constantly make it so difficult for us to keep up with you? A guard should ride before you to make certs the path is safe."

She raised her chin and met his eyes, giving him an amused smile. "I have found it advantageous in my lifetime to always take the lead. But you are always welcome to try." She winked flirtatious at the man more than half her age and began a deliberate march toward the castle kitchens.

Two scullery maids with their hair tucked up under white caps were on the kitchen's back porch scrubbing pots when they saw her approaching dressed in her riding attire.

The younger of the maids commented to the other, "Don't you think the Queen is too old to be out riding? She could have a fall and be done for."

"Shhhhh," shushed the matronly, plumper maid. "Are you daft? Let her hear you suggest such a thing and you'll be on chamber pot duty for a month. No one tells Eleanor of Aquitaine that she is too old for anything!" She immediately lowered her head, stopped scrubbing and curtsied. "Good morrow, Your Highness."

"Good morrow, Your Highness," parroted the younger maid with a curtsey.

"It is a good morning!" Eleanor declared. "I shall be down to break my fast shortly. Is Mistress Baker about? I wish to discuss the menu for tomorrow's feast with her."

"I saw her in the pantry just a moment ago, Your Grace," the older maid replied.

"Thank you," Eleanor returned courteously. Then glancing at the younger maid's pot she pointed out, "You missed a spot," before striding through the door.

* * *

After seeking her head cook and thoroughly instructing her on the menu, Eleanor, accompanied by two ladies-in-waiting, retired to her chamber in the royal residences of the castle on the north side of the Upper Ward to change into her day gown for breakfast. Once she was satisfied that her deep red gown with gold trim and flowing sleeves was properly arranged, she dismissed the girls and marched two doors down the passage to her son's room. The high oak door being closed, she knocked vigorously then waited for a count of five before turning the knob and throwing it open.

A disheveled, sleepy eyed man with strawberry blonde hair and beard sat up in annoyance until he saw the intimidating figure of his mother in the doorway. Two young women, one with long raven hair and the other in straw blonde curls, peeped up from the sheets on either side of him.

John's expression turned to an embarrassed scowl. "Mother, what cause have you to enter my private rooms?"

"Private?" she inquired raising an eyebrow. "It doesn't look very private to me. Really, John, it is clear you have no shame, but have you no discretion either?"

"Whatever you want of me, can it not wait until noon?" he moaned.

Eleanor lost patience with him. "No," she curtly retorted.

He motioned for the two young ladies to leave, and each wrapping a sheet around herself, they scurried off leaving John in his silk under garments and a blue woolen blanket. "You love to embarrass me," he complained, with heat in his voice. "Whatever complaint or report you have for me can wait."

"I think not, son." She entered the high ceilinged chamber and closed the door behind her. "Twenty and seven years a grown man, and still you behave like a child, fooling around with servants while you have produced no legitimate heir with your wife, Isabella. And, if that isn't bad enough, there are rumors at court you are carrying on affairs with married noble women!"

John raised his chin and flashed her his most charming smile. "Can I help it that women love me?"

She crossed the room to the side of his huge walnut bed and her arms folded with a look of disgust in the line of her mouth. "I doubt love has anything to do with it. Asides, how does one go about saying 'no' to the Prince? But that is not the reason I have come."

"What then, if not to instruct me in my husbandly duties?" He relaxed back into his pillows looking bored.

Eleanor said, "You should pay more attention to Isabella; you need an heir, a legitimate one. Your behavior is not just a humiliation to her; your affairs spit in the face of the Church and lower your esteem with the people."

"The Church, the people," he mocked. "What do I care about those? I am the prince and heir apparent behind my brother; I can do whatever I please."

"Just because one can do a thing, it does not follow that he should do that thing. Being king means far more than getting your way; it is about respect, strength of character, strength of will."

At that he sat up, green eyes flashing. "I have ambitions, Mother. I will be king one day, and I will have the power to lock you up like my father before me should you stand in my way."

Eleanor took a seat on the edge of the bed. "I feel that I have failed you. Because of my imprisonment, I missed being there for your formative years. Perhaps if I could have influenced you then, we wouldn't be going around about these things now. You must understand that I do want you to be king–when the time is right; when it is your turn. But that ill-advised ploy you and Phillip of France attempted with Henry Hohenstaufen, offering to pay him to keep Richard imprisoned–that is not the way to go about it! It was cowardly, underhanded, and unchivalrous, not to mention treasonous."

"And was it not treasonous when young Henry and my brothers, with your backing, stood in rebellion against my father?"

"We stood up to him face to face, militarily and politically, in a fair fight, which your father won. But we never conspired in secret with an enemy nation!"

John returned to his childish pout and laid back onto his pillows. "You know I am not a warrior like Richard. I cannot stand up to him in a fair fight and live."

She brushed a bare hand across his forehead and cradled his fuzzy cheek. "Then be patient, dear boy. Help me get Richard back. Show him your support now, and I will give you mine later. Your brother is many years your elder and you are sure to outlive him. You need more time to mature. Take on military training, listen to your tutors, grow in wisdom, make the political connections you will need with your nobles and foreign princes, go to your wife and produce children. I need you and your King needs you. Help me raise the ransom to bring him home and one day the power will be yours—when you are ready for it."

John's sullenness deepened. He wanted it now; he wanted it all now.

He had been working on another plan... one that would take them all by surprise and prove he was strong and capable enough of a leader to take the throne. As he'd just said, he could not hope to challenge her or the King outright. So instead he nodded and kissed her hand. "Undoubtedly you are right, Mother. I will assemble a team and ride out across the land. I will help you raise the money to bring my brother home from his captivity. Then, will I finally have your blessing?"

She smiled a proud and doting smile at him and kissed his cheek. "Son, you may not always have my approval, but know that you do always have my love."

* * *

AFTER PARTAKING of the morning meal of manchet bread, cheese, and fruit, Eleanor sought out the leader of the castle's troupe of troubadours, a fancifully attired musician from her native Aquitaine, Alberic. His colorful costume of green and yellow paneled tunic belted over red tights added to the flair that was part of the troubadours' appeal.

"Alberic, has the new hurdy-gurdy I ordered arrived yet?" she asked.

"Yes, Your Grace," he replied with an obligatory bow. "Just yesterday, along with a musician to play it, Gilbert de Anjou. They say he is the best, and I had to bribe him with a teaching position to lure him away from his previous post. I trust Your Highness can find a post for him. You demanded only the best, so..."

"Do not fret; that is exactly what I asked for." Eleanor gazed toward a tapestry featuring William I and knights on horseback as she pondered. "The University at Oxford is expanding and I have long wanted it to include music among its courses. Compose a letter informing the institution that I wish this Gilbert de Anjou to be hired on as a professor of music. Since London is only a day's ride from the castle, it should not interfere with his obligations here."

"I shall see to it right away," he declared with a bow.

"Not so fast, Alberic." She held up a hand to stop him. "I wish to consult with you on the music selections for the feast tomorrow evening. Naturally, all selections should be in the Courtly Love style, consisting first of music for dining followed by tunes suitable for dancing." Eleanor produced a piece of paper from a small pouch tied to a cord around her waist. "I have taken the liberty to make a list of titles that I especially want to have played."

He took the list and glanced over it. "Excellent choices, Your Grace. Some of these will feature Gilbert on our new hurdy-gurdy."

"Precisely. As you see there is a mix of instrumentals and tunes with vocals. I am determined to bring culture to this island if it is the last thing I do!" Eleanor smiled at Alberic who beamed back, very pleased to be the lead musician in the court of the leading patron of the arts in all of England. He bowed once more and scurried off, list in hand, to prepare his troupe for the upcoming event.

As Eleanor continued down the stone walled corridor with its narrow cross-shaped arrow-slit windows, she happened upon William Marshall, the Earl of Pembroke.

"Good day, Your Highness," William said with a courteous smile, a sweep of his arm, and a deep bow. He wore a royal blue surcoat with white ermine trim. At forty-seven years of age, gray had crept into the brown of his beard and temples, but he was still as strong and fit as ever with eyes the deep bay of a destrier. The famed knight who had bested over 500 opponents in tournaments and never lost a bout was the living embodiment of chivalry, a code and conduct that Eleanor promoted. Because he had gained the respect of all the people, Richard had placed William, along with Eleanor, on the board of regents he left in charge of the kingdom while he was away.

"Good day, Sir William," she returned with a slight nod. "I have been meaning to speak with you on a matter of import. Have you a moment?"

"Certainly. How may I serve you?"

"This is about how you may serve your King. Perhaps you will escort me on a walk about the grounds," she suggested as they were passed by a young lord with an attractive blonde on his arm.

"'Tis a lovely day for a stroll," he agreed and held out his arm for her to take. Together they exited the castle and all of its prying eyes and ears.

Encompassing over thirteen acres, Windsor Castle was one of more than eighty bastions erected during the reign of William the Conqueror, and one of a group of strategic fortifications constructed around London. One day's ride from the city and each other, these castles held garrisons that could easily be reinforced and protect the capital. Most were originally motte and bailey style wooden structures, but many, including

Windsor, boasted stone keeps. In fact it was William I who introduced stone castles to the British Isles.

Windsor was of particular import due to its commanding posture overlooking the River Thames, its location along a major overland road to London, and its proximity to the Saxon royal hunting grounds. Henry II, Eleanor's late husband, had established his royal palace there and embarked on a fourteen year building project which included renovating the keep and replacing the old wooden palisade with formidable stone walls interspersed with towers and turrets. Henry had Bagshot heath brought in from quarries to the south supplemented with Bedfordshire stone from the north to complete a castle he intended to stand for a millennium. He constructed the massive King's Gate and two sets of royal residences–one for his family in the Upper Ward and another for important guests and courtiers in the Lower Ward. His finished work rivaled any of the great castles of Europe.

"I trust you and Isabella de Clare will join me for the feast tomorrow evening," Eleanor began as they leisurely passed various grounds workers.

"We would be most honored," William answered as he nodded toward her.

Once they were away from any others, Eleanor began. "Richard trusted you. Surely after that debacle between John and Longchamp, you know well John does not always support his brother."

"Indeed. Rest assured that my loyalty to King Richard is without question. I allowed myself to be caught up in the affair only because I failed to see John for who and what he is." Then William shook his head. "One day, I may need to pledge John my allegiance–a pledge I would indeed keep. But as long as the Lionheart lives, I am his man, and yours, Your Grace."

"I appreciate you, William. Not only what you stand for, which is far and above the standard for all who would call themselves knight, but for who you are; I am pleased to consider you my friend."

"As am I, Your Highness. I sense something troubles you," he perceived and gazed at her in question.

Eleanor sighed. "It is John, as one might guess. I suspect he is up to something."

"Truly?" William asked. "Again? And so soon after trying to pay Emperor Henry to keep Richard captive?"

"Oh, he was much too quick to agree to help me raise the remaining ransom," she explained in an exasperated tone. Her keen eyes scanned the castle yard to ensure they were still alone. "No, he is sneaky and under-handed and definitely up to no good. He is taking off to tour the country, supposedly to collect tax money himself, along with his new friend Sir Guy of Gisborne. What can you tell me about Sir Guy? He is much older than John; I don't see what they have in common."

William stroked his beard as they made a turn at the castle wall. "He is my age, Your Grace, and twenty years ago was a strong contender in the tournaments. He inherited his father's estate and has been profitable with it. However rumor has it that his success comes at the price of cruelty to his serfs. About fifteen years ago he was banned from competing in any sanctioned events because he was caught cheating. It seems he substituted his official ash lances for identically painted ones made from maple."

Eleanor furrowed her brow. "I don't understand."

"You see," he explained. "The tournament provides lances for all jousters that are the same size, weight, and hardness, fitted with blunt ends to protect competitors. Invariably there are accidents. Sometimes a knight is killed, but that is not the aim. The point is to knock a knight from his horse. Lances made of ash are flexible and splinter fairly easily, so if a strike is indirect, the lance will break and the rider remains in the saddle; only a direct hit will unseat him. But Gisborne was substituting his lances with ones made of maple, a much harder wood, which does not splinter. That allowed him a greater chance than other competitors to unseat his opponent with only a glancing blow. Subtle, but still cheating."

"So he wanted to win unfairly," she mused. "That is what he and John hold in common. My guess is that Gisborne has pledged his fealty to John seeking advancement and reward from my youngest as soon as they place him on Richard's throne." She shook her head and looked to William. "I truly wish, I could trust my son John to be loyal to the King and wait his turn for the crown, but I fear I cannot. He has undermined the authority Richard left with us at every turn. And now that we are charged with collecting this 100,000 marks from a country barely more than a century old, from Saxons who distrust us and Normans who cannot spare the funds, we must become taskmasters of a people we would rather inspire to greatness than crush with taxes. The truth is, Richard is a better king than John would be. My prayer is that my baby will one day grow into his role; he can be more than he is–I know he can be."

"Only if he wants to be, Milady."

Eleanor moved her gaze to the castle and nodded her own agreement.

"I already have a few spies in London, Warwick, Cambridge, and another in Nottingham," she stated matter-of-factly. Then paused looking up into his honest eyes. "But I think a little insurance is in order."

"Your Grace?" the Earl questioned.

"There is someone I feel I can count on who may be able to elicit exactly the information we need. I will speak with her about it on the morrow."

"Her?" Surprise lit his expression.

Eleanor's mouth twisted into a knowing smile that strained to hold back laughter and she flashed dark eyes at her companion. "Why, Sir William, surely you know better than to under estimate the power of a capable woman."

* * *

MAID MARIAN FITZWALTER sat at the long elevated table at one end of the great hall along with the royal family and high nobles of the court. Her long, honey colored hair was divided into two braids interwoven with a blue ribbon and arranged in a fashionable chignon. The ribbon complemented the indigo trim of her otherwise azure, full-sleeved bliaut, accented by a silver necklace set with a sapphire stone. Her eyes were the pastel blue of robins' eggs set beneath delicate brows on either side of a straight nose. Her bowed lips and apple cheeks were subtly colored with strawberry rouge to set them ever so slightly apart from her alabaster skin.

Marian's seat was between Isabelle de Clare, who was near her age, and Sir Guy of Gisborne, who was considerably older and a recent widower. Also at the table were Queen Eleanor, Prince John and his wife Isabella, Sir William Marshall Earl of Pembroke, Sir Aubrey de Vere Earl of Oxford and his wife Agnes, Sir Henry FitzCount Earl of Cornwall and Bishop Richard Fitz Neal, the nation's treasurer. At the other tables were dozens of lesser lords and ladies who had been invited to the St. Mary of Magdalene

The hall was a spacious rectangular room with a high ceiling that served many purposes, including feasts. Several large picture windows faced out onto Eleanor's beautifully landscaped gardens letting in daytime light. The wall behind the dining tables had but tiny arrow slit windows bearing a long row of wall sconces for light and various tapestries for warmth and decoration. Across the expanse of floor, used for dancing, was a wide entry door beneath the minstrels' gallery where Alberic and his troubadours played a selection from Eleanor's list. In the center of the room was a tremendous hearth with a square stone chimney displaying the red and gold Plantagenet coat-of-arms, two facing rampant lions, and Eleanor's Angevin single gold lion on a red shield with one paw raised. Because the summer evening was warm, the great fire was not lit. Instead, round candelabras hung from the ceiling, brightening the room.

Squires and servants in sharp, clean attire scurried forth from a side door leading from the kitchens bearing platters of delightful delicacies to satisfy both the eye and appetite. There was thick pottage served in bowls made of bread, a roasted peacock arranged with its feathers on a silver platter along with a swan that was similarly displayed, a roast boar with an apple in its mouth, platters of cheeses, bowls of fruit, plates piled high with aromatic pastries, and goblets of wine. Everything was as Eleanor had designed.

Marian was sampling a beef fritter with plum sauce when Sir Guy turned his attention to her. "'Twas such sad news about the Earl of Loxley and his son," he said between bites of sautéed eel.

Suddenly Marian went still. She no longer heard the music nor considered the food as she turned her full attention to Sir Guy. "What about them?" she asked with concern. "I haven't heard."

"Oh dear," he replied in feigned concern and washed his morsel down with some French wine. "Word has recently arrived from the crusade. I'm afraid they both were killed." Marian's fair face paled with shock. "I understand your family was friends with the Loxleys."

"Yes, yes," she uttered. "I grew up in a nearby manor and we visited each other regularly. This is such distressing news." Marian found herself no longer in a mood for celebration, but she wanted to find out more about what had happened. "Have you heard anything of Robyn, Sir Loxley's daughter?"

Isabella, William Marshall's young wife, replied, "She seems to have disappeared. No one really knows what happened to her."

Though less beautiful than Marian, the young brunette came from a vastly more wealthy family as her wardrobe and jewelry attested. The two had developed a quick friendship during the week of William and Isabella's visit to Windsor from Kilkenny Castle overlooking their substantial holdings in Ireland.

Marian's expression went blank as she stared at the green-eyed Isabella. "What do you mean nobody knows?"

"Sweet Marian, do not upset yourself so!" Isabella put down her food and laid a hand on Marian's arm. "I heard one rumor that she has gone to a nunnery."

"A nunnery?" Marian couldn't believe it. "Why wouldn't she still be at Loxley manor? Was she so distressed by her loss?"

"I am sure it was a considerable blow, especially after losing her mother and younger siblings," Sir Guy concluded. "But you realize that, as an unmarried woman, she had no claims to the estate." Both his wavy copper shoulder length hair and his trim pointed beard bore streaks of gray. His mid-section had bulged with age, but his weight was also considered a sign of wealth. He gazed at Marian through hungry hazel eyes. "You should take note, my dear. A maid of your age must think about marriage yourself."

"You know I must wait for my father's return from Germany," she repeated, as she had many times before over the past four years. "Verily, I cannot marry without my father's approval. Now that the ransom for King Richard has almost all been collected, I feel sure he will return home with the King quite soon. But about Robyn..."

Sir Guy sighed an impatient breath and added, "Actually, I heard she has run off to Scotland."

"Scotland!" Marian was more confounded than before. "I can't believe she would commit herself to a nunnery or leave the country without telling me." Now Marian was not sure which new turn of events hurt her heart the most.

"She has always been rather strange," Isabella noted in as compassionate of a tone as she could muster. "I suppose it can't be helped, what with her being a Saxon and all. Why, I don't think she has been back to court since the summer of her coming out."

"What does her lineage matter?" Marian asked in derision. "She has not been to court because she has been busy managing the Loxley lands alone while her male relatives were giving their lives to defend our Christian faith!"

Sir Guy had gone back to eating but managed to squeeze a nonchalant word in between bites. "That is what a steward is for. I have one myself."

"It takes more than one person to run an entire estate," Marian noted, adding quietly, "to do it properly, that is."

Sir Guy changed tactics. He set down his knife and cup and turned his full attention to the eligible and desirable beauty beside him, attempting to comfort Marian in her time of sorrow. "Maid Marian, I have already arranged a trip to Nottingham for tomorrow and I promise to personally look into Maid Robyn's whereabouts." He used his most sincere tone, softening his eyes as he placed a broad well-manicured hand over hers. "I will find out what has happened to her for you and send word immediately so you will not be so distraught."

Marian smiled at him in gratitude. "Thank you, Sir Guy."

She had her suspicions about Gisborne's motives, as she did about every unmarried man who called upon her, but she did not think of him the way he thought of her. She regarded Sir Guy like an uncle or grandfather, or other such masculine relative, but not as a husband. While he always displayed chivalric manners to her, she had heard from peasants and serfs on her own family's manor that he was cruel and heartless, not even properly mourning his own wife's passing. They said he was more concerned with profits than people, with promoting his own political success than in honor, and that he could not be trusted as far as one could pitch a millstone. And while she had a propensity to believe such stories, there was always a chance folks exaggerated. For here was Sir Guy displaying empathy for her feelings... or did he simply want under her skirts?

"Don't mention it," he answered with a kind looking smile and patted her hand. "Anything I can do for the beloved goddaughter of the King will be my pleasure."

* * *

MARIAN COULD THINK of nothing all night save what had become of her childhood friend, even when dancing the galliard and roundel. She was an excellent dancer and, though her mood was dark and pensive, she was compelled by her station to join in the evening's activities. She danced with several partners including Sir Guy, but became distracted to the point of desperation. After a pavane, Marian excused herself to the garderobe, and feeling slightly more relieved set out to speak with the Queen. As it happened, Eleanor had also been looking for her.

They found each other just outside the hall doorway from which music and laughter poured. "Your Highness," Marian greeted with a curtsey. "I must ask for your leave to return home as soon as Your Highness may grant it."

Eleanor, seeing her distress, took the young lady by the arm. "Come, Marian. Have you seen the hybrid rose I have been cultivating in the gardens? I call it the Plantageitaine Rose."

Marian was baffled by the abrupt change in subject, but went with Eleanor outside. The Queen was in a regal verdant gown with long swooping sleeves adorned with gold and a thin gold band around her forehead. The moon was high overhead, and the garden was also lit by torches, so maneuvering the grounds was easy.

"I love the gardens," Eleanor said with a dreamy look in her dark eyes and a sigh in her voice. "So peaceful and private." Once they were thirty or forty yards from the festivities Eleanor stopped in front of a bed of roses.

Marian looked at them and commented. "They are indeed lovely."

"Tell me, child; why do you suddenly wish to return home?"

Marian straightened but was still much shorter than Eleanor. "I must find out what has happened to my friend, Robyn of Loxley. They are saying her father and brother were killed, and that she has disappeared. I cannot have peace until I know what has happened to her."

Eleanor studied the maid's sincerity and then fondled one of the roses. "I grafted cuttings from a rose variety I brought with me from Aquitaine to a bush native to this land. I think the result is a stronger, more beautiful and fragrant sort." Then she looked to Marian. "There are those who say Normans are superior to Saxons, but I have learned a secret; like the roses, each has something to offer the other, and we are indeed stronger together."

"I fail to understand why so many hold ill opinions of our fellow Englishmen more than a hundred years after the war," Marian voiced, puzzled again by the Queen's change in subject. "It has been at least three generations, yet some want to judge others based on their ancestry from before our nation was even established."

Eleanor gave her a bemused glance. "Some people consider what they have in common with their neighbor, while others see only what is different. My dear, I fear I must confirm what you heard this evening: the latest casualty report listed the Earl and his son as killed in battle. I regret not knowing what has happened to the daughter, nor did I know anything was amiss. She is your friend?"

"Yes, Your Grace," Marian replied choking back the tears that had been threatening all evening.

"Tell me, what is the nature of your relationship with Sir Guy of Gisborne?"

The burgeoning tears stopped in their tracks and a confused expression emerged on Marian's face. "What? Sir Guy? I have no relationship with Sir Guy."

A twisted smile crossed Eleanor's mouth. "That is not what court gossip says. My dear Marian, do you not know when a man is wooing you?"

"But I told him that I cannot even consider courting anyone until my father returns home to give his consent."

"Merely ascertaining the truth of the matter," she said and led them on a farther stroll. "You are Richard's goddaughter because your father, Sir Robert FitzWalter, is my son's dearest, oldest and most loyal friend. Even now, he sits encamped outside Trifels Castle in Germany, waiting to escort Richard back home upon his release. Despite the urgings of members of our court and warnings by the Holy Roman Emperor, he refuses to leave without his King. That is the loyalty of your father. What about your loyalty, Maid Marian?"

"I do not understand. I am unconditionally loyal to the King, and will challenge anyone who would say otherwise. In fact, I am very much my father's daughter," she declared.

"I thought as much," Eleanor replied as she paused beside some white flowering shrubs. After a careful glance around she explained. "There are those in England, even at court, even in my own family, who are not so loyal. I believe Sir Guy is among them."

Marian registered the line of conversation and the tour around the gardens. The Queen's words rang true for her. "I do not intend to wed him, Your Grace, nor any man regardless of his wealth or title if he does not love King Richard as my father does."

"It is fortuitous that you wish to return home, though not for such a grievous reason, as I would ask it of you anyway. Sir Guy and Prince John are planning to leave for Nottingham Castle to plot some scheme with the Sheriff there–I am sure of it. Both your manor and Loxley are located in the vicinity, so you can take time with your family, check on Maid Robyn and keep an eye on Sir Guy. I am not suggesting you promise him anything, but as long as his attention is fixed upon you, you may find yourself privy to what may otherwise be considered private conversations. It is imperative we discover what John, Gisborne and the Sheriff are about."

"I see," Marian said. "As long as I am there, I will do whatever is necessary to secure the return of my King, and my father with him."

"It could be dangerous," Eleanor warned, "especially if they become suspicious of you. Can you play at courting Sir Guy while holding him at arm's length with the excuse of waiting on your father's consent?"

"I believe I can; I will surely do my best. But how will you and I communicate?"

Eleanor smiled at Marian and took both of her hands in a firm, warm grip. "I will send you back with a crate of pigeons that fly only to my loft. When you learn something of import, write a short note and secure it in the little case that ties to its leg. If I need to get word to you, I will send a personal courier." Marian nodded and gave Eleanor's hands a little squeeze. "I am sorry to hear about the Loxleys, and I hope you find your friend safe and well."

"Thank you," the young lady said and bowed her head.

Eleanor moved one hand to stroke Marian's cheek. "Thank you."

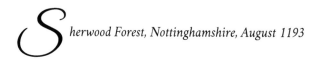

herwood Forest, Nottinghamshire, August 1193

"YOU'LL NEVER GUESS who I saw strollin' 'round Nottingham Castle this mornin'," Alan A Dale challenged the others as he rejoined the camp with a smile on his youthful face and a spring in his step.

Little John scowled disapprovingly. "I told you to stay out o' town lest you be recognized and caught. We won't be able to save you from a hanging now, lad."

"He can't help it," Will teased with a gleam in his own sparkling blue eyes. "Alan's got hisself a lady friend–that buxom young Liz what works at the tavern, right?"

Allen's cheeks flushed, and he winked a clover green eye at his comrade. "She's an energetic lass, high-spirited, and she calls me her Honey Sop," he said beaming and took a seat on the log beside Will and Robyn near the campfire under the protective branches of the ancient tree. "But I saw someone else in town today." All eyes turned to him. "Ah, come on now, somebody has to guess!"

"King Richard!" exclaimed Much as he joined the youngsters and Little John. "Oh, please let it be King Richard!" He folded his hands as in prayer as he fell to his knees.

"Sorry, Much, but not today," Alan said. Not waiting for guesses, he continued, "I saw that beauteous Maid Marian back home from court. She was just strollin' about shoppin' at the market and keepin' company with Sir Guy of Gisborne."

Robyn perked up at the news, raising her head to look Alan in the face. She had been with the outlaw gang for a fortnight and had constructed her own dwelling of sticks and canvas. She knew they laid wagers about why she always kept her hood raised. Some bet it was to hide a scar or disfigurement while others said it was to conceal her true age. Long odds were on her being someone famous. Fortunately, no one had entered the possibility she was female. She was pulling her weight with chores and had proven to them all to be a good hunter and a sure-shot with her bow. Robyn enjoyed the company and engaged in more conversation, but was ever cautious about revealing any personal information. Sometimes she overheard the lads whisper and stare in her direction, wondering why she visited the latrine at odd times and never removed her cloak despite the midday heat.

Robyn had concluded that it was becoming too difficult to keep hiding her identity, and thought the time might be close to leave, but now that Marian was back... well, that changed everything!

"Mmmmm," Will vocalized brightly. "That is one luscious woman! I'd love to sop her honey!"

"Bugger that, Will!" Robyn snapped, tensing with bridled anger. "You shouldn't talk that way about Maid Marian."

Will's mouth fell agape in shock, his blue eyes widening beneath his length of black hair while Alan rubbed a hand over his sandy facial fuzz and shook his head.

"I think Robyn is sweet on Maid Marian, boys," Alan declared.

Arthur Bland ambled up with two rabbits for the pot. "Then he's out o' luck," he said joining in. "People in town are saying she's courtin' Sir Guy, not that any o' us could even lace her shoes."

"What!" Robyn cried incensed. "That is a vicious rumor and I demand you take it back! Marian would never court that fat, old, pompous arse!" Will and Alan exchanged glances and snickered. Robyn's mouth pursed in irritation. "She is far too good for the likes of him."

"Aye, that she is," Little John agreed. "I for one am happy to see a kind, noble lady like herself back in these parts. Mayhap she will provide a civilizing effect on Sir Guy and the Sheriff."

Robyn squeezed her hands together and bounced her knee nervously, but nodded at Little John's words. "But she is NOT courting him," she added in a low, determined tone.

"Whatever you say, Robyn," Will allowed. "Alan, did you think to bring your mates any hum back from the tavern?"

Alan reached into the bag that hung from a strap over his shoulder, withdrew a dark tinted bottle, and grinned with pride.

Robyn sat oblivious to the strong spirits, brooding over the rumor of her dearest friend and a man she loathed. She tried to imagine them kissing, but the idea disgusted her too much and she closed her eyes.

I need to go see her, talk to her, find out for myself what's going on, she determined. With Marian frequenting the Queen's court and Robyn occupied managing her manor lands, they had not actually seen each other in... Has it truly been years? Robyn realized as she counted up the months and seasons. And while they had not been in each other's physical presence, not a day had passed that Robyn did not regard Maid Marian tenderly, remembering their childhood escapades, their vows of undying friendship, the laughter and the light Marian had brought into her life following the death of her mother and younger siblings. She doubted she would be the person she had grown into had it not been for Marian.

As through a fog, Robyn perceived voices approaching.

"And here we are," Friar Tuck announced. "The Heart of Sherwood Forest and Grandma Oak." Robyn turned curious brown eyes toward Tuck's voice to behold a group of about a dozen peasants and serfs, judging from their rags and frailty.

"What have we here?" Little John demanded as he marched over to meet the newcomers.

"I'm sorry, Little John," the Friar apologized as he leaned on his walking stick. "They were wandering in the woods, lost and starving. I couldn't just leave them there."

"Who are they and why are they wandering around in our forest?" the outlaw leader asked in a private aside to Tuck.

But the Friar spoke loudly in reply for all hear. "These good Christians come from Loxley and Nottingham. Those from Nottingham were sacked and blackballed by the Sheriff and, unable to find work, had begun a journey to the next shire in search of employment when they ran into these folks from Loxley. There, they banded together." Holding a hand to his mouth, he spoke to Little John in a hushed tone. "Remember the law of hospitality, Little John. We may be thieves, miscreants, and tax evaders, but we are also Christians; we cannot turn away people in need."

Despite the dissatisfied twist of his features, the outlaw leader nodded in reluctant agreement.

Robyn had risen, aroused from her personal musing when she caught the name 'Loxley'. She stood beside Little John, hood hiding her face, and looked out at the dozen refugees. She recognized some faces.

"Why leave Loxley estate?" she asked.

An emaciated man with short mud brown hair who appeared older than his thirty-five years replied. "After word of the good Earl's death, the Sheriff came and seized the manor. He brought harsh taskmasters and armed men. They increased our workload and rummaged through our homes to collect Prince John's new taxes. We couldn't even keep enough food to live on."

Robyn felt a jolt of remorse like an arrow to the heart as he spoke. She knew this man. His name was Isaac. She knew him to be a hard worker and a cheerful family man.

He continued. "Roger, here," he motioned to a somber looking fellow in his twenties with straw-colored hair and beard and a ruddy complexion. "The Sheriff overheard him saying that things were better while Maid Robyn was running the manor and the Sheriff..." Isaac stopped, sparing a sympathetic glance at Roger while he swallowed. "Sheriff Godfrey Giffard of Nottingham, soon to be named Earl of Loxley, cut out his tongue."

A shocked silence fell over the outlaw band for a moment before murmurings and the shaking of heads began. The knot grew tighter in Robyn's stomach and she feared she would be sick.

Then Isaac led a young girl recently passed puberty to the front of the desperate group of sunken-eyed souls. She stood to his shoulders with a scarf over strawberry-blonde hair and small, tender breasts just budding. "My daughter, Christina, is a sweet, pretty girl. Unfortunately, the Sheriff thought so as well. A few nights ago soldiers came to our cruck and took her. They said she had found favor with the Sheriff and would be well treated. At first Beatrice, my wife, and I thought mayhap he had chosen her to be a household servant, but when they returned her the next morning..." This time he was unable to stop the tears. The gaunt Isaac hugged his little girl.

Beatrice stepped forward. She was a slight woman in a patched dress with searching gray eyes and two small boys clinging to her. "I don't understand," she stated, looking from one of Little John's men to the next. "Why would Lady Loxley abandon us? Why would she leave us to that monster?"

Robyn closed her eyes, pressure bearing down on her chest like an iron anvil. She couldn't breathe. She couldn't think beyond, What have I done?

"Now Beatrice, we can't blame Maid Robyn," another woman in the party said patting the grieving mother's shoulder. "I was there; the Sheriff evicted her. He even declared her a traitor for opposing his takeover of Loxley. What could she have done?"

Beatrice sighed and shook her head, her shoulders slumping like those of one carrying a heavy burden. Isaac regained his composure and wrapped his other arm around his wife in comfort. "So Friar Tuck tells us you are the leader here," he said looking up at Little John's grizzly visage. He nodded. "Since we abandoned our duties to our manor and fled our obligations as serfs, we are now outlaws, too, and wish to join your gang."

John looked them over then turned to Robyn, but she was no longer standing beside him. "I am saddened to hear of your trials, and the Friar was right to bring you here. Alan, please see to our guests; I'll return anon," he said and strode across the camp.

* * *

ROBYN WAS in the privacy of a thicket she frequented when she wanted to be alone; there John stopped, stood, and waited. He heard a sniff before she gazed up at him through guilt-ridden eyes.

"I know these people," she began as streaks of tears ran down her cheeks. "Roger worked in our stables. He would sing to the horses to calm them. He possessed a lovely voice and mayhap have been a minstrel, had he not been born tied to the land." She paused a moment, wiping her face with the back of her sleeve. "And Christina, Isaac's daughter... I remember attending her christening. I remember Mother explaining to me what the priest was doing and what it meant. These are my people, Little John, and Beatrice was right; I abandoned them. I was so busy thinking of my own situation that I didn't even spare one thought for them!" Robyn's chest heaved and more tears poured down her cheeks.

"How were you to know? What could you have done?" Little John wrapped an arm around her shoulders in comfort.

"Marry the Sheriff," she said and sniffed again. "Then at least I might still hold some sway, still watch out for them. He wouldn't have raped Christina."

"Child, if the Sheriff's tastes run to young girls, marrying you would have only postponed his actions."

She wiped her face with both hands and steeled her voice. "Then I should have killed him. I had an opportunity; I should have jabbed a dagger into his excuse for a heart."

Little John sighed and enfolded her in his arms. "Robyn, you are no murderer. You could no more have done that than given yourself to him in bed."

"But now he is extending his cruelty to my people. I was responsible for them and I just ran away and left them to him! What's happened is my fault," she said immersed in guilt and buried her face into his shoulder.

"Is everything that happens in the world your fault?" he asked. "Is it your fault King Richard was captured? Is it your fault your father and brother were killed? Is it your fault that evil men carry out their intentions? I'm sorry, Robyn, but in truth you just aren't that important," he added with a laugh.

Robyn, catching the joke, tried to release some of the burden she had heaped on herself. A slight chuckle found its way out. By then her sobbing had ceased. It was time to take action. "Gramercy," she replied and looked up into his fatherly face. "But what shall I do now? I have to take care of them, John. They are my responsibility. There is only one person I can turn to for help, one person whom I fully trust."

"Maid Marian?"

Robyn nodded. "I need to visit her straight away, but shall return tomorrow. I will not abandon them again, nor you and the boys. Marian is very clever and I'm sure she will offer to lend her aid. I know you didn't count on having women and children in your camp, but if you can suffer them for one night–" Her glistening eyes pleaded with him. She knew that he'd likely be hesitant to do so. How would they take care of so many people, especially the women and children? But, if Marian could help out, maybe that would change things. Would Little John feel better about inviting them to stay in the camp in that instance?

"What choice do I have? Turn them out to starve? I trust you to return with a plan." He loosened his embrace and Robyn took a step back with a deep breath.

"Thank you; you are a good leader and an honorable man, John Naylor. Once I collect my bow and quiver I'll be off. Can you make an excuse to the others for me?"

He nodded, and she was away.

* * *

ROBYN ARRIVED at the FitzWalter manor in the cool, quiet of the predawn morning. A lark had just begun its song and the air was damp with fog as she moved with precision to a particular niche in the rough stone wall. Pushing a white rock aside, as she had done innumerable times before, she dropped to her knees and squeezed through the hole. After looking left and right, Robyn began her sprint across the yard toward a familiar tree adjacent to the house. A dog barked in the distance, but rather than the sound of alarm, it was like a greeting from an old friend; no one stirred. She passed a chicken coop with hens nestled wing to wing on their roost. They, too, sounded their greeting with subdued clucks coming from deep in their chests. Grabbing hold of the lower branches, Robyn climbed the Rowan ash like she did as a child. Then holding on for balance, she traversed onto the branch that led to Marian's window.

She was suddenly struck with a disconcerting prospect; Is this still Marian's bedchamber? Has she changed quarters? But why would she? While possible, it is too late to think about that now, she told herself and stepped over onto the windowsill. The shutters had been left open to invite in the summer air.

Robyn recalled the last time she had snuck through Marian's window. It had been their last escapade before heading off to be introduced at court. How long ago was it? she wondered. With a balance of stealth and caution, Robyn now placed a silent booted foot inside the window on the laths of the bedroom floor. After taking another step into the dark room, she was startled by the sharp edge of a thin steel blade pressed to her throat. Her first thought was, Oh, no! She's changed rooms. But then a familiar melodious tone touched her ears, even though it emanated from a seriously chilled voice.

"Do not move, thief. I will not hesitate to spill your blood."

Robyn relaxed at Marian's voice and the tension evaporated out into the night. "Glad to see you're still keeping that dagger under your pillow," sounded her amiable reply.

"Robyn!" Marian exclaimed in a hushed tone and hastily tossed the knife onto the bed. She stepped out from the shadow at the edge of the window and embraced her friend with unveiled enthusiasm. Robyn wrapped her arms around Marian, laying her cheek to rest against hers. "I was so worried!" Marian gushed. "No one knew what happened to you. They said you had gone to a nunnery, or some nonsense."

Robyn lingered a moment in silence, enjoying the warmth of their touch. It had been far too long! She breathed in the scent of Marian's hair and was keenly aware that only a thin linen nightshift swathed the fullness of her breasts, the curve of her hips, and the smoothness of her skin. "And I heard you were courting Sir Guy," she replied in a whisper, her mouth to Marian's ear.

"Rubbish!" Marian loosened her hold on Robyn and stepped back to look up into her face. Reluctantly, Robyn allowed her to pull to arm's length, but kept one hand on her shoulder and another at her waist. "Why are you in these rogue's clothing?"

Robyn sighed, trailing her fingers away from the warmth emanating beneath that linen gown. She lowered her hood, unfastened the cape, and placed bow, quiver, and all on the floor. "There is so much to tell," she began, "and I fear I have two favors to ask of you."

Marian led her farther into the room, the pale light of dawn catching her golden strands and dancing over them like sunlight on a lake at midday. Robyn drank in her honest beauty, her soul filled with contentment; but she also felt a stirring, deep within her core, recalling vivid dreams involving herself and Marian in this same bedchamber. She tried to push the images to a distance and focus on the matter at hand.

"I was so sorry to hear about Thomas and your father," Marian empathized. Her eyes relayed the depth of her feeling. "You must be devastated."

"Your father is well, I trust?"

"Yes, for now," Marian said. "We receive letters from his camp in Germany where he awaits the King's release."

Robyn nodded and smiled. "I am glad to hear it."

Marian continued to give Robyn puzzled looks and finally blurted out, "What have you done with your breasts?"

Robyn bubbled over with subdued laughter. She was pleased that Marian had noticed. "My favorite bed sheet," she explained. "I tore it into a long strip which I then bound snugly around them under my clothing.

At first I found it tight and uncomfortable, but it allows me to run and fight much more effectively. That combined with this doublet is sufficient for hiding my more feminine assets."

"I don't understand," Marian said. "Why are you pretending to be a boy?"

A somberness replaced her light visage. "Then you haven't heard the whole story. You are fortunate, Marian; your father lives and you've younger brothers who can inherit for you. I had no one, and when the Sheriff showed up with his proclamations of how I had no rights to Loxley and I could marry him or be thrown out; well the reply I gave is not suitable for polite company. He took such great offense as to declare me a traitor and an outlaw. I suppose I could have gone to a nunnery," she mused. "But the possibility never crossed my mind."

"But disguising yourself as a highwayman did?" Marian wondered aloud.

"It seemed to be the most expedient course of action. But now I have reached a turning point," she said in all sincerity, fixing her gaze onto Marian's eyes of passionate blue. "Either I fully embrace my new role, or I keep on running."

"What are you saying?" Marian tilted her head to one side and gazed back at her.

"I joined a band of outlaws in Sherwood Forest and I can make a go of it with them; however, they think I am a boy. Then yesterday other people arrived, those who have been treated unfairly by the Sheriff, who were tortured, and starved, and stolen from by him since he took over Loxley." There was smoldering heat in her voice–not the kind she wanted to share with Marian, but the kind that seethed with hatred toward the Sheriff. "I must take care of them," she stated with determination. "I must redeem my failure in running away and protect them now. But I need your help."

"Absolutely," Marian vowed, "anything you need."

Robyn took a step closer, into Marian's personal space, a space she had always been freely allowed to enter. "I want you to cut my hair, like a boy's. If I am to make this work, I must commit entirely to my new persona, Robin Hood. And I can't be wearing that bloody hood twenty-four hours a day." She drew her long, brown braid from her back over one shoulder where it dangled down to her waist. She couldn't help but gaze longingly at it. As much as she knew this was the right course—the only course—to take, she couldn't wholly shake the idea of it being further punishment. But she had to set those thoughts aside.

Marian had no such lead in to Robyn's decision to purposefully cut her hair. Her eyes popped wide as she looked at Robyn. "Not your beautiful hair! Are you sure cutting your hair alone will be enough to convince people?"

Her words did give Robyn pause, however. She lowered her head as she pondered. "I have thick brows, a strong chin, am tall and slender hipped, and they already think I'm a boy. Verily, people tend see what they expect to see."

"I suppose you are right," Marian consented and reached one hand to stroke the long, acorn brown braid. Her hand traveled the length from just below Robyn's chin past her shoulder, knuckles brushing over her bound breasts. Robyn felt a sudden tingle, a tightness, a longing. Then Marian said, "If this is what truly you want, I will do it. Come, sit here at the dressing table."

Dawn's radiance streamed through the window, casting the room in strong contrasts of light and shadow. Robyn took the seat while Marian withdrew a pair of shears from a drawer in the dressing table. "There's no going back from this," she warned. "It would take ten years for your hair to reach this length again."

"I'll be lucky to live ten years," Robyn replied with a resigned sigh. "I'll never have my life back. Everything that I've ever known was swept away in an instant. The question now is how to proceed. This is the best scheme I could devise."

Marian untied the leather cord at the base of Robyn's braid and wove her fingers through her hair loosening it. "And the second favor?"

"I need to feed the poor, the homeless, the refugees, those that have come to us for help. I confess that I do not know how to accomplish that," Robyn admitted. "If I still had my lands and family resources, then it would be no problem; as it stands, I am as penniless as they are."

With the braid loosed, Marian combed her fingers through Robyn's hair. For Robyn, it was an immensely pleasing sensation that drew away every bit of tension and apprehension leaving only calm serenity. Robyn relaxed her shoulders and leaned her head placidly into Marian's hands.

For a moment it was as if there was no one else in the world—no war, no sheriff, no loss. Just Robyn and Marian and whatever was between them. In that instant, Robyn reasoned she could let it all go. If she and

Marian ran away together and left everything behind, that would be fine by her. For just a twinkling, her world became everything she had hoped for.

"I can give you some money to buy food for them," Marian offered as she continued to massage her fingers through Robyn's silky strands, "but it would only be a temporary remedy." And there was reality smashing the dream. Robyn had stopped running; she'd determined to take a stand and do right by her people.

"Your charity is greatly appreciated, but I need your ideas," Robyn said, snapping back to the moment as Marian reached for the shears. "You always came up with the best schemes, the grandest pranks, and each one a greater success than the last."

Memories brought a smile to Marian that touched her eyes. "Yes, but you were the one bold enough to carry them all out."

"Only because I had faith that your plans would succeed and succeed they did."

"Remember the time you poured ink in the town bully's ale? It turned his teeth black for a month!" Marian bubbled over with laughter.

Robyn joined her lightness of spirit. "And the best part is he never learned who did it."

"Well, you shall have my donation," Marian confirmed. "Come to think of it, I know quite a few nobles and merchants in these parts with deep pockets who could easily contribute to the cause. Why, they could feed your refugees for months and not even miss the coin."

A look of dismay returned to Robyn's face. "Like I'll convince any of them to be charitable?"

"Well." Robyn recognized the tone of Marian's voice at once; it meant she had a devilishly clever plan in mind. Brightness gleamed in Marian's intelligent eyes and a grin tugged at the bow of her lips. The shears went about their cutting and a woman's crown of glory fell unceremoniously to the floor. "Your band of outlaws, some swords, and some bows may convince them to part with their purses."

And then the spark passed from Marian to Robyn. "Are you suggesting that we rob the rich to feed the poor?" She couldn't quite help the grin on her face as she said the words.

"It's not like they will miss any meals, and I'm sure you can make better use of their excess blunt than they could. But you had better hurry," she added seriously, snipping the last bits of Robyn's hair. "Prince John is traveling about, raising more taxes. Queen Eleanor has raised two-thirds of the ransom from her holdings on the continent, but without the remaining portion she cannot secure the King's release. So you will need to hit them before the tax man does."

"And Sir Guy?" Robyn asked, narrowing her brow. She raised her chin bringing her eyes to catch Marian's.

"Sir Guy has recently lost his wife and is in search for a replacement. He seems to believe that I will suffice, but I assure you I have no intentions of accepting a marriage proposal from him, or anyone for that matter, until my father returns home."

Robyn let out a sigh of relief, joy beaming in her eyes and her soul at the certainty she was right, that there was nothing to this rumor about Sir Guy.

Then Marian took her by the hand and led her to a large looking glass. She stood beside her, showing off the results of the haircut. Robyn was rightly impressed. "I even look like a boy to me!"

Marian laid her head on Robyn's shoulder reaching one arm around her waist gazing at their reflections. As Robyn peered into the mirror, she thought of what a lovely couple they made and how, if things were different, they could be together. She realized she yearned for that more than ever in her life, even as she inwardly quivered. Then Marian continued.

"But I must consider marriage. After all, I will turn twenty in December. Most maids of our age are already wed. People are already saying, 'Marian thinks she is too good for anyone, how vain she is, and no man meets her expectations.'"

"Bollocks," Robyn uttered darkly, and like a mist, her dream disappeared. "With the likes of Giffard and Gisborne to choose from, a nunnery sounds like a fine idea."

"I doubt either of us would survive in a nunnery," she said as she continued to linger at Robyn's side staring at the two of them in the looking glass. "We both love our freedom too much for that. And what of you? You turned twenty-two in May."

She remembered my birthday, Robyn thought and smiled a little despite herself. "I think I have just laid that question to rest," she replied as she scrutinized the face, hair and dress of a pageboy in the mirror.

"I wish I had options," said Marian gravely and lowered her chin casting her eyes to the floor.

Of course she has options, thought Robyn. She can do whatever she wants. Then, without letting her brain have time to register the words, she blurted out in a playful manner, "Well, you can always come live in the forest with me and the outlaws." She meant it to sound like a joke, but in her heart she longed for nothing more.

"Oh, Robyn." Marian let out a disappointed sigh. Her hands dropped to her side, and she stepped away, glancing around her room as she spoke. It was completely light by then. "I have responsibilities. I have my family and my station to consider." Marian avoided eye contact as she spoke.

Robyn turned from the looking glass, her head lowered in regret at her own lost family. In that instant, Marian turned to Robyn, stepped close, and reached a hand to caress her cheek. Gently, she guided Robyn's chin so that their eyes met.

"I am so sorry," she began with heartfelt tenderness. "I didn't think, I didn't mean…"

"Do not fret," Robyn replied. "I know what you meant." She lifted a hand up to stroke Marian's where it rested on her cheek. "Anyway, I am getting used to being alone now. Naturally you have obligations to your family. They expect to arrange a fine marriage for you with a young man from a noble house."

"No, Robyn," Marian corrected her. She interlaced her fingers with Robyn's, which were already becoming rough from manual labor. Then she peered through Robyn's eyes straight into her soul and stated with absolute authority, "You are not alone; you are never alone. You will always have me." Marian stretched up and kissed her cheek.

A moment passed between them, and Robyn wondered if Marian felt what she felt–the energy, the passion. The room was so silent Robyn could hear the pulsing of both their hearts. But before another word could pass between them, there came a frantic knock pounding at the door.

Buy Heart of Sherwood today to discover what happens next!

ABOUT THE AUTHOR

Edale Lane is the author of an award winning 2019 debut novel, *Heart of Sherwood*. She is the alter-ego of author Melodie Romeo, (*Vlad a Novel, Terror in Time*, and others) who founded Past and Prologue Press. Both identities are qualified to write historical fiction by virtue of an MA in History and 24 years spent as a teacher, along with skill and dedication in regard to research. She is a successful author who also currently drives a tractor-trailer across the United States. A native of Vicksburg, MS, Edale (or Melodie as the case may be) is also a musician who loves animals, gardening, and nature. Please visit her website at: https://pastandprologuepress.lpages.co/

Made in the USA
Columbia, SC
10 November 2021